THE
UNDISCOVERED
DESCENDANTS

Book #1 in the Nordri Series

Jo Visuri

Pohjola Press

Pohjola Press
Solana Beach, CA
For information on bulk orders, contact info@pohjolapress.com.

Library of Congress Control Number: 2021918090
ISBN 978-1-7377639-0-1 [paperback]
ISBN 978-1-7377639-1-8 [hardback]
ISBN 978-1-7377639-2-5 [ebook]

First edition 2021 printed in the United States

Cover design by Lena Yang
Illustrations by P. J. Visuri

*For my parents, whose love and support
brought Auor and the Clans to life.*

Contents

Prologue

A fter the earlier chaos, the still of the night sent nervous shivers racing down my spine. The cold bit at my cheeks as I stepped down the porch steps and turned to take one last look.

The light shining brightly on the snow reflected the innocent merriment inside the house. My family was safe. How I longed to be enjoying myself with the rest of them, but I knew I was different. I'd always been like a lone birch in an evergreen forest. Now it was just tangible—and dangerous.

My heart cried a little with each crunch of snow as I hurried away. I hoped I'd see them again soon, but for now, it would have to be silence. I had no choice. It was my fault after all—I had to go. Some would argue that where I was now going was impossible or imagined—a fantasy—and until a few months ago, I would've agreed with them.

To be found and invited to join was unexpected. Learning their secrets was beyond my wildest imaginings. Landing in the middle of a brewing conflict was never part of the plan.

ONE

A new neighbor

ELIN

The wind played with my hair, tying it into knots as I searched the beach for seashells with my sister. She was the beautiful one. Blond hair, brown eyes, curvaceous at eighteen in a way that would make most mature women jealous. I, on the other hand, was gangly, long-legged, and slim as a twig, with amber eyes and auburn hair. I was the odd one, given our Nordic roots.

The beach had been a childhood friend. It was a small sandy inlet with tall reeds growing around the edges and a floating dock just big enough to accept a skiff or two canoes during the summer. We'd learned to swim in the lapping water when it was actually warm enough to try.

As I bent down for a particularly large clamshell, I saw movement out of the corner of my eye. It was so quick that I could've easily mistaken it for a reed or a tree branch, except for the flash of silver that reflected off it under the autumn sun.

"Maria, did you see that?" I asked my sister.

"See what?" she replied.

"Over there." I pointed to the edge of the tall reeds where the forest began. "There was something over there." She glanced in the direction I was pointing.

"I don't see anything." She turned to look at me. "What'd you see?"

"I'm not sure. I thought I saw...something move," I answered, realizing that I sounded stupid. Maria's mouth turned upward into a wide smile.

"You saw something move." She laughed as she continued. "Oh, that's a good one! Elli, it's one of the windiest days we've had so far, and you saw something move in the bushes. Come on...help me gather these shells so we can get the next jar done."

With a long glance at the spot where I'd seen the silver flash, I stooped back down for the shell that I'd dropped. I knew my sister was in a hurry to finish our decorate-the-porch project, but I moved a little more slowly than she probably liked, as I couldn't shake the feeling of being watched. Whatever or whoever it was that I saw must have left some sign behind—a footprint or broken reed. I purposely moved towards the reeds on that side of the beach as I continued gathering shells. As I got closer, a tingling feeling rose inside me. I was nervous but not frightened—and my curiosity was stronger than my apprehension.

I reached the edge of the beach. My breath quickened as my senses heightened. The wind blew a little more strongly. The reeds shuddered. Goosebumps formed under my long-sleeved shirt.

"What're you doing?" my sister asked. "I need to be back in a half-hour, and we haven't filled the last jar. You know I've got a date with Erik tonight. I don't want to be late, and I haven't even picked out what to wear yet. Or figured out how to do my hair... what do you think, up or down?" Fighting the wind, she twirled her golden hair into a French twist as she looked expectantly at me.

Whatever my senses had reacted to was gone. My heartbeat

returned to normal as I listened to my sister prattle on when I didn't immediately respond. I walked back to the glass jars on the beach and deposited my load of shells.

"There, that finishes off the last one," I said, hoping that would distract her from asking more fashion-related questions.

"Oh, good! Let's head back, then. If we hurry back, I'll have time to figure out what shoes go best for tomorrow's party," she said, smiling.

"The party," I groaned as I remembered that my sixteenth birthday had been planned in excruciating detail. I didn't see why it couldn't be a small get-together—just our family and perhaps a few school friends...low-key. But my parents were determined to be equitable in every way between my sister and me. Maria had had a Sweet Sixteen party with pink streamers and at least fifty guests, so that was what I deserved.

The thought of it made me a little queasy—having to make an entrance at the party and everyone staring at me. It just wasn't my idea of a good time. And who knew what kind of dress my sister and mom had picked out. It was supposed to be a birthday surprise, but my sister had spilled the beans a week ago when the package arrived by delivery boat at the island dock. I guessed I should be glad that I hadn't had to tromp through all the dress stores, modeling their favorites.

The glass jars slipped a little in my hands as we walked back towards our house. I bent down to place them on the dirt road so I could blow on my cold hands. It was already cooling down, even though the sun was still sending its last rays through the atmosphere. As I straightened, the wind sent another gust our way, blowing my loose hair into my face. At that moment I felt the same senses heighten. Goosebumps blossomed on my arms. Something was close by. My senses knew it, but as I turned to look around me —there was nothing. All I could see were autumn leaves and rocks exposed in the dirt road by recent rain.

I shook it off as I saw my sister turn around, ready to express her annoyance at the delay. With a final warming blow on my hands, I picked up the jars and hurried after her.

"So...Mom wanted me to ask you, was there anyone special that we should've invited for tomorrow?" my sister asked with a coy smile.

"What do you mean, 'special'?" I asked, trying to avoid the question by posing another. "We already invited half the island, and Derek, Mia, Sam, and Betty are coming from the mainland."

Derek, Mia, Sam, and Betty were my closest friends from growing up on Auor Island. We'd all been in the same kindergarten class, although our mutual friendships had been slow to form. Mia and I had been instant friends from our first disagreement about which block should be on top of the pyramid we'd built. Luckily, we'd never had to choose, since Derek had knocked over our masterpiece—uniting us in our common anger towards him.

"I never did understand why they all changed to the mainland boarding school," my sister said, momentarily distracted from her earlier question.

"I don't think it was their choice," I replied. "Their parents made the decision based on schools and college-acceptance rates. They think their kids will have better opportunities applying from a private boarding school."

I frowned to myself. As much as I wanted to join my friends at the mainland's private boarding school, it was definitely out of my reach. My family didn't have the same financial resources as my friends' parents. Making ends meet for college would be hard enough.

My brother had earned a college sailing scholarship that had covered his tuition, while my sister had been working at a local fashion boutique since freshman year to help offset some of her impending higher-education costs. She had a gift for fashion that made the job more of a pleasure than a chore. Given my lack of skill in team sports or music and the sparse year-round job openings on Auor, I'd have to rely on my good grades and testing aptitude to find a scholarship or two.

My parents always said to follow my talents and passions and things would work out. But I had no idea what mine were. It seemed like all my friends and family had a natural ability or affinity for something. Mia was a math whiz, Derek was interested in medicine, Sam was an expert rock climber, and Betty could bake like no one else. Yet, at nearly sixteen, I hadn't figured out what I was good at.

Interrupting my thoughts, Maria mused, "Whatever happened to the idea of a big fish in a small pond? It worked for me."

"I think this pond was feeling a little crowded for their parents...or so at least Derek said," I replied.

"Oh, Derek—now there's somebody 'special,'" she teased. "You know he's got a humongous crush on you."

"No, he doesn't. We've known each other since we were five years old. We're good—" I started to explain.

"He's turned out to be quite good-looking too, Elli. And he works out, from what I can tell...although he hides it well under those hoodies of his," she interrupted, smirking at me as she bounced up the back stairs and opened the porch door.

"FRIENDS," I yelled as she flitted into the kitchen. "We're just good friends!"

Why did everyone make these assumptions about my love life? As if I wasn't dating someone, it was a crime. I just hadn't found anybody of interest. Plus, Auor Island was a natural barrier. It kept our community small and unchanging. Besides the summer influx of mainland vacationers, the same year-round people had lived on the island for my entire life.

I followed my sister through the porch door and put the jars with the collection that was forming on the windowsills. The back porch was perhaps my favorite place in the house. It was a glorified mudroom but had enough space for an indoor bench-swing that looked more like a couch, given the army of pillows my mom had heaped on it. Nobody sat out there for very long during the colder months, since the room wasn't heated, so it was a perfect place to escape when I needed some space.

I arranged the jars from the windowsill so that each window had one. My sister's idea involved several more jars on each so it would start looking like a picture she'd seen in a home-decor magazine. I frowned as I thought of what my weekend involved—a Sweet Sixteen party and seashell-picking—oh, such fun things.

At least my mainland friends were coming. It would be good to see them. A few weeks ago, with summer coming to an end, they'd all left to go back. It had meant an end to beach bonfires, rock climbing, and a united front against nosy parents.

I braced myself as I entered the kitchen. I loved my parents, but their endless stream of questions was invasive and made me want to either hide or explode. It was anyone's guess as to which would get the better of me.

"Hi, honey," my mom twittered as I walked in. "How was the beach?"

"Fine," I answered as she turned to look at me.

"Your hair! It's a mess. You should've tied it up. You're such a beautiful girl, but the way you let yourself walk around! It makes it hard to see that gorgeous face," she said. My mom had always been biased. She thought my auburn looks were unique.

"Did you know we have new folks moving to the island? They're going to be our neighbors. It's so exciting! I met the parents this morning at Nilsson's. They were picking up a few grocery items," she continued. I was grateful that the inspection was over, but internally I grimaced at the thought of how long I was going to have to hear about our new neighbors. "They were so nice and warm that I thought it was rude not to invite them to your party—especially since they don't know anyone here. You don't mind, do you? They have three kids. I think one of them is roughly your age, Elin. He's going to start school here on Auor next week. Won't it be nice to have someone new in the class? And you get to meet him first."

Her eyes twinkled as she spoke. I could already see the matchmaking happening in her mind. It only made me more determined not to see our new neighbor in that light.

"Sure. Sounds great, whatever," I said as I made a move toward the dining-room door.

"Don't forget that we start getting ready for the party tomorrow at 3pm! I need you here an hour before that so we can get you dressed and ready. Oh, I can't wait! It's been such a long time since I've seen you in a dress." She glowed as the thought enveloped her.

"Mommm! I was going to meet Derek, Mia, Sam, and Betty at the dock at two. We were going to hang out and catch up. The invite said the party wasn't until four. Why do we need two hours to get ready?" I squirmed at the thought of two hours of primping.

"Oh," she said. "I guess I understand...although you'll have the whole weekend to see them." She thought for a moment and then said, "We'll compromise and say 3pm on the dot."

That would give me only about a half-hour with my friends, since it was a fifteen-minute bike ride to the ferry dock, but I knew that this was an argument I wasn't going to win. I also didn't want to disappoint my mom when I knew she was so excited about the dress.

"Okay, fine—3pm it is," I replied as I slid out of the room.

"Hi, Elli," my older brother said as I entered the hallway, heading for my upstairs bedroom. "Mom giving you the scoop on the new neighbors and how you're going to marry their son?"

I gave him a good punch in the arm. My brother Anders liked

nothing better than to tease me. Any new material was as good as gold in his book.

"Ouch, s o r r y! Maybe Maria is right and it'll be Derek instead." He smirked as he danced away from my next blow.

"What is it with you people! Your lives must be so empty, since you have to concentrate so hard on mine," I quipped back.

I regretted the last part a little as I saw that I'd hit a sore spot with Anders. He was twenty-two and back at home after college, still trying to figure out what to do with his life. As much as Anders teased me, I got along with him the best out of my entire family.

"Sorry, Andee. I didn't mean it that way," I said, trying to soothe the blow.

"When you're right, you're right, Miss Bodil," he said in a quiet tone. Then a grin appeared on his face. "Although at least I'm not the one getting married." He headed for the front door as I chased after him, grabbing an umbrella from the stand to hurl at him.

The sun had almost set, and the first whispers of darkness were appearing. The wind had knocked down many of the golden and red maple leaves, although plenty still clung to the branches. Anders had disappeared down our driveway behind the curve before it met the road. He'd always been a good sprinter.

I stood in the middle of the dirt drive, breathing in the cool air, and closed my eyes. The umbrella was still in my hand in case Anders reappeared. Just as I was relaxing, the goosebumps on my arms began to rise. My heart started to beat faster. My eyes opened in a flash, but all I saw around me now were the gray shapes of trees and bushes, as the sun had finally set.

Then I heard my brother laugh as he spoke with someone. They sounded like they were coming closer to the house. I let out my breath as they rounded the corner and came into the sphere of the light from the house. Anders was walking with a boy I didn't recognize. He was tall—almost Anders' height—with jet-black hair and sea-blue eyes that seemed to be taking everything in. A pair of earbuds dangled around his neck, with the cord disappearing into the pocket of his navy-colored jacket. His eyes came to rest on me, inspecting me from head to toe and landing on the umbrella in my hand.

"Oh, hi, Elli. Still out here?" Anders greeted me with nonchalance. "Meet Aedan Grady...one of our new neighbors." Anders held a large bouquet of white lilies in his hands. "He's dropping off these flowers for Mom for tomorrow. Aedan, this is my baby sister, Elin."

Aedan held out his hand for a shake. I extended mine and placed it in his warm hand. I felt something like a small electric current run through my body as his hand closed on mine—not uncomfortable, but disconcerting. He looked equally disturbed and quickly dropped my hand.

"Preparing for rain?" he asked, looking pointedly at the umbrella in my hands.

"What? No, um...this was for Anders," I answered as the color rose into my cheeks.

I'd never been good at talking to good-looking boys, and Aedan definitely fell into that category. His face could have been out of a magazine cover, with all the rough edges in the right spots and proportions to match. His build was strong but not bulky. His movements were easy, almost like he practiced yoga twice a day, but there was also something slightly awkward or different about him. I couldn't quite put my finger on it. However, my own feelings of being gangly and ungraceful grew very evident in his presence. The need to hide became strong.

"Hey, cool bracelet," Anders said, admiring a well-worn leather cuff around Aedan's wrist.

In the middle of the cuff was a medal carved with intricate detail that gave it an almost-3D appearance. The symbol in the center looked like four interlinked sectors that formed a complete circle. Around it, like the points of a compass, were distinct embossed lines that made four different shapes.

"Thanks. It's a shield-knot cuff. Kind of a family tradition," Aedan offered as an explanation.

Anders and I nodded in interest. With none of us having anything further to say, there was a moment of silent awkwardness.

"Andee, I can take those into Mom," I said, pointing to the flowers that Anders had received from Aedan. "They probably need some water."

"Great, let's all go in. I'm sure Mom would like to meet Aedan and say hello," Anders said as he led the way into the house.

Aedan followed Anders. As I ascended the steps into the house, a cool breeze lifted my hair, and my little neck hairs stood up. I took a final glance into the yard, but nothing was there.

I walked into the warm house. I could smell that my mom was making a stew for dinner. Anders and Aedan were standing in the entryway, watching as Maria made her entrance from the top of the stairs. She looked beautiful in a pale-blue fitted dress that accentuated her curves and made her brown eyes look darker and deeper. As her mouth curved into a warm smile, I could see that she was appraising Aedan and liked what she saw.

"Hello," she said as she reached the landing and extended her hand toward him.

For a small second, I thought I saw apprehension flash across his face as he put his hand out to meet hers. But his face relaxed as their hands met, and he shook her hand enthusiastically. I could hardly blame him. Maria looked great in her date attire.

"When's Erik coming?" I asked. As if right on cue, there was a knock on the door frame. Erik walked in through the still-open door.

"Hi all," he said with a wide, easy smile—although a small

shadow flickered across his face when he saw that Aedan was still holding Maria's hand.

Erik was an easygoing, handsome jock. He'd been the captain of the high school hockey team and popular at school given his looks and laid-back attitude. He and Maria had dated on and off over the past two years. They were due to start their first year at separate colleges in a few weeks. Nobody knew what that meant for their relationship, but for now, it seemed like business as usual.

"Hi there," Maria chirped. "Erik, meet Aedan. I was just being introduced. Aedan is one of our new neighbors."

She talked as she moved to Erik's side and looped her arm through his. I could see Erik's shoulders relax as he took in the information.

"Nice to meet you," Erik said as he reached out his hand to shake Aedan's.

"Likewise," Aedan responded, smiling as he shook Erik's hand.

"There you all are," my mom said as she bustled into the entryway from the kitchen. "You must be Aedan. I'm Annika Bodil. Your parents said to keep an eye out for you. Oh, those lilies are beautiful! You must thank your parents for me. The flowers will be perfect for tomorrow's party." I watched as she took in the rest of the crowd. "I see you've met everybody—well, of course, except for Mr. Bodil. He's running late from the mainland office tonight. Erik and Maria, are you having dinner here or heading out? You're welcome to stay—the more the merrier. And of course, you must stay for dinner, Aedan. It's all ready to serve, and I'm sure your parents won't mind if we call them." Annika Bodil had always been a hostess first and knew how to steer people in the direction she wanted.

Aedan politely declined, not knowing what he was up against. "Oh, I couldn't impose on you, Mrs. Bodil. Plus, I should get back to helping my parents unpack."

"Heavens, I'm sure that you'll be so much more productive,

going back with a full stomach. And I'm sure that Anders will give you a ride home now that it's dark. A couple of miles in the pitch black is a long way. You haven't experienced our small-town life yet...it's very different from the mainland at night. The only streetlamps are on the main road, and they're few and far between. Now, I won't hear another protest. I'm calling your parents right now." She quelled any further argument by steering Aedan towards the kitchen.

"Thanks, Mrs. Bodil, but Maria and I are headed out for dinner," Erik answered, grabbing Maria's hand.

They started for the door before their plans could be changed. But they had nothing to worry about because my mom was too busy sorting out Aedan. Anders, still holding the large bouquet of lilies, looked at me.

"Guess it's just you and me, kid," he said as he moved toward the swinging kitchen door. "After you."

I did a quick mock curtsey, acknowledging his display of chivalry, and entered the kitchen. My stomach rumbled at the smell coming from the stove. The heat in the kitchen made me push up my shirt sleeves. I was suddenly very hungry. My mom already had Aedan setting the table. I chuckled to myself over her unassailable abilities.

Anders heaped the flowers into my arms, smirking. He was obviously glad to have passed the flower-arranging puck to me. He made a move for the door but was promptly stopped by my mom's voice.

"Andee, why don't you help Aedan set the table?" my mom asked, although it was more of a command.

I grinned and stuck out my tongue at Anders. His escape had been foiled. Aedan saw our exchange and quietly smiled in camaraderie.

As I arranged the lilies into vases, I noticed Aedan glancing my way with an inscrutable expression on his face. I couldn't tell what he was thinking, but his expression seemed like curiosity combined with fear and excitement.

I had gone to place a large vase of lilies on the dining table when my foot caught on a fold in the rug and I lost my balance. I was about to have crystal-vase pieces and lily petals for a new floor covering when Aedan was there to steady me. The electric current that sizzled between his hand and my bare arm was undeniable this time. I almost dropped the vase a second time. Aedan quickly grabbed it and placed it on the table. His breath and mine had quickened. We stared at each other, not quite sure what to say.

"*Whoa!* What happened here?" Anders said as he walked into the dining room and saw the splashed water and a few escaped lilies on the floor. "Elli, snap out of it! Get some towels before Mom comes in."

I came to and rushed out of the room for some towels. My mom was nervous about the dining-room floor since it needed refinishing. She felt that any spill, no matter how minor, would instantly soak into the wood.

When I came back, Anders and Aedan had finished collecting the stray flowers into the vase. All three of us dropped to the floor and started to mop up the water. Aedan was purposefully avoiding coming anywhere near me, although his eyes kept meeting mine. He seemed concerned.

My brother asked again what had happened. I admitted my clumsiness and mentioned Aedan's help but didn't say anything about the electric shock. I wasn't sure why except that I felt like too many weird things had happened that day. I didn't feel like explaining another. Aedan looked relieved.

The rest of the evening progressed uneventfully. We ate my mom's stew, laughed at Anders' jokes, and tried to find out more about Aedan's family. He wasn't exactly a Chatty Cathy about them. His answers were short but polite. His parents had decided to enter early retirement after selling off a successful company and investing wisely in the stock market. They wanted a less-hectic life than the mainland offered and had seen a golden opportunity when the perfect house came on the rental market on Auor Island. And that was it—we learned nothing more during the whole meal.

The darkness grew thicker outside, and yawns were starting to circle the table. It had become later than we thought. The conversation had flowed, and the candles had flickered. We'd all enjoyed ourselves, but the hour was long past ten.

"Thank you, Mrs. Bodil, for a delicious meal, but I need to head home," Aedan excused himself as he began to rise from the table.

"Our pleasure. It was great having you here. Andee, why don't you go pull the car around while Elin and I walk Aedan out?" my mom replied.

"Sure, no problem," Anders answered as he got up from the table and headed for the front door.

Aedan tried to mutter some protestations about being driven home, but my mom quickly silenced them. The three of us made a slow exit toward the front door. A cool breeze greeted us as I opened it.

Anders was just pulling the truck out of the garage and into the driveway. My mom turned to say goodbye to Aedan, who held out his hand to shake hers but was quickly drawn into a pat-on-the-back embrace.

I caught my breath when I thought that he'd have to touch me again to say goodbye. He must have been thinking the same thing, because when he approached me he smiled, and instead of holding out his hand, he launched himself into a full-body hug with me.

The whole thing was surprising—even my mom looked a little caught off guard. First, I expected to die from the full-body electrocution headed my way, but I felt only a small zing when his cheek brushed mine. Second, he'd been polite and reserved all evening. This was just plain weird in comparison. Anders must've been startled as well since I saw his elbow slip from the top of the steering wheel where it had been resting and inadvertently beep the horn.

Aedan let go and hurried toward the passenger side of the truck. With a quick wave, he and Anders were off. I stood there in shocked silence as my mom muttered something about a strange boy and went back into the house.

Once I'd gained my composure I turned back towards the house. All the events of the evening and the day were swirling inside my head. It had been a day full of odd sensations. Yet none of it frightened me. It was just perplexing. I was tired. I needed the comfort of my warm covers and quiet room.

"Goodnight, Mom! I'm going to bed," I called out as I started up the stairs to my bedroom.

"Goodnight, sweetie! Big day tomorrow, so get some good rest," she responded from the kitchen, where I could hear her clanging the pots around as she washed the dinner dishes. Thanks for the reminder, Mom, I thought to myself as I climbed the stairs. Now I'll be sure to sleep well, with that on my mind!

TWO

A physical reaction

AEDAN

The minute I'd shaken Elin's hand I'd forgotten to be vigilant —and being aware of my surroundings was paramount to survival. What *was* that electric current I'd felt with her?

I knew I hadn't imagined it, because it had happened again when I helped her with the vase. What was weirder was that none of her other family members had induced the same reaction. If they had, it might've been easier to chalk the whole thing up as a fluke.

Now, I really wasn't sure what to make of my evening with the Bodils. The one thing I did know was that I'd never met anyone like Elin Bodil. She was attractive for sure, but I'd met beautiful girls before and never had a physical electric jolt been a part of the package. That wasn't one of my abilities. I tried to remember if anyone in our family history had awakened a latent ability later in life. Nope, no one came to mind.

Argh, now to make sense of it all, I was going to have to tell my parents about my earlier beach expedition. I had thought I'd be able to bury that one. Exposure wasn't something we could risk, and I'd come very close to being caught...although clearly, it was not my fault, given all that had happened. Elin Bodil was definitely not a normal *Mannlegur* girl.

As we pulled up to my new home, I hopped out of the truck, thanked Anders for the ride, and hurried into the house. My parents had made tremendous progress in unpacking everything that the delivery truck had left behind. This was our fourth home in a year. My parents had chosen Auor Island as our next residence because of its isolated nature and mix of wealthy and middle-class households. It was somewhere we could blend in and not draw suspicion over our lifestyle. I mean, where else could we have been more off the grid than in the middle of an archipelago way up north? The thought-out camouflage and seclusion were absolute necessities—our lives depended on it.

Everything was new, of course, so I was curious to see how the furnished house looked. I noticed two large suitcases labeled with my name by the staircase. They were all that I'd been allowed to bring from our previous home. At least I was getting better at packing light.

My parents were sitting on the family room floor with three remote controls in front of them, discussing which remote would turn on the new TV. I walked into the room and sat down on the couch. The un-removed plastic protector rustled.

"Hi, Aedan. We were just starting to wonder if Mrs. Bodil was keeping you overnight," my father teased.

"Yeah, me too," I replied, chuckling a little. "You guys having trouble with the remotes again? Shouldn't you have enough practice by now?" It had always perplexed me, how with all of my parents' abilities and knowledge, it was the little things that stumped them.

"We finally got all the wires sorted out, but now the remotes don't want to work." My mother sighed, clearly exasperated by the process.

I could see how tired she was—all of the bouncing around and setting up new homes seemed to be taking a toll. I hated to put another problem on the table, given the larger issues we faced, but I needed some answers.

"I can take a look tomorrow, Mom," I volunteered. "I have something else that I need to tell you both."

My parents looked up, their faces showing some concern. I guessed the tone in my voice betrayed what I felt. I told them about my day's adventures at the beach. I confessed to my mistake, at which my mother had a slight intake of breath, but she relaxed when she understood that nothing had been revealed. I went on about the uncanny way Elin had been able to sense my presence— almost as if she could see me, which was impossible. My medallion cuff had been on my wrist and turned to the appropriate setting for the *leynasking* to work to conceal myself. My parents shared a glance but said nothing. I dove into recounting the evening's events and finished by telling how I'd almost tackled Elin while saying goodbye in order to avoid touching her skin.

"Liam, do you think it could be..." My mother's voice trailed off as she sat there with a look of slight disbelief on her face. "Could we be so lucky?"

"Now, Dara, don't get ahead of yourself. We don't know anything yet. There's no proof one way or the other," my father replied.

My father started to pace the floor—his way of thinking—while my mother peppered him with half-baked questions that went unanswered. Their reaction wasn't what I expected. There was no reprimand for the beach incident and no musing on how strange the electric shock between Elin and me had been. Instead, it felt like they understood what the electricity meant and were excited about the possibilities.

"What are you guys talking about?" I almost yelled. My father stopped pacing and looked at me.

"Aedan, how'd you know not to touch her bare skin?" he asked.

"What—um, I don't know...I guess I brushed against her in the doorway as we were setting the table. I didn't feel anything when I touched her clothed body," I replied, slightly annoyed that my father was not answering my question.

Maybe I wasn't being quite truthful about not feeling anything, being that close to her, but it didn't seem relevant to the conversation. She'd smelled good, like fresh apples. I shook the thought out of my head and turned back to my father.

"Tell me what it means," I said, looking my father directly in the eye.

"We haven't seen one or known of one in many years, but there's a chance that Elin could be a Dormant Descendant," he said with a thoughtful expression. Reading the question in my face, he continued, "Dormant Descendants are *Mannlegurs* who can become like us. They're carriers of a dormant Clan gene that can be woken through an ancient ritual."

I was stunned. I'd never heard of the possibility. I'd always believed that our gifts were directly passed down from the Clan generations above—no awakening needed. I looked at my mother.

"It's true, sweetheart," my mother said. "The prevailing theory is that the Dormants are descendants of a Four Clan member and *Mannlegur*—a sort of hybrid phenomenon. However, nobody has found one in such a long time that people eventually stopped talking about it, and it became a myth. It's whispered that some of the greatest people in Clan history have been Dormants."

The wheels in my head were turning quickly. The Four Clans were the original source of our *megin*. The legend was that long ago, four societies from earth's cardinal points were granted supernatural abilities by their moon god or goddess to help guard humanity against oblivion. Over the hundreds of generations, the clans themselves had intermingled, leaving behind multicultural descendants—but it now seemed that there was an added twist. My mother anticipated my question.

"How do you know when a person is a Dormant Descendant?" she said. "Well, based on what we know, there's a reaction between us and them. What that reaction is...hasn't been documented well. All we know is that it's something physical. I've never heard of it described as quite so strong as what you experienced, but again, there isn't a lot of material on this."

"It's late, son. Why don't you head upstairs, and we can talk more tomorrow?" my father said.

I glanced at my watch. It was nearly midnight. I couldn't stifle an insistent yawn. My head was humming with the insights I'd gathered from my parents, but my body was definitely fatigued. I reluctantly nodded. I said goodnight to both my parents and went to heave my two suitcases upstairs.

I could no longer make out their words as I reached the top landing, but I could hear my parents' voices undulating between excitement and concern as they continued their discussion. I stared down the hallway, trying to remember which door was mine. The snoring from behind the first door on the right definitely told me that my older brother, Edvin, was fast asleep in there. The next door was a little way down the hall on the left. Oops, definitely not mine. I quietly re-closed the door on the chaotic scene of a chair knocked down under the weight of women's clothing. That would be Claire's room. Only my sister would start by unpacking her clothes first.

The last door was all the way down the hall. I opened it and was relieved and thankful to see that someone had set up a bed for me, including sheets and a comforter. The rest of the room's furniture was still in packaging. I noticed labels with "desk," "chair," "bookcase," et cetera.

I laid my suitcases on the floor. It was dark in the room, but given my abilities, it was easy for me to find what I was looking for in my bags. The moonlight streaming through the square windows also provided cool, helpful light in the room. It looked like I'd scored the corner room this time. Edvin, Claire, and I were on a rotational program for who got the most-coveted room in the new house, excluding my parents' room.

I found my toiletries and shuffled towards one of the remaining doors in the hallway, hoping it was a bathroom. It looked like Edvin and I were sharing. Better than sharing with Claire. There never seemed to be enough cupboard space when she was involved. I played with the idea of turning on the light but decided against it and proceeded with my nightly routine. As I re-entered the hallway I could see the lights from downstairs still crawling up the staircase. My parents were still talking.

I tried to quiet my mind. It wanted to join them in ruminating on what it all meant. I forced my feet in the direction of my bed. My body sighed in contentment as I pulled the covers over my head. The last images flipping through my mind before I succumbed to sleep were of the strange girl I'd met that evening.

I woke up to sunlight streaming through the windows. Priority one: curtains. I tried to stuff the pillow over my head to block out the light, but it was too late—I was awake. I rolled over with a groan. It felt like I'd just gone to bed. I reached down to the floor for my watch. It read 8:33am. The sounds coming from the hallway indicated that I wasn't the only one awake. I swung my legs out of bed and reached for my jeans, which lay crumpled on the floor from the previous night. I rummaged through my suitcase, found a favorite t-shirt, and stretched it over my head. Looking out the window, I could see that there was white frost covering the grass where the sun had yet to reach. I walked out into the hallway and caught Edvin coming out of the bathroom.

"Nice hair," Edvin greeted, rubbing the sleep from his eyes.

He wasn't dressed yet and was standing in the hallway with just his boxers on. He was tall, dark-haired, and muscular. He would've been a great rugby player if my parents had let him play.

"Yeah, you too," I replied, running my hands through my hair and trying to calm the waves that had come to life during the night.

"Morning," Claire said as she emerged perfectly coiffed and dressed. She glanced at Edvin. "You gonna put some clothes on?"

Edvin smirked at her and went into his room. You'd never guess that they were twins by their looks, but it was hard not to see a connection when they interacted. Claire had inherited my mother's more delicate features and figure but had the same black hair that united the Grady clan. She was by all accounts a beautiful twenty-something.

"Morning, Claire," I said as I stepped into the bathroom.

I rushed through my morning ritual, as I smelled the aromas of pancakes and bacon wafting from the kitchen. I knew in order to get some I'd need to make it down before Edvin.

I walked into the kitchen right before Edvin and slid into the open chair at the counter. My mother stood on the other side in front of the stove. She heaped some delicious-looking scrambled eggs and bacon along with two pancakes on my plate. Her eyes met mine. She smiled, but her shoulders were folded forward. She had dark circles under her eyes. I felt a twinge of guilt for adding the previous night's burden to what she already carried. Just then, Edvin slapped me on the back and reached over to steal some bacon from my plate.

"No way...get your own," I said as I slid the plate out of his reach.

"Good morning, everyone!" my father said as he entered the kitchen and made his way toward the coffee. He kissed my mother on the neck as he passed and gave her a gentle squeeze on the shoulders. "How did everyone sleep?"

I mumbled a positive affirmation through the scrambled eggs in my mouth.

Claire said, "Well," as she stared Edvin down, silently communicating to him, "Stay away from my bacon."

"Great, Dad," Edvin said as he finally yielded to getting his own plate out of the cupboard.

"Glad to hear it," my father said with a warm smile. "Your mother and I thought we should all go to town for lunch and stock up on some additional supplies. I know that eventually, we'll need to go to the mainland to get everything we need, but for now, I'd like us to minimize trips off the island. If you need something you can't buy here, there's always the internet."

I never had completely understood why the internet was more secure than a trip outside our "safety zone," as my father liked to refer to it. However, he believed our purchased alternate identities were secure for online use.

"Oh, one other thing..." he continued. "Aedan brought something to our attention last night that concerns us all."

He went on to relate what I'd told them and shared the same information about Dormants. I watched as Claire and Edvin absorbed the news. They were clearly having a silent dialogue with each other. Sometimes I wished I could even just listen as they telepathically spoke, but they'd never been able to include anyone in the discussion—not even with my mother's help. I'd concluded that it was a twin thing.

"So, we need to stay cautious around Elin for now until we know for certain what we're dealing with," my father concluded. "There's a lot to consider about this situation. The first thing we need to establish is that this electricity isn't just with Aedan. The Bodils' party this evening will be the perfect opportunity for all of us to 'connect' with Elin, but we need to do it as subtly as possible. We don't want to alarm her."

I frowned at this last statement as I considered the sensations from the previous night. That might be hard if the five of us were electrocuting her all evening. I shared my thought.

"That's why it's important that we all find different ways to make contact, and not at the same time. Clearly, we can't all just line up and hold out our bare hands. We'll have to be stealthier than that," my father answered.

"Can't we just *leynask* and then reach out to her? She won't see us," Edvin suggested, fingering the shield-knot medallion hanging around his neck.

"From what Aedan saw at the beach, I don't think that'll work. We can't risk her sensing us," my mother replied.

We spent the rest of breakfast plotting how to make and not make contact with Elin. It was also determined that I should definitely avoid touching her. Once we'd woven some basic rules, each of us returned to our normal tasks of unpacking and organizing for the rest of the morning.

Around one o'clock, as the first tendrils of hunger were making their appearance, my mother collected us for our trip to town. As I recalled from our arrival, "town" had appeared to be a handful of tourist shops and restaurants crowded around the main harbor where the ferries landed. Apparently, it also included a reasonably well-stocked grocery store and hardware shop, but I'd yet to experience either. We climbed into my father's new prized possession—a brand-new Land Rover. He was still in the process of convincing my mother that it was the only choice for a 4-wheel drive vehicle. She had her doubts about needing that much car on a fairly small island, even if it did have two mountains.

As we entered the town, my mother listed the options for

lunch. We decided upon a small red restaurant by the water. It had at least two doors and a slew of windows, which made for several potential exits should we need to make a hasty departure. The menu was basic fare, but the restaurant had been recommended by a few of the islanders that my parents had met. We received a few stares as we entered, but the hostess quickly found us a table near the windows.

Fish seemed to be the ingredient of choice on the menu. We all went with the flow and ordered some combination of seafood as our meal. Our lunch was uneventful and tasty. As we rose to leave the restaurant, we saw that the ferry had docked.

"That's the last extra ferry to the mainland. Summer is officially over," the waitress woefully informed us, looking at the large boat through the window.

"I guess the weather has been turning cooler," my mother responded, commiserating.

The waitress nodded. We thanked her for lunch and turned to walk out of the restaurant.

We stopped outside to discuss how to tackle getting everyone's errands done. I mentioned my need for curtains. My mother turned sideways to point out a shop that she'd seen that might work. I looked in that direction and saw Elin Bodil standing with a group of what seemed to be friends. She was at ease, laughing with them as they shared a humorous moment while eating ice cream cones. There was a taller boy standing next to her in a hooded sweater, who put his arm around her as he said something to her that made her laugh harder. I felt a knot tighten in my stomach. I gritted my teeth a little.

"Aedan, did you hear me?" my mother asked.

"Huh, what...? Um, no. What'd you say?" I tried to focus on my mother.

"I asked, would you mind looking for a shower curtain for the upstairs bathroom?" she repeated.

"Uh-huh...yeah, no problem," I replied. Claire slid beside me and followed my distracted gaze while my parents continued their discussion.

"Is that her?" she whispered as she looked in Elin's direction.

I nodded slowly. We continued to watch as their merry party started to break up. They walked up to the square and four of them got into an old blue Volvo station wagon. The boy in the hoodie slid into the driver's seat. Elin continued across the square, heading for the bicycle rack.

"So that's the Dormant Descendant," Edvin said, grinning widely. Before either Claire or I could stop him, he'd made it to the other side of the square at a speed that would have lifted eyebrows had anyone been paying attention.

"No," Claire ground out under her breath as she read his intention.

Ignoring her protests, Edvin ducked into a sheltered doorway, reached under his shirt for his medallion, and in a small shudder of air became part of the background. I was too stunned by the risk he was taking in *leynasking* so publicly that I couldn't utter any words. The doorway had shielded his bulky frame, but if anyone had been staring directly at it, they would have witnessed a large man disappear before their eyes. I quickly scanned the square. No one's jaw seemed to have unhinged to their feet. Everyone seemed to be preoccupied with his or her errands. I let out my breath.

"What's he trying to do?" I asked Claire, annoyed.

She shrugged in response. We stood nervously, unsure of what to do. We watched as Edvin, now imperceptible to everyone but us, moved closer to the bicycle rack.

At that moment, my parents clued into the fact that none of their children were paying any attention to them. Somehow Claire was able to find words to relate to them what was happening.

"It's Edvin. He's at it again." She subtly motioned towards him.

The muscles in my father's face tightened, and his eyes became razor-sharp as they focused on Edvin. My mother started to fidget with her hands, turning them over and over within each other. Claire must have communicated this to Edvin since he threw a glance in our direction as he settled between the two bicycles at the stand.

Elin was nearly there. She was about twenty feet away when she froze to a standstill. Her body became rigid, and she seemed to be contemplating whether she should move forward. Then I saw her square her shoulders as she closed the distance to her bicycle. She was now within an arm's length of Edvin. At first, she seemed determined to unlock her bike as quickly as possible, but then she straightened from her bent position and turned around, facing Edvin head-on. All of us were holding our breath. Edvin had to take a few steps back to avoid Elin as she stepped in his direction.

The initial thrill must have worn off for Edvin since he started to backpedal a little more quickly into the road. Claire let out a loud gasp as a car came down the cobbled street toward him. He must have received her warning because in the same instant he crouched and sprang into a backflip over the car. Elin must have heard Claire's gasp because her gaze was now directed towards us. Trying to think quickly, I waved at her feverishly.

"Wave! Everyone smile and wave," I muttered under my breath.

My parents and Claire complied and tried to act as normal as possible. Elin looked puzzled but then lifted her hand and hesitantly waved back. I could hear my parents let out their breaths. She turned, finished unlocking her bike, and then rode off with a final wave.

"Why do I *always* have to look stupid to save Edvin's skin?" I grumbled as I turned and stomped off to look for the curtains. I left my parents and Claire to chastise Edvin.

By the time we got back to the house from our errands, it was close to three o'clock. We wanted to get to the party on the early side, so all of us rushed around, getting ready within forty-five minutes. Given the uncertainty of how the evening was going to unfold, my parents decided it was best to take two cars. They were going in the Land Rover, and Claire, Edvin, and I piled into the smaller Audi Q5.

I glared at Edvin as he made a move for the driver's side. "I'm driving."

He quickly acquiesced, still clearly feeling a little apologetic about the afternoon. Whatever talking-to my parents and Claire had given him, it had clearly worked.

The drive to the Bodils' place was short, about fifteen minutes over dirt roads. My parents pulled into the driveway ahead of us. As we rounded the bend, I saw that a few cars had already arrived. The blue Volvo station wagon from earlier in the day was amongst them. I felt the same knot in my stomach tighten a little. I purposely pulled in right next to the Volvo and parked the car. I wasn't sure why, but I already knew that I was not going to like the boy in the hoodie.

The three of us let my parents exit their car and enter the house first. The Grady clan, with our distinct dark looks, was known to attract attention when we were together, and that was the last thing we wanted tonight. It had been decided that it was best if we made our entrances in batches.

Once my parents had been in the house for a few minutes, we opened our car doors and headed for the front steps. The sound of laughter and people talking merrily echoed from the house as we approached across the lawn. With the sun dipping lower in the sky, the breeze was starting to get frosty. We were almost at the front steps when I happened to glance at the second-floor windows. For a slight moment, I thought I saw Elin's face in the window, but the curtain fell back into place, so I couldn't be sure.

Edvin, Claire, and I entered the house and were warmly

greeted by Mr. and Mrs. Bodil. Mr. Bodil was a tall, lanky, blond-haired, brown-eyed gentleman in a dark suit. He seemed reserved next to the robust and bubbly Mrs. Bodil, who had curled her blond hair into tight ringlets for the occasion. From the hallway, I could see that the dining table had been taken over by a massive smorgasbord of food. The rest of the house was decorated in a variety of white flowers and pale green streamers. Even the banister of the stairs had gained a green-and-white garland. As I looked around I could see that Maria was proudly explaining to a few other female guests her ideas behind the decorating scheme. She looked great in a tightly fitted red dress that gracefully highlighted all her assets. Edvin was clearly salivating. I gave him a quick elbow in the ribs to get him to focus on the task at hand.

After shaking hands with Mr. Bodil, the three of us fanned out in the house. I headed for the kitchen to get something to drink while Edvin beelined into the living room, where Maria was holding court. Claire made her way into the dining room, where my parents had congregated. I swung the kitchen door open and stepped into the warmly lit room. There, standing by the island counter, was the boy in the hoodie, but without his hoodie. He was talking to a red-headed, freckled boy, and he was obviously enjoying the conversation. I'd stopped inconveniently in front of the swinging door, and it bumped into me as a person struggled to come in. I quickly moved a few steps forward and turned to apologize.

"Oh, so sorry," the brown-haired girl said as she managed to get the door open.

"No, no...that was my fault. I was standing in the wrong place," I replied. She smiled warmly and put out her hand.

"Hi, I'm Betty," she said. I took her hand and shook it as I introduced myself. "How do you know the Bodils?" she asked, making conversation. She was a nice-looking girl with dimples in her cheeks when she smiled.

"My family moved in next door—a couple of miles down the road. How about you?" I answered, smiling back.

"Oh, right. I think I heard mention of the new neighbors. Welcome to Auor Island," she said. "My folks own a house a couple of miles down the main road from here. I went to school with Elli starting way back in kindergarten."

She continued chatting about island life, and I half-listened, making agreeable utterances when called for. I scanned the crowd as it swelled, looking for signs of Elin. I wanted my parents to have the opportunity to experience what I had so we could get some more clarity on the situation.

Betty was laughing and gently touching my arm as she narrated a particularly funny story about growing up on the island. The red-haired boy had been glancing our way for some time, and this was enough impetus for him to squeeze over and slide his arm around Betty protectively.

"Oh, hi, Sam. Have you met Aedan yet?" Betty giggled as she turned to face him.

"No, I don't think I have," Sam said as he reached his hand out, keeping his other arm wrapped around Betty's waist. I grasped his hand in a friendly manner and shook.

"Sam grew up on the island as well and was part of our kindergarten club," Betty related, giving me some more context.

"Sounds like quite the time, growing up here. Betty was just telling me some choice stories," I said, smiling, hoping that my friendly tone would ease some of Sam's concerns.

"So where're you from?" Sam asked.

"Well, that's a bit complicated...we've moved around a lot, the last couple years. But most recently we were living on the mainland some ways south of here," I replied.

This wasn't an easy question for my family to answer, since relating all the places we'd lived would be incomprehensible to most people. Luckily, I escaped having to answer any more follow-up questions, because a loud gong sounded from the hallway. We could hear people being encouraged to move in the direction of the staircase.

"Oh, it's time for the big reveal!" Betty squealed. "Elli was dreading this part more than any other tonight. She hates the attention. This whole party has been like pulling teeth for her." Betty shrugged as if brushing the thought out of her mind.

Being closest to the kitchen door, we were able to squeeze through before the rest of the crowd tried getting through the cow chute. We stationed ourselves by the front door with a clear view of the staircase. The boy in the hoodie joined us.

I felt a cool, delicate hand on my shoulder. I turned my head to see Claire standing behind me. She flashed me a smile. I quickly scanned the crowd for the rest of my family. Edvin was standing like an obedient lapdog, a few feet away from Maria—although he was now blocked from going any closer by Erik's frame. And my parents were on the other side of the staircase.

Mr. Bodil stepped up to the first riser on the staircase and cleared his throat. "I'd like to take this moment to wish a very happy sixteenth birthday to my daughter Elin. Please, let's welcome her down the stairs to join her party." The crowd burst into applause as low music started to play in the background.

At first, you could see only her feet, placed in black patent heels. Next came her legs, followed by the appearance of the pale-green fabric of her dress. It seemed to match the decorations on the banister.

As Elin came fully into view, she was bravely wearing a smile on her face, but it didn't quite reach her amber eyes. They darted up and down and avoided looking at anyone for too long. She did, however, look great in her dress. It flattered her slim figure, falling simply from her shoulders to just above her knee. The color actually brought out more variants of the red in her hair.

Her eyes met mine for a moment. I smiled, hoping to convey

encouragement. They seemed to brighten. Before I had a chance to take in the moment, her eyes turned to the boy in the hoodie, who had broken into a mock dance and was making funny faces. The attention in the room shifted to him.

With the guests distracted, Elin quickly hurried down the remaining steps. She laughed unreservedly at the show as she made it to the safety of the crowd. My father had strategically positioned himself so that he'd be only a few steps away when Elin was mingling with the other guests. With a larger male guest between Elin and himself, he reached out and brushed her bare arm as if reaching for another guest. I watched his face intently and saw surprise flicker across it as he made contact. I didn't observe a reaction on Elin's part, but her mother had just appeared beside her, whispering something in her ear, so it was difficult to say whether she'd noticed the interaction.

My father was back at my mother's side, talking to her with a very small amount of space between them. He looked toward where Claire and I were standing and gave a quick nod. Claire smiled.

"Looks like you were right, Aedan," she whispered.

"One down, three more to go," I replied.

"Well, I'm next," Edvin said with a large grin. He'd left his post by Maria and was now sidling up to us. He'd clearly gotten the news from Claire.

"This isn't a competition, Edvin," I reminded him.

"Nope, but I've never touched a Dormant before," Edvin said, smirking.

I punched him in the upper thigh, hoping no one would notice. As the pain vibrated through my hand, I silently cursed, having forgotten that Edvin was built literally like a tank.

"Aren't we touchy?" Edvin responded.

"I just don't want you to ruin this with some crazy antics. You already had a close call today," I retorted.

It might not have been an expression of everything I was feeling, but hopefully, the comment would curb Edvin and help protect the family—and Elin. He mumbled something under his breath about never living it down as he headed for the smorgasbord in the dining room.

I looked at Claire, whose eyes had been focused on Elin during the conversation. She turned and smiled at me when a group of girls clustered around Elin, admiring her dress. Without another word she floated over to where they were standing and joined in the admiration. As a few girls were touching the fabric, Claire reached over as well and grazed Elin's hand in the process. Whatever Claire felt was well hidden behind her warm, affable smile and easy chatter as the girls continued discussing the dress.

I realized that I was awkwardly standing alone at the door, watching the girls discuss Elin's outfit. The crowd in the entryway had thinned after the hoodie-boy's show concluded. I decided it was time for some food and started in the direction of the dining room. A hand in the crook of my elbow stopped my progress. I turned and found Elin at my side. She looked almost as surprised as I was.

"Hi," she said. She seemed to be at a loss for words.

"Hi...um...happy birthday. Great party. Lots of folks," I stuttered, shocked that she'd approached me.

I felt my usual composure leave my body while a million thoughts raced through my head. She had touched me. Thank goodness I'd worn my corduroy jacket. The thick fabric was good in this case. She'd sought me out. Why? I felt a little flutter at the thought. I couldn't let her touch my hand. I instinctively straightened my arm and her hand fell off it. She looked even more uncomfortable.

"Um...you look great in your dress," I said, hoping to break the awkward moment.

"Thanks, my mom and sister picked it out. Have you, uh...have

35

you tried the food yet? The fish cakes are really good." She finished the last part of the sentence a little faster and tried to smile.

"I haven't yet, but I was just heading that way. Would you like any?" I replied.

"No, uh, no...I'm good—thanks." She almost swallowed her words as she turned around and headed back to her friends. A brown-skinned, dark-haired girl gave her a quizzical look as Elin motioned her into the kitchen. I stood there for a moment, contemplating our interaction, and then continued into the dining room.

Edvin was in the process of seeing how many fish cakes he could stuff into his mouth at the same time. I saw my mother pondering how to best reproach his eating method.

"Hey! Leave some for the rest of us," I said as I got closer to Edvin, cocking my head towards our mother.

"You've got to try these cakes. I'm not sure what's in them, but they're delicious!" Edvin responded as he bit into another.

"I would if you weren't hogging the entire plate—and by the way, they're fish cakes," I answered.

"Oh, sorry. Didn't realize I was blocking your way," Edvin said as he grabbed one more cake off the plate and headed towards the drink section. I took a plate from the stack and was mulling over the best strategy for filling it when my father came to my side.

"Aedan, your mother and I think that we should leave now. She's fine not connecting with Elin, and I don't want to risk another unforeseen touch between you and her. We saw your conversation," he said, giving me a knowing look.

"Dad, it was nothing. She touched my clothed arm. I can handle it," I whispered back, annoyed at the change in plans. "Besides, Edvin isn't going to want to leave before he's had his contact."

"Edvin and Claire can stay."

"Seriously? Edvin can stay, but I can't?"

"They haven't had the same interactions or experiences as you've had with Elin. Claire's and my connection with Elin were more on the static electricity level rather than a full sizzle. And Claire will keep an eye on your brother," he insisted. I could see that this wasn't an argument I was going to win.

I acquiesced. "Fine."

"You take your mother to the car, and I'll say the necessary thank yous and goodbyes for the three of us," he instructed. I nodded, placed the empty plate back on the stack, and went to collect my mother from the other side of the room.

Through the side door, I could hear the activity in the kitchen starting to increase, which usually meant only one thing—the birthday cake. They were starting to light the candles.

My mother was engrossed in conversation with an older woman, and my attempts to gain her attention from a few feet away were proving to be more difficult than expected. I wanted to make our exit before the cake was delivered so it would be less awkward. I quickly closed the distance to her and placed my hand upon her elbow.

"So sorry to interrupt, but Dad would like you to come *right now*," I said, hoping my mother was in the loop already.

"Oh, okay...please excuse me. It sounds like my husband needs me. It was so nice to meet you. I enjoyed our conversation," my mother said, so sweetly that anyone would have been completely disarmed and ready to accede to her every wish. The older woman nodded agreeably and waved us off with a smile.

I tried to guide us through the maze of people as quickly as possible. Several people turned their heads and tried to engage my mother in conversation, but I ignored their puzzled looks as I kept a firm grip on her elbow, not stopping to acknowledge them.

As we reached the door, the singing began from the kitchen. I could see people gathering around Elin in the living room. She was standing in front of the coffee table with the roaring fireplace behind her and a direct view of where my mother and I were standing by the door.

Our eyes met. I felt something stir inside me. However, the moment was broken as the boy with the hoodie walked up to her side and gave her a shoulder embrace as he broke out into a loud rendition of "Happy Birthday." I opened the front door with a little more force than necessary. The door let out a slight groan in protest. Luckily for me, the singing covered the noise.

Once we were outside, my mother turned to face me. I could tell she was gauging my emotional state. "Are you all right?" she asked. "I've sensed about five different emotions from you in the last few minutes."

"Mom, *please* don't read me right now. I'm fine. Just tired from all the excitement and anticipation." I really didn't want my mother using her ability on me right now. I wanted my emotions to be my own and not have to explain them.

"Okay, honey, but you know if there's anything you want to talk about, both your father and I are here," she said, warmly squeezing my arm. We continued to the car. I hopped into the driver seat of the Land Rover and pulled the car in front of the house in expectation of my father's arrival.

The car was warm by the time my father made his exit from the Bodils' home. He must have felt a little guilty about our hasty exit since he climbed into the back seat without comment about my driving the car home.

"Well, I think we can conclude that Elin is a strong potential Dormant. All of us who connected with her felt the electric vibration. We clearly won't know for sure until the actual awakening itself." My father sighed deeply as he announced his thoughts. His previous excitement seemed to have vanished.

"Isn't that good?" I asked. "Wouldn't another one of us be a good thing?"

"Normally, I'd be beyond excited at the prospect of discovering a Dormant Descendant, but what can we offer her right now? Given our circumstances, if we help her convert, we're introducing her to a life of perpetually looking over her shoulder. Is that a fair trade? Or what happens if she inadvertently exposes us and we have to move again? We can't take her away from her family. Or what if she isn't a Dormant at all? What do we do then? These are weighty matters, and I am not sure we've thought through all the scenarios and risks," my father answered lost in thought.

"Shouldn't she be allowed to be part of those decisions? It doesn't feel right, making them and keeping her in the dark. It's her life, after all," I argued back.

"We'd have to introduce her to our world, and that's a significant amount of trust to place in someone who isn't a part of it," my mother pointed out.

"But how can she make a choice without knowing the options? Besides, Elin is sensing our world already. She hasn't given it away yet, and she doesn't even know what she is dealing with," I stated.

The possibility that my parents were going to ignore Elin's choice in the matter and decide without ever consulting her made me feel desperate. I also had to admit that the thought of being able to share our secret with someone outside of our family was intoxicating. It had been so long since we'd interacted with any of our own kind beyond our immediate family. The cost of trying to find others could result in loss of life or the disappearance of entire families. Thus, it had been deemed too dangerous. Being dispersed and out of contact was a much safer alternative.

Although it hadn't stopped the Hunters...now they were just going after us one by one. I shuddered at the thought as I pulled the car into our driveway. The rest of the ride home had been quiet, as each of us had been lost in our thoughts.

"Aedan, I do understand your perspective. Normally, Elin

should absolutely have a choice, but I'm just not sure yet what the right path forward is in the current circumstance. This is a complicated matter. If we share our world, we might place others in danger. But if we hold back, we might miss an incredible opportunity. I wish I could speak with your Uncle Quinn. He'd have further insights and access to the old books," my father lamented as he got out of the car. My mother placed her hand on his shoulder as they walked up the path. My father turned and gave her a thoughtful and loving gaze.

From just that one look alone, it was obvious how much they loved each other. It made me wonder if Edvin, Claire, or I would ever have what my parents had. Our constant moving and fear of exposure made romantic relationships with *Mannlegurs* impossible.

I pulled the car into the garage and climbed out. The moon was almost full, casting bluish-white light on the front lawn and the wide porch. It was still early evening, but darkness came swiftly after sunset. I breathed in the cool, crisp air and felt the wisps of cold working their way through my coat as I moved. What had Elin wanted at the party? Why had she sought me out? I didn't really believe that it was just about fish cakes. No, there was definitely something else.

I climbed the stairs into the modern-looking house. My parents were in the kitchen, clanging pots around in an effort to create something for a late dinner. I needed to busy myself. Do something to drive the questions from my head. I pounced up the stairs two at a time.

I'd made great progress with furniture assembly in my room that morning and already had a desk, chair, and a bookcase forming. I'd also gotten my newest acquisitions for the windows in place and felt thankful that I might have a chance of getting more sleep before the morning light woke me. I dug through my bags and found my running clothes and shoes. I changed as quickly as possible, wanting to take full advantage of the moon. I found my iPod on my nightstand where I'd left it charging earlier and grabbed my earbuds from the drawer. With the frequency with which we had to change cell phones, the iPod functioned as a practical solution for storing my music collection. I pulled on a wool hat as I hurried down the stairs.

"I'm going for a run. Don't wait on dinner for me—I'll just get something later. I'll probably be a while," I shouted as I headed toward the front door.

"Be careful, Aedan," my mother responded.

I closed the front door before I heard the rest of her response. I just needed to stretch my legs and clear my head from all the noise. I did a quick stretch on the wide porch before jumping down the stairs in a single bound. It felt good to let go of my guard and use my full abilities. I selected my running playlist from the iPod, and The Rolling Stones' "Start Me Up" began to stream through my earbuds.

In an instant, I was off. I was faster than any normal person— we all were, especially Claire, who could easily run circles around any of us. That was her unique gift—grace and speed.

I didn't want to *leynask*, so I ran in the woods out of sight. The earth felt good under my shoes. It seemed to spring me forward as I navigated fallen trees and other obstacles. My body snapped the small dead branches of trees as I pushed through. I guessed the good news was that the way back would be easier to find. I didn't have a destination, so I let the forest guide me. When a thicket of trees or branches got too dense, I changed direction.

I got to the top of a large hill that had an open clearing of granite that stretched toward the sea. The view was breathtaking. I stopped. Breathing hard, I took it in. The moonlight played on water glistening as the small waves reached the rocky shoreline below. In the distance, I could see the dark form of the next island over, which was uninhabited. There were so many islands out there. I wondered if anyone had ever counted them all.

Closer to shore was another island. It was very small—in fact, it looked more like a very large boulder. The moon reflected off the cut stones that were stacked on top of the boulder. They looked like the ruins of an old tower. The lower part of the tower had remained intact while the years or something more violent had demolished the top.

The tall grass growing between the cracks in the granite swayed in the breeze. I took out my earbuds, closed my eyes, and listened. All I could hear was the crackling of the reeds and the lapping of the waves below. It was peaceful. I drank in one more glance at the view and then turned to head back.

I ran at a slower pace, without my music, letting my mind wander as my body performed its mechanical actions. I saw lights up ahead. Thinking it was our house, I ran toward it. As I came to the edge of the woods, I realized I'd somehow ended up at the Bodils' house. All but one car had left. To my irritation, the blue Volvo remained in its previous spot.

Voices grew louder as five people emerged from the house. I recognized Betty, Elin, Sam, the boy in the hoodie, and the dark-haired girl. Elin had wrapped a large, colorful blanket around herself instead of a coat as she walked her friends out. They were laughing and saying their goodbyes with hugs. I could overhear Betty and Sam lamenting the fact that they had to leave early the next day and would miss hanging out. The boy in the hoodie, Elin, and the dark-haired girl seemed to be talking over their plans for the following day, although I couldn't make out enough to understand what they were saying.

Once they'd finished, Sam, Betty, and the dark-haired girl climbed into the Volvo. The boy in the hoodie hung back and talked with Elin. One of Elin's curls had come loose. The boy in the hoodie reached over and swept it back, caressing her cheek at the same time.

I could feel the knot in my stomach twisting, and I knew I didn't want to see what happened next. I turned the shield-knot medal in my cuff to *leynask* and disappeared into the background. Then I turned on my heel and sprinted back into the woods. I ran as fast as I could until my lungs burned.

THREE

A mishap

ELIN

As I stood there in the cold wrapped in my grandmother's quilt, talking with my friends, the goosebumps returned. The feeling that someone was out in the darkness crashed over me, causing me to involuntarily shudder.

"Come on, guys. Let's let Elin go back inside. She's freezing out here." Mia had noticed my sudden movement. Sam and Betty said their goodbyes with strong hugs and climbed into the Volvo.

"I'll see you tomorrow. Do you wanna call when you wake up?" Mia said as she gave me a quick hug and headed for the front seat.

I nodded. "See you tomorrow!"

Derek hung back, letting Mia shut the door before turning toward me. A strand of my hair had gotten loose and hung softly by my face. Derek reached out his hand and gently tucked it behind my ear. His hand brushed my cheek as he pulled it back. I couldn't help thinking about Aedan and the shock that his touch had ignited. In the same instant, the goosebump sensation grew overwhelming, and I stumbled forward into Derek, breaking the moment he'd created.

"I'm so sorry." I cringed as I removed my foot from Derek's toes. "I must be really tired."

"No problem," Derek said, grimacing as he took a step backward on his assaulted foot. "I should let you go back inside and get some sleep."

"Come on, Derek! What's the hold-up? Betty and I gotta be up early," Sam said as he poked his head out the car window.

Derek shrugged and grinned at me as he walked toward the driver's side. I smiled in response and gave a little wave as I turned toward the house.

As quickly as they'd come, my goosebumps disappeared. I gave a final glance out into the darkness as I mounted the porch steps. All the lights inside the house were out. It looked like everyone else had already gone to bed. The light from the remaining coals in the fireplace gave a soft yellowish-red color to the living room.

I walked over to warm my hands in front of the embers, watching the red glow slowly die in the darkness. I thought about all the weird sensations I'd felt in the last two days. Maybe it was just all the birthday chaos and hitting what most people considered a milestone date. Adults always seemed to be talking about what a confusing time the teen years were. It especially seemed like a favorite topic when a teenager was present.

Their version implied that we didn't know our own minds, our hormones were in constant flux, and we didn't have enough "adult" information to make good decisions about our lives. I wasn't convinced about the other two items, but maybe I *was* experiencing a weird hormonal imbalance. Note to self: research hormonal imbalances: causes and symptoms.

Maybe Derek was experiencing some hormonal instability as well. I felt like he'd been glued to my body all evening. I'd known him for such a long time that this shift in his attention level was confusing. I understood what everyone was hinting at—that Derek's feelings had progressed to something more than those of childhood friends. I just wasn't sure whether that was what I felt. Of course, it would have been easy, natural. We knew everything about each other, and Derek was a good person. My parents liked him, my friends clearly knew and liked him...it should've been a simple decision.

The embers in the fire crackled, breaking further apart. I cringed when I thought about my fish-cake conversation with Aedan. What had I been thinking? I pulled my grandmother's quilt over my head. Fish cakes—really? I'd had an overwhelming urge to connect with him, to talk to him about our previous night's electric shocks, but it had all come out so wrong. He must've thought I was an idiot—that is if he'd even given it a second thought. There was something in his sea-blue eyes that sent a tingle down my spine when he looked at me. But I was sure he barely knew I existed, besides my being the neighbor's youngest daughter whose birthday he'd been forced to attend. No wonder he left early with his parents.

"Elli, what're you doing up?" I could tell it was Anders by his voice.

"Um...just warming up by the fire," I replied, feeling too sheepish to pull off the quilt.

"With a blanket on your head? Come on—time for bed. Did you have a happy birthday?" Anders asked as he steered me, blanket and all, toward the stairway.

"Sure. I guess—haven't really processed it all yet," I responded.

We'd reached the stairs. Anders pulled the quilt off my head, tousling my hair into a static frenzy.

"I've got one last surprise for you," Anders said, holding out a small brown paper bag. Looking up at him in surprise, I took the bag and opened it, to find a silver charm bracelet with one small, intricately carved bird charm attached.

"It's a Nordic bird. They say birds have special meaning and the ability to guard your soul. I thought you'd like the design. Happy birthday!"

"I love it! Thank you, Andee." I smiled and hugged him.

"Okay, okay...let's get you to bed," Anders said, clearing his throat and shifting uncomfortably in my tight embrace. With one final squeeze, I let him go.

The flight of stairs suddenly felt like a climb to a mountaintop. My face stretched into a giant yawn as I contemplated the ascent. Anders helped me get started by gently pushing me toward the first step.

"Too much partying for you, young lady," Anders said, mimicking our dad's voice. My concentration was fixed on making it up the last couple of stairs, so my only retort was a halfhearted huff.

I made it up all the stairs and, with a final shove from Anders, into my room. I collapsed on the bed, pulling the quilt on top of myself. I knew my mom would kill me, but I was too tired to change into pajamas from my dress, so I just closed my eyes and was asleep a moment later.

I woke up to the sun shining directly in my eyes. I'd forgotten to pull the blackout curtains. I shielded my eyes as I struggled into a seated position. My previous night's dress was tangled around me in a wrinkled mess.

I heard my mom making her way down the hall, chirping about how it was time to get up. It meant only one thing—she'd be entering my room in a minute, barely pausing to knock. If she saw the state of my dress, I wouldn't be going anywhere today.

I scrambled to my feet, desperately reaching for the back zipper. She was now talking about breakfast, and her voice was nearly at my door. I prayed for a miracle. With one last effort, I managed to get my hand to grasp the zipper. I pulled it down as fast as possible and reached for my robe while letting the dress fall to the ground. I slipped the robe on, becoming a giant pink-terry marshmallow. It was a hand-me-down from Maria. Using my feet, I shoved the dress under my bed. The door opened at the same time and my mom poked her head in.

"Hello, sleepyhead. Glad to see you're up. It's time for breakfast," my mom said in greeting. "Did you have a good time last night? Oh, you looked so pretty! Everybody thought your dress was just perfect." She was about to launch into reciting who "everyone" was when Maria saved me by calling out a question to her.

"Just coming, dear. Okay, Elin, I'll see you downstairs in a bit," she said while pulling me into a quick morning hug. I prayed that the marshmallow robe was blocking any telltale signs of the dress that hadn't quite made it under the bed.

"Okay, Mom. See you in a bit," I said, giving her a warm smile and no argument...at which suspicion flashed across her face.

Luckily, Maria called out again for her to hurry, and I was left in peace to close the door. I breathed a sigh of relief as I grabbed the dress and stuffed it into my hamper, a problem for another day.

My hair was a tangled mess from sleeping with bobby pins and hair spray. A shower and hairbrush became the next orders of business.

After a tasty Sunday family breakfast, my stomach protested at the thought of exercise as I climbed on top of my bike. Having coordinated with Mia, my plan was to meet her at the bottom of Witner Hill. We'd hike to the large granite opening where we could gaze at the sea while picnicking. I had a good half-hour bike ride ahead of me, even with taking the shortcut between Auor's two mountains, Aldinn and Hamar. I adjusted my backpack and zipped my windbreaker as the cold breeze reminded me that autumn had indeed arrived.

Given that many of the roads on the island were dirt, most people used mountain bikes to navigate the potholes and uneven gravel. Derek had insisted on adding a few extra upgrades to my hand-me-down bike. It now had a full suspension system and disc brakes that made my ride more comfortable and safer, but heavier.

The air was crisp and fresh. I breathed in deeply as my body loosened up into its mechanical motion. Before long, I was pedaling down the valley road between the two mountains. I looked up to see a white dusting on Mount Aldinn's shady side. The snow must've fallen overnight, and the mountain air was now cold enough where the white coating was sticking to the ground even during the day.

I'd just rounded the sharp corner on the Witner Hill Road when I heard a loud roar and skidding behind me. All I had time for was a quick turn of my head to see a large object hurtling towards me. Somehow, I managed to direct my bike off the road into the ditch beside the woods to avoid the impact.

Thanks to Derek's upgrades I was able to maneuver the bike to a decent stop before falling over. I lay stunned on top of the moss-covered embankment, trying to assess which part of my body hurt the most. After convincing myself that nothing felt broken, I tried to lift the bike off my left leg.

A shadow fell across my face. I looked up to where a few moments earlier had been only sun and blue sky. A figure in a black motorcycle helmet stood looking down at me.

"Wow, I'm so sorry. I did not mean to drive you off the road," the figure said, scrambling down the embankment. "My bike skidded rounding the corner."

The voice was definitely male, I thought to myself as I continued my efforts to raise my bike off my leg. It was a difficult angle, and I was making little progress. The figure was now beside me, removing his motorcycle helmet.

I'd been correct, for now in front of me stood a boy roughly my age, with dark olive skin, sandy hair, and pale-green eyes. His features were delicate yet masculine, and charming in a slightly too-handsome way. He lifted the bike off my leg as if it weighed nothing and knelt down, removing his gloves. He felt my leg with his hands, gently moving them up as he squeezed. I winced as he made it to my knee, where my torn pants exposed a sizable gash from the bike pedal.

"Nothing feels broken here, but that gash on your leg looks bad. Anything else hurt?" he asked, staring at me with concern.

My usual handsome-guy shyness took root as I searched for words. "Ummm...no... umm...nothing feels broken," I managed to stammer out.

"Good. I'm going to lift you up now and get you out of this ditch," the motorcycle boy said as he rocked back onto his feet.

He slid his hands under my knees and around the small of my back, hoisting me into his arms. He moved so quickly and seemed to lift me with so little effort that I was too stunned to protest. He carried me back up to the main road and still had me in his arms when a familiar blue Volvo appeared from around the corner.

I can only imagine the picture we painted for Mia and Derek... the motorcycle boy cradling a disheveled me in his arms. He set me down and reached into his saddlebag. He pulled out a red bandana, which he then started to methodically wrap around my injured knee.

The Volvo came to a quick stop. Both Mia and Derek jumped out of the car. "Elli, are you okay?" Mia asked, hurrying over to where the motorcycle boy knelt, attending to my knee. He rose, his hand grazing mine as he stood. A now-familiar tingle of electricity passed between us. Our eyes met and a flash of surprise seemed to ignite in his eyes.

"I'm fine, Mia. Just a few bumps and bruises," I said as Mia wrapped her arms around me for a hug.

As I explained to Mia and Derek what had occurred, the

motorcycle boy scrambled down the embankment to retrieve my bike, his gloves, and his helmet. When he returned, he joined Derek and Mia in their huddle around me.

"Again, I'm so sorry for driving you off the road. I am new here and completely misjudged the turn," the motorcycle boy said, looking sincere. "On the positive side, your bike seems to have survived the experience, but if anything is broken, please let me know." He rolled the bike towards me.

Derek stopped the motion of the bike with one hand while the other protectively encircled my back and said, "Thanks. We'll take it from here."

Mia, being more polite and quick on her feet, said, "It's a dangerous curve. Most accidents that happen on the island happen right here. I'm just happy everyone's okay. I'm Mirai Arya, Mia for short, by the way. This is Elin Bodil and Derek Eiker." She gestured to each of us respectively.

"It is nice to meet you all. I'm Tristan Rees," the motorcycle boy answered back, his mouth curving into an easy smile.

Derek, clearly unhappy, said, "Well, we should probably get Elin to Doctor McCaw to get checked out."

"I'm fine, Derek—nothing's broken," I protested, embarrassed by the signs of possessiveness that Derek was exhibiting. "Thanks for your help in getting back up the hill, Tristan." I smiled and our eyes met again. The pale greenness seemed to search my amber for something more.

Once again Mia came to my rescue. "Where can we reach you? I mean, if there's anything wrong with the bike." She subtly probed for more information.

"I'm staying with my Aunt Adis on Sparrowhawk Lane," Tristan responded.

"Ms. Haugen, the librarian, lives on that street. Is she your aunt?" Mia asked.

"Yes, that's right. Well, you should probably get Elin to that doctor. Derek is right. She should get checked out—especially that knee," Tristan said. "I'm sure I will see you around." His eyes pierced mine as he completed his sentence.

I'd barely been able to put three sentences together to address him, yet I felt like he meant something more with his last statement. I was probably imagining things. He was right. I needed to get checked out.

Derek guided me towards his car with one hand while steering my bike with the other. As I walked I turned my head to watch Tristan climb back onto his motorcycle. Before he flipped the visor on his helmet down, he turned his head towards me and flashed a smile. I felt my insides squeeze.

FOUR

The Hunter

TRISTAN

I could not believe it. Had I found one? Had all my training actually paid off? What a place to find one—a small island in the middle of nowhere.

My growing excitement was quickly replacing the lingering annoyance of being forced into a skid. Her rare potential outweighed her infraction of clumsily being in my way. Otherwise, I would have never lost control of my motorcycle.

I already missed the orderliness of Falinvik, the home city of the *Stór-menni*, but this was becoming a real opportunity, not just another hunting mission. I needed to make sure before I could contact the Clan Council. Dormant Descendants were very rare, and the Clan Council had plans for them. False reports were not tolerated.

My motorcycle roared as I accelerated into a turn. I needed to get to Aunt Adis's as quickly as possible. I would have to submit my initial report to the Clan Council without mentioning the possibility. But if it was true and I could bring them a Dormant Descendant on my own, then my independent, efficient results would be like gold.

Sparrowhawk Lane was now visible. The lane was a small turnoff from the Witner Hill Road, with only a few homes at great distances apart. Aunt Adis's was the last one on the right. It was a typical island home—painted red, with an A-line roof, a generous front mudroom, a mosquito-proofed porch that wrapped around the side and back, and plenty of windows.

I pulled into the large car shed on the side of the house. My 1950 BSA Gold Star motorcycle was one of my prized possessions, so storing it in the proper way was of extreme importance. I could still hear my mentor repeating to me, "Take care of your things and they will take care of you."

Once I had the kickstand in place, I carefully inspected the motorcycle for any damage from the afternoon's skidding incident. A few scratches were apparent, but nothing that a few hours of buffing would not clear. I placed the tri-max polyester all-season cover on the bike, making sure that everything was perfectly aligned.

I closed the shed doors, which rolled easily in their well-oiled grooves. I walked up the path towards the house between well-manicured landscaping. There was no squeak when I opened the screen door to the back porch. Aunt Adis's shoes were precisely lined up, with matching pairs next to each other. All were perfectly clean and polished—even her gardening shoes did not show a speck of mud. I used the stationary shoe brush next to the door to wipe down my motorcycle boots before pulling them off.

I had not seen Aunt Adis since the Clan Gathering three years earlier. She was my mother's sister and undeniably Norse. My mother's family descended from the Nordri Clan, whereas my father's heritage originated from the extinct Sudri Clan. It was his Egyptian roots that I had to thank for my complexion and the long stares I elicited, especially outside of Falinvik in *Smá-menn* society. Everything else I was, I had earned. After all, I had not lived with my parents since I was a toddler.

My aunt was a well-respected advisor to the Clan Council on all historical items and exhibited their most prized qualities—mastery, control, self-sufficiency, and productivity. I entered her house through the back door, which brought me into her spotless kitchen. I could hear my mentor's words echoing in my mind: "Cleanliness and orderliness are the marks of true self-sufficiency."

I continued through to the hallway and then towards the front entrance. I came to the doorway of my aunt's office and saw her sitting at her desk. She had a small, wiry frame that was a deceptive façade to the true nature of her power. She looked up from her work when I cleared my throat to make my presence known.

She gave a quick nod. "Tristan, you have arrived. Upstairs, first door on the left. You will find your bags in the correct room."

And then she shifted her steely eyes back to the work in front of her. I headed for the stairs without saying a word. My aunt was a very productive person and distractions were not looked kindly upon. The Clan Council had often cited her as an ideal society member.

I reached the top of the stairs and approached the first door on the left. Aunt Adis was used to hosting the occasional Hunter as they tracked fugitives, so the room had little personality but did contain the required items—a bed, desk, chair, lamp, and bureau. My luggage sat neatly in the corner by the desk, waiting to be unpacked. I grabbed the top bag and easily swung it onto the bed. Being a Hunter required you to be in top shape. Our enhanced abilities were not enough to capture a desperate fugitive who was bent on escaping—especially when we did not know what their personal ability was.

This was my first solo hunt. I had been ordered to track a married pair of fugitives. They had proven to be difficult to find, particularly since little was known about their family besides the pair themselves. They had refused to register their children with the Clan Council as was expected of every Clan member. The registration was required so that each child could be enrolled in the mentorship program and tracked through the process of becoming a productive society member.

My previous trips had been with my mentor Henric, who had provided clear guidance on numerous subjects, including tracking. Now my first trip on my own was already rapidly changing into something much more complicated and potentially dangerous. The value of finding a Dormant far outweighed the potential capture of a pair of fugitives. Their time would come, but right now I needed to concentrate on how I would get proof that Elin was an undiscovered Dormant Descendant.

FIVE

Ash Park

ELIN

I limped out of Doctor McCaw's office with the help of Mia and Derek. The good news was that the wound was superficial, but the bad news was that it still required a few stitches.

"So much for our hike to Witner Hill," I mumbled, frowning.

"Doesn't mean we can't still make a day of it," Mia said. "In fact, now that we're in town, we're closer to Ash Park than Witner Hill. We could picnic by the ash tree and Torne Stream. We already have sandwiches and drinks. It'd be a shame to waste them."

"It sounds like a good plan...except, the ash tree isn't that close to the parking lot. I'm not sure I can do the walk with these stitches," I replied, frowning.

"That's no problem. I'll carry you," Derek offered.

Sensing my increasing hesitation, Mia piped up, "We can both help you. It'll be fun...a five-legged race of sorts!"

Picnicking did sound like fun. It had been a strange morning—no, a strange couple of days. Spending the rest of the day with my oldest friends would be the perfect remedy.

"Okay, let's do it. Hope you guys know what you're in for!" I said, half-joking.

"It'll be fine, Elli. Derek's been working out...and I'm used to carrying your weight around," Mia teased. My accident-proneness had often left Mia lugging my bags around the school while I hobbled on crutches.

"I've gotta work out, given how injury-prone my friends are," Derek said, smirking. Our old camaraderie was coming back. It felt good—normal.

The conversation kept the same lighthearted tone and teasing all the way to the great ash tree. The walk over was a bit painful with the fresh stitches pulling at the skin around the gash, but they held. I groaned in relief as I finally sat down in the grass in the shade of the tree and stretched out my leg. A nice, cool radiance emanated from the gurgling stream as the water rushed over the stones, making its way from the mountains to the sea.

"I wonder how old this ash tree is?" I pondered as I leaned back on my arms, tilting my head to admire the tree's girth and its multitude of branches.

"Hundreds of years—I think. I read something like that on the informational signpost by the parking lot," Derek answered as he started to unfurled our sandwiches and lemonade/ice teas from Mia's backpack.

"Yeah, some people believe it's actually thousands of years old, which is highly unlikely since ash trees don't live that long. But the same people who do believe that also think the tree has mystical powers," Mia said as she hunted for her veggie sandwich among Derek's and mine.

"What do you mean, 'mystical powers'? Like magic?" I asked.

"Well, it's not really clear from what I've read and heard. 'Magic' and 'mystical' have slightly different meanings. It's a thin line, but magic means generally a more active form of energy, whereas mystical power can exist within an object without actually having to be active. Does that make sense?" Mia responded. I nodded. She'd always been a voracious reader of anything to do with legends and magic.

"Well... I know one thing that does seem to have magical powers... and that's your car. I mean, it's the only rational explanation to why it behaves so strangely whenever you're behind the wheel," Derek teased.

Mia crumpled up her napkin and threw it at him in response. For all of Mia's good sense and logic, somehow her driving skills left something to be desired. It was a well-established fact and one that we all shared in teasing her about.

The rest of our picnic was spent laughing and talking about shared memories, inside jokes, and secrets of growing up together. We lamented not having Betty and Sam there since they were also an integral part of our little pack.

Derek had looked over at me when we were speaking of Betty and Sam's growing relationship. "You know...they've spent almost the entire summer together. And now they'll be able to start at Breckhaven together."

"Yeah, they're really lucky," Mia said with a dreamy look. "I wish I could find *my* person so easily."

"Yeah, they're a good match," I said, avoiding Derek's gaze. "I just hope it lasts... for all our sakes."

A slightly awkward pause hung in the air. Mia broke the silence. "So, guys...I think we may need to pack it in. Those storm clouds are growing by the second. We'll be lucky to make it to the car dry at this rate."

I glanced up at the menacing clouds. "Oh, wow...you're right. They do look bad."

Mia was in the process of stuffing the remnants of our lunch into her backpack as the first droplets of water hit the ground. Derek jumped to his feet and rushed to help me stand up. "Elli, no time for fussing," Derek said as he picked me up in his arms, ignoring the beginnings of my protest.

Mia was already starting down the path, motioning for us to hurry as the skies opened and the rain came pouring down in what seemed like buckets. I reluctantly wrapped my arms around Derek's neck as he hurried into the woods after Mia. I tried to maintain some sort of distance between Derek's body and mine, but it was impossible with the rain pelting us and making the ground slippery. I gave in and tucked my head into his shoulder, trying to avoid the wind that was now causing the rain to come in sideways.

We finally made it to the Volvo in the parking lot. Mia was throwing the backpack into the trunk of the car and hurrying to the driver's side to unlock the rest of the car doors. Derek set me down by the back-seat door. Our eyes met for a moment as he steadied me on my feet.

He was so close to me. He reached towards my face to push a wet bundle of hair out of my eyes. I instinctively pulled back. I grimaced internally and dropped my gaze. I'd dodged one awkward moment by creating another.

Derek busied himself with opening the door as the rain and wind whipped at us furiously. He helped me inside without saying a word. He then quickly got into the passenger seat, shaking the water from his jacket. Mia was sitting in the driver's seat. They exchanged looks, realizing the problem.

"No way! You're not driving in this. Chinese fire drill—go!" Derek said as he pushed the door open.

Mia scrambled out her side. As they were rounding the car, lightning flashed across the sky, momentarily lighting the parking lot. I squinted. I could've sworn I saw someone standing at the edge of the parking lot staring at us, but I couldn't be sure. A cold shiver ran up my spine.

Another crack of lightning and thunder rumbled. Mia and

Derek, now in the correct seats, quickly shut the doors. My eyes were still searching the edge of the parking lot, but I could see no one.

The three of us looked at each other and burst out laughing. We were drenched to the bone—not a dry article of clothing between us. Our hair was plastered to our faces. We looked like we'd taken a swim in the stream instead of a picnic beside it.

"Where'd that come from? I forgot how fickle island weather can be," Derek said as he started the engine. Mia reached over and turned the dial on the car heater up to combat the teeth-chattering that was settling in amongst us. "Where to, ladies?"

"Not sure I'm fit for anything but home and a hot shower," Mia said. "And, Derek, we probably need to figure out if we can get to the mainland tonight with the weather. School starts tomorrow." A little bit of sadness crept into my heart as I remembered that I'd be starting my junior year without my closest friends.

"Right. Let's drop Elli off first, and then we can figure out the ferry at your house," Derek answered, putting the car in gear and heading for the main road. "Elli, can you hand me that towel in the back seat? The water from my hair keeps dripping in my eyes."

"Sure," I replied as I searched for the towel in the twilight. Finally locating it, I extended my hand with the towel towards the driver's seat. "Here."

"Thanks," replied Derek.

He kept his eyes on the road since it was nearly impossible to see between the rapid movement of the windshield wipers and the heavy rain pelting the glass. As a result, he first ended up grabbing my hand before finding the towel. Out of instinct, I braced for the electric shock...that never came. I guess subconsciously I'd assumed that every guy who now touched my hand would give me a jolt of electricity. But Derek hadn't. Why?

Now that I was thinking about it, plenty of boys and men had shaken my hand during my birthday party—even Dr. McCaw, today. Nothing. The only two instances I could think of where the shock had been present were with Aedan Grady and Tristan Rees.

~

"Elin! What happened? You're soaked and limping," my mom exclaimed as Mia and Derek helped me through the front door.

"Mom, I'm fine. Just had a bit of a biking accident, but Dr. McCaw has me all patched up," I replied, hoping my nonchalance would help diminish whatever concerns my mom felt.

"Elli got run off the road by this new kid on a motorcycle," Derek expanded. He wasn't helping.

"What! You got run off the road?" My mom looked truly shocked.

"It was an accident, really," I insisted, throwing Derek a dirty look.

Mia tried to assist. "She has a couple of stitches in her knee, but otherwise Dr. McCaw said she's fine. All's well that ends well, right, Mrs. Bodil?"

"What do you mean, stitches! I can't believe that Dr. McCaw didn't call me. I'll have to have a talk with him," my mom said. "Well, you two had better help her towards the sofa. I'll get some towels for you so you can dry off, and some fresh clothes for Elin." My mom gave me a careful hug and hurried towards the laundry room, shaking her head.

"Crisis averted?" Derek asked.

"I doubt it. I've got a feeling that this may lead to some privileges being revoked," I responded frowning.

In hindsight, I probably should've stopped and called my mom. But I'd gotten caught up in all the events and still trying to enjoy the remaining time with my friends.

My mom returned with some towels for all three of us. "Here

you all are. Elin, on second thought, you'll be better off getting into a hot shower right away. You are soaked through. Say goodbye to Mia and Derek. I'm sure they need to get back home. Doesn't school start tomorrow for you as well?" my mom asked as she handed out the towels to each one of us.

"Thanks, Mrs. Bodil. Yes, school starts tomorrow for us as well. Although I'm not sure how Derek and I will get there with this crazy storm," Mia said as she toweled herself off.

"Well, we better get going," Derek said as he gave a final toweling to his hair and arms. "It'll take a while to get home in this storm."

Mia turned to me and gave me a good squeeze. "I'll talk to you soon, Elli. I still can't believe that we'll be starting at separate schools tomorrow. I'll miss you."

"I know—it'll be really weird, not having you guys there. Plus, I'll have to face Mr. Shard for math by myself...and without Mia's wizardry with numbers. I don't know how I'm gonna survive it all. I'll really miss you guys." I sulked at the prospect of school without my friends.

"I'll miss you as well, Elli. Will you come out to Breckhaven to visit?" Derek asked.

"Yeah, of course," I replied, shrugging off the comment as obvious.

Mia and Derek smiled, and both encircled me with their arms for a big group hug. There were a few more assurances of quid pro quo visits and phone calls. Then Mia and Derek ran back out to the Volvo in the storm.

As the evening progressed and the full story came out, my mom was not happy with me. It was bad enough that I'd shown up soaked to the bone, but to have been run off the road, gotten stitches in my knee, gone for a picnic, and not called her, was very thin ice on the road to getting grounded. To layer on top, school was starting the following day. She was worried about how I'd hobble through the day now that Mia wouldn't be there to help me. I was putting on a brave face, but I was nervous about my friends not being there as well. My banged-up knee made the situation even worse. I could already see the nightmare my first day would be. I tucked myself into bed early, hoping the next day wouldn't be as bad as I thought.

SIX

First day of school

AEDAN

It was going to be my fourth first day at a new school this year. Edvin was dropping me off since the family was sharing two cars. They all had more errands and unpacking to do during the day. He hadn't hesitated to express his annoyance at having to get up early to drop me off, but it was either that or be left carless for the rest of the day. Not that there were too many places to go on the island.

"So, have a good day, sonny. Give us a kiss now!" Edvin teased as he puckered his mouth into a kissy face. I punched him in the arm instead. Edvin loved to rub in the fact that I still needed to attend school. "Hey, numskull, don't forget the family discussion—stay away from Elin."

"Yeah, whatever," I said as I climbed out of the car. We'd had one of our famous family convenings to decide how to handle the Elin/Dormant situation. My parents had decided that at this point, our life was already way too complicated and dangerous to involve a third party. We wouldn't be able to protect her or have her run with us when the time came. It was best for her to stay oblivious to her gifts.

I wasn't sure if I agreed with them. Was it really in her best interest and safety to be left fending for herself? What if she could help us? We knew Dormants were special—even if the details were a bit murky. But my arguments had fallen on deaf ears. Edvin and Claire had agreed with my parents that right now was not the time to start exploring a new phenomenon that we knew nothing about. We needed to stay as inconspicuous and hidden as possible. Majority ruled.

I grabbed my bag from the back seat of the Audi and closed the door, reminding Edvin that I'd need a lift home after school. He mumbled an acknowledgment and, as soon as the door closed, drove off.

I put my earbuds in my ears and pressed "shuffle" on my iPod. The opening notes to "Norwegian Wood" by the Beatles immediately began strumming through the earbuds. I turned to face the brick building. It wasn't as large as some of the schools I had attended, but it was more imposing than I'd expected. I knew the layout from the architectural drawings my father had acquired and on which he'd marked all the potential exits with red circles. "Safety first" was his motto.

The school had rectangular wings that led to a central tower structure with a large clock. It was hard to see with the autumn sun gleaming from behind the tower, but the black hands of the clock seemed to indicate the correct time of a few minutes before eight.

I saw Elin climbing out from her father's white Volvo SUV on the other side of the drop-off zone. She seemed to be moving a little more slowly than normal and with a slight limp. She waved her father off and started heading across the grass towards the front doors. She hesitated a little when she encountered a group of girls standing between her and the building, but then she squared her shoulders, adjusted her book bag, and moved forward. When she got closer to the group of girls, one of them addressed her.

I was too far away to hear what was being said, but I could tell Elin seemed uncomfortable. I was about to make my way to her when a roar seemed to catch everyone's attention. A motorcycle and its driver had just entered the school parking lot. The display drew the attention of the girls who had been speaking moments before to Elin. They seemed to be enthralled as the motorcycle driver took off his helmet, revealing himself as a good-looking boy that I judged to be about a year older than me. After making final adjustments and securing his helmet, he headed toward the group of delighted girls.

Elin had taken the opportunity to start making slow progress towards the front doors. I started to head that way myself. The motorcycle guy had now made it to his eagerly awaiting fans, but instead of stopping, he pushed past them, almost as if not seeing them. He quickened his pace until he reached Elin, at which point he greeted her as if he knew her. She smiled at him and chatted back. He pointed at her knee, asking her something. She shook her head and laughed a little, seeming to brush off the comment. He reached for her book bag, clearly insisting on carrying it for her. All of this was carefully being scrutinized with shocked faces by the group of girls he'd ignored.

The bell rang, which snapped everyone out of their stupor and conversations. The remaining students headed for the front doors. In the shuffle, I lost sight of Elin and the motorcycle guy.

Being a new student, I needed to head to the registrar's office to get my class schedule. I followed the arrow for "Registrar Office," which pointed left toward the main entrance. The ins and outs of being a new student were becoming second nature to me. I'd already lost count of how many schools I'd gone to over the last twelve years. With all the uprooting, my parents had taken to homeschooling us on top of whatever school we attended to make sure we didn't fall behind. This meant that most of the time I was ahead of whatever curriculum my new class was working through. I reached the registrar's office, took out my earbuds, and went in.

"Hi. I'm Aedan Grady and I'm new. I think you have a class schedule for me," I said to the woman sitting behind the tall counter that separated the administrators from the students.

The woman let her glasses slide to the edge of her nose as she inspected my face and said, "Aedan Grady—junior, right? You were supposed to be here fifteen minutes before school started. Now you'll be late for your first class." She paused for disapproving dramatic effect and then continued. "I think Marion has your file. Wait here."

She removed her glasses, slid off her stool, and walked through a back door. I stood there, in no hurry to start another new class.

I hadn't waited for too long when the door behind me opened and in walked the motorcycle guy.

"Hey—is this the registrar's office?" the boy asked.

"Yup. She just stepped out but should be back soon," I answered.

"Great." He stood behind me in line, not bothering to say anything further to break the silence.

After several minutes, to cut the awkwardness, I said, "I'm Aedan. Just starting here—you new as well?"

"Tristan. And yeah, I'm new," he responded, giving the impression that talking to me was boring him.

I let the silence descend again. Clearly, this guy had some issues.

The woman with the glasses reentered the office. "Here it is. Aedan Grady—your first class is history with Mr. Hutchinson." She looked up from the paper and handed it to me. She seemed surprised when she saw Tristan standing behind me. "Who are you?"

"Tristan Rees—transfer student. My old school should have sent my records," Tristan responded.

"No, we had only one new student starting today and that was Mr. Grady there. Mr. Grady, you can move along now to class," she said as she noticed my curiosity and my attempt to delay exiting.

The last thing I heard as I left the office was Tristan trying his best to charm the woman behind the desk with a story of lost paperwork and about having to move here on short notice right before his senior year. I glanced down at the paper I'd been handed. Room 162, Mr. Hutchinson, History. That was the first class listed on my schedule. Now I just needed to figure out where the classroom was. If only I'd paid more attention to the room numbers in the building's blueprints when I'd memorized the exit locations.

"You lost?"

I glanced up to see a boy about my age, dressed in an oversized pair of jeans, a hooded jacket, and a baseball cap, slightly askew. What hair could be seen sticking out from its edges had the appearance of its owner having just rolled out of bed.

"Lost for words or just generally lost?" he continued, as my appraisal of him had caused an unnatural pause.

"Um, no. Just new—Do you know where room 162 is?"

"Well, it's my lucky day," he said with a widening grin. "I'm headed there as well. Follow me."

Without further comment, we proceeded down the white hall with lockers and doors on either side. At the T-intersection, we turned right, and the boy confidently opened the first door on the right.

"Mr. Larson, how kind of you to finally join us," the adult standing at the whiteboard remarked as we entered the room.

"Ahh...Mr. Hutchinson, it's not my fault. The new kid took longer to get his paperwork at the registrar," the boy answered.

"And when did you join the Welcoming Committee, Joel?" Mr. Hutchinson responded.

"Um, today...community service for tardiness," Joel replied without hesitation. A few snickers escaped the classroom audience.

"Well, then please introduce us to our new classmate," Mr. Hutchinson said as he motioned for me to enter the room more fully. I could see Joel swallowing uncomfortably as he realized that we'd never actually exchanged names.

"Aedan. Aedan Grady," I said as I approached Mr. Hutchinson to give him my class schedule for sign-off. I heard Joel sigh with relief behind me.

"Well, Mr. Grady, welcome to world history. Joel, I suggest you take your seat before I change my mind about your tardy slip. You can save the rest of your theatrics for drama class," Mr. Hutchinson said with a raised eyebrow. He signed my class schedule and handed it back to me. "Aedan, please find any open seat. We'll get you sorted with the reading materials later. Perhaps you can share with someone in the meanwhile."

I turned to search for an empty seat, facing the classroom for the first time. There in the front row closest to the door sat Elin. Her hair was pulled back into a ponytail with a few strands having already escaped to frame her face. Her amber eyes looked up at me for a moment as I scanned the room for an empty seat. The only desk that seemed vacant was in the opposite corner of the room, second to the last row, next to Joel. He grinned at me as I approached the desk.

"Hi, comrade," he said, smirking, as I slid into the seat next to him. "Here, I'll share my text. Oh, and thanks for the save! One more tardy slip and the principal will want me to visit again."

"No problem. I get it," I replied.

"Boys, do you have something you want to share with the rest of the class, or do you mind if I finally get started on the lesson?" Mr. Hutchinson asked, interrupting our dialogue. Joel and I exchanged a glance but neither of us spoke. "Good. I'm glad you understand a rhetorical question. Please turn to page 107, Chapter 3, 'The History of Island Formation.'"

The rest of the class session proceeded without incident. Every once in a while, I couldn't help but steal a glance at the back of Elin's head, wondering about what I'd seen that morning in the school parking lot with Tristan. How did she know him and why was she limping?

"You still boring a hole in her skull, or do you think you can turn the page?" Joel asked as Mr. Hutchinson referenced a chart on the next page.

"Um...what? Oh, yeah, sure," I mumbled, lifting my hand, which had been resting on the book, and flipping the page.

"I don't think that's how it works," Joel continued with a smirk. "If you want her to notice you, that is. You might actually have to say something. Staring her down will get you only so far."

"Very funny. And that's not what I'm doing."

"I beg to differ. If you had Superman's abilities, she'd now be feeling a breeze through her skull. You've been staring at her nonstop through the entire class," Joel said. Not having a ready retort, I simply mocked him with a silent, sarcastic laugh.

"It's not like that," I said. "I know her from before."

I was saved from having to explain any more by Mr. Hutchinson. He was asking us to find partners for a semester-long research project that would be a significant portion of our final grade for the class. There was a flurry of discussion amongst the other students as they paired up with their usual partners. I looked at Joel expectantly.

"Sorry, comrade. I already have my ace in the hole for this project," he said, indicating a bookish-looking girl with a heavy pair of glasses.

"Does everyone have a partner?" Mr. Hutchinson asked. I slowly raised my hand to indicate that I didn't. Two other students raised their hands—a petite-looking boy in the teacher's-pet seat and Elin. "Oh, I see. Well, in this case, Elin, why don't you partner with Aedan. Jeffrey and I'll sort something out as an individual study project. Everyone, please move closer to your partner and start discussing project ideas."

I was stunned. This was not supposed to happen. I had a clear directive from my parents to try to avoid Elin. How was I supposed to do that if I was partnering with her on a semester-long research project? A small flutter went through me as Elin approached my desk.

"Hi," she said.

"Ah...hi."

"So, any ideas?" she asked. I was still in my head, trying to figure out a solution to my current predicament.

"Ah, none," I blurted, thinking about my situation. "I mean, I'm not sure. Do you have any topics in mind?" I tried to recover my bearings. I'd just switch partners later.

"Well, I was thinking about religion and war. There's a lot of material to work with, given all the wars through the centuries," she answered, looking at me expectantly.

"Sure, that sounds good," I said. At that moment the class bell rang. "Why don't we get together later to figure it out? Do you have a cell number? I can text you."

"Okay, sure. Here's my number." She wrote her number on a scrap of paper torn from her notebook. "Talk later, then."

"Great, thanks. Yeah, talk later," I said, taking the piece of paper that she offered.

SEVEN

Lunch

ELIN

W here and, more importantly, with whom was I going to eat? All my usual friends were no longer there. I'd known lunch would be the really uncomfortable part of the day. At least I'd packed my own food, so there was no awkward lunch line to endure.

I glanced around the crowded cafeteria for an empty table. The eating area was organized into two rows of variously sized rectangular tables, with a few odd smaller tables by the large windows that looked into an outdoor courtyard.

A social hierarchy existed at the tables in the main rows. There was the "mean girl" table, with Candice holding court over her besties Gretchen and Madison and some younger social butterflies who were drawn to the flame. Then there was the jock table, which was overflowing with hockey players ogling the short skirts and low-cut tops at the table next to them. The alternative indie group was on the other side of the cafeteria along with the nerds and potheads, which was an interesting dichotomy of intelligence and spaciness.

Normally, I'd have headed outdoors to find a spot under a tree to avoid the social exclusion that confronted me in the absences of Mia, Derek, Betty, and Sam, but the weather had turned to a drizzling gray.

As I stood there pondering my limited options, a voice behind me said, "Hi, Elin! Will you rescue a new student from eating alone? There is an empty table by the window."

I turned to find Tristan looking expectantly at me. "Um...sure," I replied, surprised by the turn of events.

Apparently, I was not the only one. The jaws at the mean-girl table nearly fell to the floor as Tristan and I walked by, heading to the table.

"Oh, Tristan! You can eat with us," Candice cooed in her most siren-like voice.

"I'm good. Thanks, though," Tristan replied, smiling, as he kept walking.

Candice's face puckered at the response, reminding me of my sister's face when she ate sour lemon candies. The rest of her minions looked shocked at their queen's rejection. Candice quickly recovered, brushing off the snub and saying something that made the rest of the table giggle and snicker.

"So, Elin, how is your leg doing? I really do feel bad about the other day. Sorry again for knocking you down," Tristan said, looking up at me as I gingerly slid into the seat opposite him.

"It's definitely improving, and you don't have to keep apologizing. It was clearly an accident," I responded. He'd already apologized once this morning in the school parking lot.

"Well, nobody deserves stitches from a first meeting, so I definitely owe you one," he said.

"Really. It's fine. The doc said I get the stitches out next week, so I'll be as good as new in no time."

"Oh, I'm so glad to hear that! So, you will be all recovered in time for the school dance next month," Tristan said as more of a confirmation than a question.

"Yeah, but I still probably won't go. It's not really my thing," I said, crinkling my nose.

The idea of facing the Harvest Dance without my trusted friends was not a pleasing thought. Getting through the next year of lunches and other awkward moments at school was going to be punishment enough. I silently prayed for the prompt return of my friends.

"Why not?" Tristan asked.

"Well, all of my closest friends started school on the mainland this year so...I'm...um, trying to find my bearings again," I explained, trying not to sound like a complete loser after being put on the spot.

"Got it. Well, it sounds like we are in the same boat, then... establishing new friendships. Why don't we go to the dance together?" Tristan replied.

I nearly choked on my sandwich. Had he just asked me to the dance? Surely he was just teasing me—but the earnest look on his face left little doubt. The hot new senior guy in school had just asked me to the Harvest Dance. Before I could reply, Candice swooped in, having grown tired of being ignored.

"Hi, Tristan! What are you guys talking about so intently?" Candice asked. "I mean, you're missing out on the funniest story that Zack was just telling us..."

She prattled on, sitting kitty-corner on the table with her back facing me and gazing at Tristan. Tristan kept trying to peek around Candice to see me, but Candice was determined to command his full attention. After a few moments, she called for reinforcements from her troops. The rest of lunch became an uncomfortable squeeze as more people joined our small table.

I quickly finished my sandwich and placed my hand on the table to support myself into a standing position. Tristan reached across the table, placing his fingers on top of my hand. A small electric current quickly established itself between our hands.

"Think about what I said, Elin," he managed to say before being swallowed up by the adoring crowd again.

I left the table, happy to escape the crush of human beings, and headed to the trash cans to throw out the leftovers of my lunch. I didn't know what to make of the whole situation—the dance, Tristan, and the persistent electricity that seemed to be following me around recently.

I noticed Aedan sitting with Joel Larson at the alternative-indie table. He seemed to sense my presence as I came closer and looked up. He smiled. I gave a small hand-wave and smiled back. It had certainly been a surprising day.

EIGHT

An ancient book

TRISTAN

E nrolling in high school was not a task that I had envisioned or wanted as part of my mission. But I hadn't been able to think of a better way to get close to Elin. At least it was already paying off. I was starting to establish a relationship with her. Granted, it was still early, but the whole thing was easier without her friends around—especially that boy in the hoodie. His protective stance at the biking incident, and then how he carried her, running through the thunderstorm in the parking lot...It was definitely fortuitous timing.

I had realized that the only way to prove to the Clan Council that Elin was a Dormant was by getting her to do the awakening ritual. As far as I understood, the process was complicated and required guidance. I needed to access my aunt's library—and to win Elin's trust.

The teacher's prolonged silence and intent stare brought me out of my contemplation.

"Mr. Rees, do you have an answer?" she asked.

I quickly glanced at the textbooks around me, trying to

determine the subject at hand. The teacher walked back to the whiteboard and pointed to an algebraic equation. In Clan society, these subjects were taught to students at a much earlier age, since time was not wasted on play or other unproductive activities. Thus, the equation presented little challenge to me. I promptly solved it. The teacher seemed slightly surprised but continued the lesson and her attempt to find another, more unprepared student.

Candice, who was seated beside me, leaned over, suggestively tilting her head to expose her neckline. "Tristan, you're so good at algebra. Maybe you can help me with my homework later?"

The last thing I needed right now was to be distracted by a *Smá-menn* girl. She provided no opportunity for productive advancement—she was just a regular girl. In fact, she was hoping I would expend my own time teaching her. Clan rules were very clear on what was considered a productive use of time. *Smá-menns* did not figure into the equation.

However, my mentor Henric had always reminded me about the importance of blending into *Smá-menn* society during a hunt. *"Commingling is the gift of camouflage."* While efficiency was a core Clan edict, a broken perception could hinder the main mission, and exposure must be avoided at all costs. *Smá-menns* were not like us and could not be relied upon to understand our ways.

"Sure, but not today," I said, smiling back at her.

Candice looked slightly taken aback. She was not used to being deflected. She moved a little closer. "Why not?"

"I have to help my aunt with a few things after school," I replied, having no idea where my aunt was or if she needed help.

"Oh...I see. Well, another day then," Candice said. She straightened back up to refocus on the teacher's lecture.

I glanced at my watch. Five more minutes until the school day ended. I thought of all the different classes and subjects I had attended that day. The workload would be bothersome. However, I couldn't afford to fail out of the school. I would need a plan...perhaps Candice could be helpful after all.

"How is Wednesday after school for you?" I asked. Candice turned to me with a wide smile of satisfaction.

"Perfect," she answered.

I could already hear the boasting Candice planned to discharge on her followers later. *Smá-menns* were so predictable. But now, at least, appeasing her attentions would serve a purpose. The school bell rang its final dismissal. I smiled at Candice, said goodbye, and hurried out of the classroom.

I walked out of the school entrance towards my motorcycle. There on the side walkway stood Elin, engaged in conversation with a boy. It looked like that boy from the Registrar's Office this morning. What was his name again?

A Volvo SUV that had pulled up close to the side walkway honked its horn. Elin turned to acknowledge the driver with a quick wave. She then said something more to the boy as she turned to walk towards the vehicle.

Not wanting to waste an opportunity, I yelled, "Elin!"

She turned towards me, smiled, and waved but continued to the car, opening the door. If exposure had not been a risk, I would have used my abilities to catch up with her. Two leaps and I would have been by her side. Instead, I returned her wave and smiled as I continued walking. I had more important matters to attend to for now anyway.

I remembered that my aunt had given a lecture on Dormants at the Clan Gathering. The talk had been based on an ancient book she kept in the Clan library. I needed to find that book.

I swung my leg over the motorcycle seat and turned the key in the ignition. The machine roared into life under me as the vibrations passed through the handlebars and into my arms. I sat down in the leather seat, pondering the same question I always did. Which would be faster—a Clan hovercraft or my motorcycle? I sped out of the school parking lot, much to the admiration of the schoolgirls and the annoyance of the parents in search of their children.

I reached Aunt Adis's house in record time and went through the usual routine of covering my motorcycle and cleaning my boots before entering. It had occurred to me on the drive that I had never actually seen, let alone been inside, my aunt's coveted library. The need to consult a book had never arisen during a hunt.

Given that a hunt was my reason for being there, I was stumped as to what compelling excuse I could conjure to access it now. Certainly, I didn't think I could just ask my aunt for the book about Dormants, as that would prompt a series of questions leading to a report to the Clan Council. All of which I was trying to avoid at this stage.

Aunt Adis's electric compact car hadn't been in the shed when I arrived. I was hopeful that this meant that she was not at the house.

"Aunt Adis?" I called out as I walked the first-floor rooms.

She was not in her office, the living room, kitchen, or dining room. I called out again as I climbed the stairs to the second floor. Nothing.

I had no idea how long I had to search before she came home. I rushed back down the stairs, only to stop at the bottom, not knowing where to start. Where would one hide a library? This wasn't a small object that you could just tuck away in a drawer. It required significant infrastructure, given what I knew about the library. It housed not only hundreds of books but ancient artifacts and other significant items—some of which were quite substantial in size. Which meant that the actual library could not be located inside my aunt's house. But Aunt Adis would never inconvenience herself by not having direct access. This would have been inefficient and a waste of valuable time.

I slowly walked the downstairs rooms, running my hands along the empty wall space. I knocked on hopeful spots, listening for any indication of hollow space where an entrance might be located. Many of the downstairs rooms had bookshelves overflowing with books varying from small to large bound volumes. What white space was left had a few framed awards that Aunt Adis had received or the occasional drawing of a plant or flower with the Old Norse name inscribed below it. There were a few picture frames in the living room on top of a low bookshelf that ran below the windows. The pictures were of Aunt Adis with Clan Council members dressed in their dark professorial-type robes with velvet-lined openings and white collars. A *Smá-menn* could have easily mistaken them for judges or professors at a prestigious college or university.

I stood in the middle of the living room, waiting for inspiration to strike. None of the walls had produced anything worthy of further investigation. If the walls weren't hiding an entrance and going up was not realistic, then going down must be the answer. I stomped on the floor. It was definitely not cement and responded back to my effort. The floor sounded hollow underneath. Of course, the basement!

I ran to the entrance hallway where underneath the stairs was a small door that led to the basement. How could I have forgotten! It made total sense. I turned the handle and was about to open the door when I heard the side porch door close. I was in the direct line of sight for my aunt, who had just entered that house.

"Tristan, what are you doing?" she asked.

My hand was still on the doorknob since I had frozen on the spot. Aunt Adis was a powerful *Stór-menni* and Clan Council advisor. She was one of the few people that frightened me. One wrong word or action and I would be bound and on my way to the Clan reform camp, otherwise known as Ginnungagap. And trying to enter her library without permission would certainly qualify for such measures.

"Oh, hi, Aunt Adis. I was just going down to the basement," I replied, trying to sound casual.

"I can see that. Why?"

"I realized I forgot my seax and wanted to see if you had one I could borrow," I lied.

A seax was a dagger that all Hunters carried with them during the hunt. You could never be too prepared. Most of the time, a hunt was a straightforward collection of runaways who would be sent to Ginnungagap for reformation. Violence was a last resort. Usually, our training combined with our abilities was enough that none was needed. However, during the darkest point in the moon cycle when our ability, or *megin*, was nonexistent, there could be a need for extra measures. Thus, all Hunters carried a seax among their equipment.

"I see. I may have one that you can borrow," my aunt said, eyeing me with suspicion and as if taking notes. "Let me take you down, and we can see what I have available."

For a Clan Hunter not to have his or her seax was highly unusual. However, I would rather my aunt think I was absentminded than discovering my true intention. I let her pass and open the door to the basement.

The stairs circled downward into the darkness. Aunt Adis, being unabashed *Stór-menni*, didn't bother turning on the lights. We could see almost as well in the dark as in the light.

We rounded the stairs three times before stepping onto the

basement floor. I looked around the cavernous space. There were several workbenches pushed against the wall. Above them were cabinets with glass doors showcasing weapons of various shapes and sizes from different ages. If I had not known better, I would have assumed my aunt was either an enthusiastic weapons collector or preparing for the apocalypse.

Without saying a word, my aunt walked to a workbench in the left corner. She reached into her side pocket and pulled out a large key ring with multiple keys of varying dimensions. She selected a small Victorian skeleton key and placed it in the keyhole of the cabinet in front of her. Through the glass, I could see a smorgasbord of seaxes. She reached for one with a black leather handle and white braiding on the top and bottom of the leather. She placed it on the workbench and reached for the accompanying black sheath. Once she had both in hand, she expertly guided the two pieces together, barely glancing at her hands.

She handed the seax, secured in its sheath, to me, locked the cabinet door, and turned toward the stairs. All of this happened in silence. There was no commentary on the contents of her basement or the seax. Just efficiency. I had made a request, she had responded, end of story. As I followed her to the stairs, I tried to make out the basement's layout as much as possible, but it was too vast to make any useful surmises. I would need more time down here—without my aunt.

"Aunt Adis, would it be possible for you to call the school tomorrow to tell them I'm sick?" I asked, breaking the silence as we wound back up the stairs.

"Are you ill, Tristan?" she asked.

"No, Aunt, but I need to chase down some leads for the hunt."

"All right. I will call them in the morning before I leave for my conference," she replied as we reached the top of the stairs and moved into the light-filled hallway.

I had seen my aunt's calendar on her office desk during my earlier search and knew that she would be gone for the full day on Tuesday. It would give me plenty of time to search the basement and the rest of the house if needed.

"Thank you, Aunt," I said as she moved past me towards her office.

NINE

A project partner

AEDAN

I woke to my phone's alarm trilling at 6:30am. I turned to my side and knocked a few items off my nightstand as I tried to locate my phone, which was charging somewhere on its surface. After successfully quelling the noise, I rolled onto my back, enjoying a few more moments under the covers while I contemplated my coming day. Thankfully, I didn't have to compete with Edvin for the shower, since he'd be snoring away until the last second before needing to drive me.

After a quick breakfast that I could smell my mother preparing, I'd be off to school. I tried to recall my class schedule for the day and what time I'd get home. Oh, wait—I'd agreed with Elin that we would start on our history project that afternoon. I hadn't needed to text her, as we'd encountered each other in the parking lot after school the first day. The prospect of meeting her later made my insides a bit fluttery. But how was I going to explain to my mom why I wasn't coming directly home?

Not readily coming up with an answer, I rolled over to my side, swinging my legs out of bed and onto the floor. The movement was quick and seamless. We were only a couple of days past the full moon, so I could feel the *megin* pulsating through my body. I didn't have time for a run to release the energy, so I would need to find another way to consume the excess. I dropped to the floor for a quick hundred pushups to burn off the top jitters.

After a quick morning shower and throwing some clothes on along with my medallion cuff, I was surprised to see my entire family up and about in the kitchen. Claire had clearly already gone for a morning swim, her uncoiffed, wet hair giving her away. My parents had their exercise clothes on and were hydrating with water. Even Edvin was up, doing squats by the kitchen table.

"Edvin, do you *really* have to do that in here?" Claire asked, turning away as Edvin dropped into another low squat and exposed a plumber's crack on his backside.

"Well, I'd do it out in the woods on my normal obstacle course. But since I've been designated Aedan's personal chauffeur and I don't know when His Majesty will be ready, here I am," Edvin replied. Apparently, driving me to school was his penance for nearly exposing us in town the other day—although now it was starting to feel like mine as well.

"Fine, you big baby. I'll drive him today. Besides, I wouldn't want your supercharged *megin* to cause an accident on the way," Claire responded.

The moon was like a charger to the battery of our abilities. We felt most charged on the second day past the full moon, as that was when the *megin* had fully infiltrated our body's cells again. It was also the day we had to be the most careful about exposing ourselves. To dampen the adrenaline high we got with the charge, my parents had mandated an exercise program for all of us.

"Thanks, sis," Edvin said as he made a beeline to the front door before Claire could change her mind.

"Morning, darling," my mother greeted me. "Have you done your exercise for today?"

"Morning, Mom. I did a few exercises upstairs before my shower," I replied.

"Now, Aedan, you know that isn't going to be enough. You need to get in at least a twenty- or thirty-mile run," she said.

"But, Mom...I've got school. I don't have time. It starts in a half-hour, it takes fifteen minutes to drive there, and I haven't had breakfast yet. I promise I'll be careful today," I pleaded.

"Okay, Aedan, but you're doing it after school. No arguments. You know how important it is for everyone," my mother commanded.

"I'll definitely do it tonight, but I can't after school," I said, internally grimacing.

I didn't want to lie to my parents. Our family relied on trust, especially given our transient circumstances and the constant dangers we faced from exposure or the Hunters. But I also didn't agree with their strict measures regarding Elin.

The conversation had now caught my father's attention. "And why not, son?"

"Um...I have a semester history project. My group is meeting after school to begin discussing it," I answered, finding an internal compromise for now.

I hadn't exactly lied. It *was* a group project. I just wasn't expounding on the group members or exact number.

"Okay. Well, in that case, you can defer it until this evening. But then, son, you're doing thirty miles. No more excuses. And next time, I need to see some better time management from you," my father said, putting his hand on my shoulder.

"Okay, Dad. I understand," I answered, relieved that no new question had been raised over my history project.

Besides, thirty miles in my current energized state would only take me roughly an hour if I ran in the woods without *leynasking*— although, given the size of the island, it might not be possible to constrain my run entirely to the wooded areas. I contemplated this fact as I munched on the eggs and toast my mother had heaped on the plate in front of me.

My sister re-entered the kitchen about ten minutes later. "Come on, slowpoke! We have to get going to get to school on time." She was now fully dressed in jeans and a sweater, with her black hair dried and curled into soft waves.

"I still have five minutes."

"Not unless you want to run to school," she answered as she grabbed her purse and headed towards the front door. While technically feasible, running to school using my abilities had several problems, given that this was the island's version of rush hour.

"Okay, okay...I'm coming." I grabbed one last bite of toast. "Bye, Mom! Bye, Dad!"

The drive to school was quick with Claire behind the wheel. Her talent in maneuvering in and out of traffic even in a small town was something to behold—and it was not a supernatural ability. We arrived at the school parking lot a good ten minutes early. Instead of just dropping me off as Edvin did, Claire pulled into a parking space by the side walkway.

"Ah...it's okay. You can just drop me off," I said as she turned off the ignition.

"I need to run a quick errand inside," she answered as if we'd just pulled up to the local market instead of my school. Before I could ask any further questions, she grabbed a small brown paper parcel from the back seat, opened the car door, and climbed out.

A voice greeted me as I got out of the car. "Hey, Aedan!"

I closed the car door to find Joel standing there staring at my sister. His baseball cap was on backward, with the bill facing the rear. Joel's eager, transfixed face was clearly revealed.

"Hi, Joel!" I responded. Joel had obviously fallen under Claire's spell. He kept staring at her but he wasn't saying a thing.

"Joel, this is my sister, Claire. Claire, this is Joel." I made the introduction to break the awkward silence that had descended.

"Hi, Joel. It's nice to meet you," Claire said. Joel was able to squeeze out a small utterance that sounded like, nice to meet you too. Claire smiled. "Have a good day, boys! See you later, Aedan."

Joel finally snapped out of his stupor as Claire turned and walked away. "That's your sister? You didn't tell me she was a goddess! Hey, you think I should ask her out?"

"Joel! She's my sister. Plus, she is way older than you."

"Age never meant a thing to me," Joel said, wistfully looking in the direction my sister had walked.

"Let me save you from some future suffering. You don't have a snowball's chance," I said, trying to nip any of Joel's ideas in the bud.

"Okay, Mr. Downer. How you doing with Elin? Any progress there?" Joel responded, smirking and turning the tables on me.

"It's not like that with her. She's just my history-project partner."

Joel laughed. "Yeah, sure, and I'm the Queen of Sheba."

"Look, man...it's complicated, okay?" I said, brushing off Joel's implications. "In fact, I could use your help. My family can't know I'm doing the history project with her. If asked, can you be my project partner instead?"

"Sure, man. I dig it—as long as I don't have to do any actual work," he replied. Then he smirked. "Aww...now I get it. It's a secret romance!"

Joel moved out of my reach before I could respond by punching him in the arm. He was saved from any further onslaught by the school bell ringing, announcing the start of the day.

TEN

Two cups

ELIN

Aedan and I had agreed to meet at the only coffee shop in town to start our history project. Karl's Coffee was actually an old Italian restaurant that had been transformed into the local coffee lounge. It still had the green booths from the Italian restaurant running down the middle of the shop, along with a mural on the back wall that transported the viewer to the green-and-gold hills of Tuscany. The coffee bar was a long wooden counter on the left of the shop, supporting various glass containers of cookies, biscotti, coffee cake, and other baked goods. Along with the loud copper espresso machines at the far end of the bar, the new fixtures were a gas fireplace and surrounding couches that added an element of warmth and comfort.

The shop was humming that afternoon as returning commuters, harried parents, and high school students came to get their fix of the black elixir being served in a mixed collection of porcelain and paper to-go cups. I pushed my way through the crowd, looking to see if Aedan had arrived before me. Most of the tables were taken, and I didn't see a telltale sign of Aedan's black hair.

I deeply inhaled the coffee-flavored air, trying to calm the host of butterflies swirling in my stomach. Being paired with Aedan was the last thing I'd expected on the first day of school. My mind seemed to be in a tug-of-war. The prospect of spending alone-time with a Greek god of a boy was nerve-racking. How would I be able to concentrate on the history project if I was focusing on what to say to him? I couldn't afford not to do well on the assignment—it was, after all, sixty percent of our history grade. And good grades were my only path to a scholarship.

A couple of soccer moms stood up to leave from a booth in the middle. I quickly raced to secure it before someone else could swoop in. I hadn't been sitting there for too long when Aedan appeared from among the throng with two steaming mugs of what smelled like hot apple cider.

I groaned internally. He looked really good in his brown knit sweater and jeans. Concentration would be impossible. A navy windbreaker was hanging from his backpack and a now-familiar pair of earbuds dangled around his neck. His sea-blue eyes seemed to inspect my amber ones, making me more nervous than a cat on a lifeboat.

"Hi," he said, smiling. "I wasn't sure what you liked, so I just got the autumn special. Turns out it's hot apple cider. Hope that's okay?"

I tried to sound casual. "Yeah, that's great, thanks. I love apple cider." I actually really did like apple cider. Nothing marked the autumn season as well as apples—especially when they had been pressed into cider with some cinnamon.

Aedan slid into the seat across from mine, facing the door. After a few moments of awkwardness, we both began to speak at the same time.

"Go ahead," I said, nervously laughing.

"No, it's fine. You go first. You were saying something about the project?" Aedan replied, also chuckling.

"I was just asking if you'd thought more about what our topic should be," I said.

"Well...," Aedan began. "I was thinking we could focus on the resistance aspects that occur during wars."

"What do you mean? Like within the troops themselves, or the people they're conquering?" I asked, begging myself to focus on his words and not his eyes.

"Sort of...I'm thinking more of after the conquering has occurred. There are always pockets of resistance that don't adopt the new way of thinking or practicing...like with the pagans and Christians," Aedan explained.

"Oh, I get it. Sort of like in World War II...there were resistance forces in most of the occupied countries," I replied, nodding. Nothing like the subject of war to appropriately refocus the mind. "Sure, that sounds like a very interesting topic."

"Hey, guys!" Joel Larson appeared, interrupting me as he slid into the same bench as Aedan. He had a steaming cup of something cradled between his two hands. "So hard to find a seat in here."

"Um...hi, Joel. What're you doing here?" Aedan asked, looking slightly annoyed.

"Oh, you know... joining my study group," Joel answered, trying to hide a smirk that was threatening to emerge. "Oh, hey, look...it's Claire!" Aedan's sister had just appeared from between two businessmen in black coats who were standing in the coffee line. "Hi, Claire," Joel called out, blatantly sighing in the same breath.

Claire turned to look at our booth, her black waves of hair swinging to frame her face. She was wearing a thick green turtleneck sweater, which accented her light-green eyes, dark jeans, and knee-high boots. She looked as perfect as she did all the times I'd seen her.

"Hi, Joel. What are you two doing here?"

I was about to correct her, but then I noticed that Aedan had vanished. He was no longer sitting next to Joel on the bench. As I was about to check under the table, Joel stopped me with a swift nudge of his foot.

"Oh, you know...just TWO students grabbing some coffee before we study," Joel responded, with an emphasis on the word *two*. "Would you like to join us?"

Three things happened as Joel asked his last question. He suddenly lurched forward as if in pain, nearly spilling his coffee; Monsieur Tibadeau sidled up to Claire, his ebony skin drawing a contrast to her fairness; and that strange sensation of goosebumps from the last few days began to blossom on my skin again.

Normally, seeing my French teacher outside the school context would've been strange enough, but the whole situation was weird—especially with Aedan vanishing into thin air. Monsieur Tibadeau handed Claire one of the to-go coffee cups he was holding. I managed a furtive glance under the table. Aedan was definitely not there.

"Oh, how nice of you to ask, Joel, but Florent and I got our cups to go," Claire responded. Monsieur Tibadeau turned to face us as he realized that Claire was speaking to us.

"*Salut,* Elin! *Ça va?*" He greeted me with his perfect French pronunciation.

Monsieur Tibadeau came from the French tropical island of Martinique. How he'd ended up on our chilly island was a bit of a mystery, but he always insisted on speaking French with his students.

"*Salut, Monsieur Tibadeau. Ça va bien, merci. Et vous?*" I replied self-consciously, saying I was fine and asking how he was in return. I'd taken French every year of high school, but the words still felt a little foreign when spoken out loud.

"*Ça va bien aussi, merci,*" he answered, affirming that he too was well. His ebony hand grabbed Claire's fair one. He continued in a slight French accent, "We should go, Claire. There is little time left."

"Oh, yes! You're right, Florent. Nice seeing you both," Claire responded. They disappeared back into the crowd, heading towards the front door.

"Joel, what's going on?" I asked as soon as Claire and Monsieur Tibadeau had left.

"What? Everything is fine. Normal...super normal," Joel said, looking sheepish and trying to sound convincing.

I pursed my lips and gave him my most incredulous face. Joel squirmed uncomfortably in his seat.

"Now where did Aedan go?" he asked, trying to avoid eye contact and looking around the room.

"Joel," I said in my best interpretation of my mom's you're-in-trouble voice.

Joel caved, finally meeting my eyes. "Okay, fine...I...I can't take the pressure. Aedan's not allowed to date."

"Okay...but we're not dating. This is for a school project," I answered, perplexed.

"His family is...is really sensitive to even the appearance of dating," Joel explained, still shifting uncomfortably.

"Are you serious?" I didn't really buy his story. "Why would his family have an issue with him dating?"

"I don't know...something about school, sports, grades. You'll have to ask him," Joel said, deflecting. At the same moment, I heard Aedan's voice from behind me.

"Hi, guys! Sorry, had to duck into the bathroom," he said, trying to appear nonchalant as he slid back into the seat next to Joel.

"Hi, Aedan. You just missed your sister and Monsieur Tibadeau," I said, watching for a reaction.

"Oh, I did? Well, that's too bad." He glanced at Joel, who was fidgeting profusely with his now empty mug.

"Um...so, um...I think I should go. You guys probably want to get back to your project anyway. Um...Aedan? Can I talk to you for a sec?" Joel asked, unable to hide the rueful look on his face.

"Ah...sure. Sorry, Elin. Give me a minute," Aedan replied, looking a bit confused.

He and Joel stepped a few feet away, just out of earshot. What I was able to witness was Aedan looking confused, then a little angry, then resigned. Once finished, Joel slinked into the crowd with his back still towards me.

"Hey, so this place is feeling a little crowded. Do you mind if we go somewhere else?" Aedan said as he came back to the table.

"Sure, that's fine." I got up from the booth. "Let me just grab some to-go cups for the cider."

Aedan followed me through the jostling crowd to the front, carefully balancing the two mugs of cider. I grabbed two paper cups and lids from the stand by the front door and proceeded with the transfer of the hot, sweet liquid.

Once outside, we headed towards the waterfront. The sun was still out, offering some warmth on what otherwise would have been a chilly fall day. The water glistened as small waves lapped the rocky shore. The air had a briny tang to it, and a few seagulls hovering above the arriving fishing boats squawked.

We crossed the rock beach, heading to the large granite boulders that cupped the small cove on the other side of the breakwater. We chatted as we made our way, keeping the subject matter confined to our history project. Once we reached the boulders, I noticed Aedan had slipped on a pair of gloves from his pocket. He took my cider cup from my hands so I could climb the first low boulder. He then handed the cups to me once it was his turn. In such a fashion, we quickly reached the top.

We looked for the sunniest spot and then sat down between the tufts of sweet grass and lichen that had taken root in the cracks between the granite. The view before us was of the undulating gray granite sloping down into the blue-green sea. The sunlight played on the tops of the small crests formed by the wind or a passing boat. I instinctively took a deep breath, enjoying the brisk sea air.

To my surprise, a few hours quickly passed. The conversation between Aedan and me had flowed more naturally than at Karl's, as we had no interruptions and more space to fill. He was easy to talk to and had good ideas for our project. We created a solid outline and assigned each of ourselves a section to start researching and composing.

My earlier apprehension regarding the jeopardization of scholarships seemed rather foolish now. Somehow, the afternoon with Aedan had been perfectly comfortable—and, dare I say, I'd even enjoyed it. Perhaps it had something to do with the "dating option" being removed from the equation.

A cold breeze tousled my hair, and a shudder passed through my body as the cold started to snake its way through my coat. The sun had dipped lower in the sky, and its warmth was quickly fading.

"Here," Aedan said as he offered me a wool navy beanie with a white stripe he'd found in his bag. Normally, I might have felt awkward accepting a hat, but stopping the inevitable teeth-chattering had me more motivated to say yes.

"Thanks." I took the hat from his hand and slipped it over my loose auburn hair.

I did a little hair-tucking until I felt secure that most of the unwieldy bits were in place. Taking a deep breath for courage, I decided to ask the question that had been nagging me since Karl's Coffee. "Do you mind if I ask you a personal question about what Joel told me?"

"Um...sure," Aedan replied, looking a little uncomfortable.

"Why don't your parents want you to date anyone?"

"Ah, it's...it's a little complicated," he answered, but continued when I kept staring at him, hoping for more. "We've moved around a lot, so they're just concerned about my falling behind in schoolwork."

He started to get up from the rocky surface. Sensing that this wasn't a subject he wanted to further elaborate on, I got up as well.

I changed the topic. "Should we head back?"

"Yeah, I think we'd better before we lose all the light," Aedan responded, looking towards the way we'd come up.

"I know a faster way to get to the road. We can cut through the forest," I said, pointing behind us. "There's a trail that leads back to the main road. I'll just text my dad. He can meet us at the other end and drop you off on the way home." My father was acting as my driver since my knee injury wasn't quite ready for the trials of my bike. I noticed that Aedan was about to protest, so I continued, "Don't worry—we can drop you off at the top of your driveway. That way nobody will see our car." Aedan seemed to relax a little and nodded.

"Okay, thanks," he said as he reached down for his book bag and the remnants of our cider cups.

ELEVEN

Oh, deer!

AEDAN

E lin's dad pulled up to the trailhead in their white Volvo quicker than expected. I glanced in the car windows to make sure he was alone. I'd had enough surprises for one day—the last thing I needed was a Clan Hunter sitting next to me for the ride home. The whole afternoon felt like a blur to me, starting with the coffee shop. I couldn't believe that Claire had shown up unexpectedly—and who was that man with her? Elin had called him Monsieur Tibadeau, her French teacher. Was that the person to whom Claire had delivered the parcel at school?

"Hi, Aedan!" Mr. Bodil greeted me from the open car window.

"Hi, Mr. Bodil! Thanks for the ride—really appreciate it," I responded, still mulling over the day's events.

"No problem. Just climb on in and let's get going," he said in a friendly manner.

Elin rounded the car and climbed into the front passenger seat next to her father. I got into the back seat behind Mr. Bodil. Once we were in the car, Mr. Bodil began by asking Elin about her day at school and the classes she'd had. It gave me a few moments to further contemplate the afternoon.

I'd never intended on *leynasking,* especially since Claire would have seen me anyway. It had just happened on instinct. My heightened *megin* had kicked into overdrive when I slid under the table to hide from her. Thankfully, I didn't think that Claire had seen me or that my sudden disappearance had been that noticeable to Joel or Elin.

Joel had really saved my skin on my abnormal avoidance of a family member. I felt a little guilty for having punched him from underneath the table when he invited Claire and Monsieur Tibadeau to sit down...although I still couldn't believe he'd made up that story about my not being able to date. I internally grimaced and pressed my head against the cool window. There was no good way to recover from that. I just had to accept it and play along. At least it would help explain my occasional odd behavior to Elin.

Driving fast, Mr. Bodil seemed very familiar with the empty island roads. Most of the evening traffic had already subsided, with the mainland commuters now safely tucked in their homes, enjoying dinner with their families. Without streetlights, the dirt road was dark. The last light from sunset had faded a while ago.

Elin and Mr. Bodil were playing a game, trying to guess what Mrs. Bodil had made for dinner—clearly not an unusual pastime, as they both were joking and laughing as their predictions became more absurd. To be inclusive, Mr. Bodil looked at me through the rear-view mirror and asked, "So, Aedan, what are you expecting for dinner?"

At that same moment, as we were rounding a bend, Elin screamed for her father to watch out. There was a herd of at least ten deer crossing the road in front of us. At the speed that the car was traveling, it would be impossible for Mr. Bodil to stop in time. As most country drivers know, you never swerve to miss a deer. In all likelihood, the deer would also panic and jump in the direction toward which you had just directed the car. Without thinking, I tapped into my *megin.* Concentrating as I moved my hands, I carefully lifted the endangered deer out of the vehicle's path.

There was chaos inside the car. Mr. Bodil was braking hard and yelling. He wanted Elin to duck in front of the console to avoid the deer he thought was undoubtedly going to crash through the front windshield. Elin was gripping the sides of her seat and screaming for him to stop the car. The car's safety alerts were wildly beeping about obstructions ahead that were disappearing as quickly as they'd appeared on its radar. I was panting hard from the effort and adrenaline rush that accompanied using so much of my *megin* at once.

Eventually, the car skidded to a stop, its automatic safety features assisting Mr. Bodil in braking. The remaining deer on the road quickly leaped into the woods, following the intact herd. The car didn't have a single scratch on it. Mr. Bodil and Elin sat in stunned silence, trying to recover from the experience.

"Is everybody all right? Elin? Aedan, are you okay?" Mr. Bodil asked after a moment as he turned to look at each of us. Both Elin and I nodded, unable to find the words quite yet. "I can't believe we managed to avoid all of them. I shouldn't have been driving that fast. I'm so sorry! That could've been a lot worse. We're very lucky." Mr. Bodil leaned back into his seat, taking a deep breath to calm his nerves.

"Lucky indeed," Elin said as she placed her hand on her father's arm and gently squeezed. At the same time, she turned to look at me with a peculiar expression on her face.

"No harm done, Mr. Bodil. So glad that you managed to keep us safe and avoid all those deer," I said, trying to gloss over any strangeness in the event.

Mr. Bodil took another deep breath. "Okay, then. You both ready? We'll drive home at a snail's pace. I don't think I can take another run-in with deer, or anything else for that matter." He shifted the gear into drive.

Mr. Bodil was as good as his word. It took us another solid twenty minutes to reach the top of my driveway. We all were lost in our thoughts, so there wasn't much conversation in the car other than my indicating the approaching turn.

"Oh, Dad. Aedan would like to be just dropped off at the top of the drive," Elin said as her father was about to turn into the driveway.

"No, I insist on seeing Aedan to the door. I want to explain to his parents in person what happened," Mr. Bodil said.

I tried to assuage his concerns and avoid the inevitable uproar at home. "Oh, no, sir. That's unnecessary. It was really just an unfortunate incident. No one to blame."

"No, no. I really do insist. They should hear it straight from me," Mr. Bodil responded as he turned into the driveway and proceeded towards my house.

I cringed as I thought about how the evening was about to unfold. At first, there'd be confusion as to why I was with the Bodils, then concern about what happened, and finally an endless stream of questions as my parents assessed any risk of exposure. After which I was pretty sure to find myself grounded.

Elin threw me a sympathetic look as the car came to a stop in front of the wide stairs of our Scandinavian modern home. I could see my parents getting up from the sofa through the large square picture windows that overlooked the front-drive. They'd seen Mr. Bodil's car. There was no escaping now.

I was surprised when Elin unbuckled her seatbelt and opened her car door to get out as well. The three of us made our way up the front stairs, Elin and Mr. Bodil taking the lead. Before either could knock or ring the doorbell, my parents opened the front door.

"Good evening, Dara and Liam," Mr. Bodil greeted my parents.

"Hi, Leif. Everything all right?" my father replied, obviously surprised to see the three of us together.

"Yes, yes. I just wanted to explain a little incident we had on the way to your house," Mr. Bodil said.

"Oh, dear!" My mother sounded concerned as she tried to peer around Elin to see my face. "Nothing too unusual, I hope."

"No...well, in fact, it was deer." Mr. Bodil smiled and made an effort at lightheartedness. "You see, we almost ran into a herd of them on the road. I wanted you to hear it from me. It was quite a scare for everyone, and I wanted to make sure that Aedan would be all right. I was going a bit faster than I ought to have, especially with the kids in the car. We were just so lucky. The deer just seemed to leap out of the way. I've never seen anything quite like it. Fortunately, everyone is safe. There isn't even a scratch on the car. Just shaken nerves all the way around."

As Mr. Bodil paused, Elin jumped in to explain. "You see, I had bumped into Aedan walking home on the dark road, which can be dangerous. My dad was coming to pick me up anyway, so I insisted that we give Aedan a ride. That's how he ended up in the car with us."

I was astonished. Elin had just covered for me. She'd given me a rational reason as to why I was standing with them in front of my parents. And it was mostly true—we had been on a dark road together, and she'd insisted on giving me a ride. I was thankful that she was blocking my parents' view of my face, which otherwise might have betrayed my surprise.

"I see," my mother said. "Well, that was very thoughtful of you, Elin."

"And don't worry, Leif. It could happen to anyone. Deer are bound to be on the road on this island. I'm just so relieved and happy to hear that no real harm occurred to anyone—even the deer," my father continued from where my mother had left off.

"Can we offer you a cup of tea or anything to give you a moment's rest before getting back in the car?" my mother offered.

"No, no, we're fine. Annika has dinner waiting for us at home. But thank you for the offer," Mr. Bodil said.

With warm smiles, goodbyes were said. Elin and her father made their way back to their Volvo. My father put his hand on my shoulder as we turned to watch Elin and her father drive away.

"I would like to hear a bit more about how exactly those deer managed to leap out of harm's way," my father said, squeezing my shoulder.

"Oh, Liam! It sounds like it was a very necessary action to avoid a bigger harm," my mother said, wrapping me in a large hug. "I'm just so happy you all are all right. Oh, and was that your hat Elin was wearing?"

"I agree with you, Dara. I just want to understand the risk involved. Did anyone see you, son?" My father asked, missing my mother's more poignant observation.

"No, I don't think so. Mr. Bodil and Elin were sitting in the front seats. There was so much chaos that I don't think either of them noticed. Also, we were the only ones on the road. The only witnesses were the deer themselves. And I don't think they'll be talking anytime soon," I joked, happy to have avoided answering my mother's question regarding my hat.

"Well, then—we were lucky," my father said, the relief evident in his voice. "It did seem like Mr. Bodil had concluded that it was just dumb luck that no deer were hit. Did Elin say anything to indicate that she'd sensed something?"

"No, she didn't say anything," I answered truthfully. Internally, I was a little less confident about whether the same could be said of her sensing anything.

TWELVE

A concealed space

TRISTAN

It just wasn't there. I had managed to searched my aunt's basement at least three times over the past week. I had looked at every possible wall, behind all the cabinets, and even crawled under the workbenches. The only things I had learned was that my aunt had an unhealthy obsession with antique weapons and that the basement was as immaculate as the rest of her house. Not a spiderweb or dirt speck to be found.

The one corner that had looked promising, given its odd shape, revealed nothing. Instead of being a concave corner as one would expect in its outer-wall position, it was a convex corner, meaning that the two adjoining walls jutted inward into the basement. I had scrutinized every cinderblock in that corner hoping to find a button, loose block, or something else that would open a door. Yet there was nothing.

The frustration was beginning to mount. "Unproductive time is wasted time" was a Clan mantra practically chiseled inside me. I had never spent so much time so inefficiently or unproductively. My mentor Henric would be ashamed of me.

I sat down on the cold cement floor, resting my head on my

knees. I had learned that one could set a clock by my aunt's routine. In the morning, she promptly left the house at 7:50am and didn't return until evening at exactly 6pm. She was the town's librarian, which meant that during the week she tended to the books at the *Smá-menns'* library. Her job meant that I had a solid three hours after school to search for the hidden door—although now I was beginning to wonder if it even existed.

I slid onto my back, resting my head on my hands. I stared at the basement ceiling. My body was angled towards the most promising corner. I thought about what Henric had done when facing a dead-end or a cold lead during a hunt. He had always said you could not force inspiration or an epiphany to strike. It was contrary to the words' definitions. Henric believed that busying yourself with other inconsequential tasks would allow your subconscious enough room to find the answer. But I had no other small tasks with which to busy myself—not even schoolwork.

During my after-school encounter with Candice, I had promised to help with her math if she would agree to do my trivial homework. She readily agreed since the bargain gave her what she truly wanted—which was more time being seen in my company. For me, the arrangement allowed me to offload meaningless assignments. What quality she produced did not really matter as long as I did not fail.

The one part of the situation that would be trickier to manage was Candice herself. She had made it plain in every way possible, except saying the actual words, that she wanted the appearance of a romantic relationship. I did not see the harm in playing along with her as long as it produced what I needed from the equation.

Smá-menns could be so preoccupied with what others thought of them. In Clan society, straightforwardness in action and speech were valued. Everything else was considered counterproductive.

My eyes traveled along the uncovered floorboards of the upper story that made up the basement ceiling. All of the panels ran directly towards the corner and seemed to be tucked underneath the cinderblocks...except one. There was a small sliver of light leaking through a tiny opening where that board met the wall. If the room had not been entirely dark, I would have missed it.

I quickly stood up and approached the wall for a closer look. It definitely looked like artificial light. It had that warm yellowish tinge. I pulled a nearby stool over to the wall so I could climb on top for a better look. There was clearly a crack between the board and wall. It was letting the light through from the other side—meaning that there was a lit space behind the cinderblock wall.

I got down from the stool in one hop. My heart beat a little faster as I tried to imagine the outline of the house on the basement ceiling. I felt certain that the entrance was not down here. The implication, then, was that the entrance to whatever the convex corner was hiding was upstairs.

My best estimate was that the corner was located in my aunt's office. Of course! I should have known, I grumbled to myself. She would most often need access to the *Stór-mennis'* library when she was working. She would make the entrance in the most time-efficient location.

But I had combed the office walls several times and had not found anything. I was really starting to miss *Stór-menni* technology. It would have made the task of finding the entrance so much easier. However, it was strictly forbidden to take any *Stór-menni* object or tool outside Falinvik except for what was approved by the Council.

I would just need to be more patient. At least now I had narrowed the options. With one last look to make sure I had the location of the corner firmly in mind, I headed towards the stairs to climb out of the basement.

When I reached the hallway upstairs, I checked my watch. It said 5pm. I had one hour before my aunt came home. I hurried to her office. My only experience with hidden entrances or concealed spaces was during hunts with my mentor Henric. In Falinvik, having such clandestine structures was futile. Our Security Aerial Surveillance Units, or SASUs, could scan any building, object, or human in under a second, highlighting any concealed rooms or items. The units mainly patrolled our city, keeping us safe from any trespassers, fugitives, or dissidents. However, when needed, they provided other services as well. I could have used one right about now.

With Henric, his main tool in searching for hidden objects during a hunt was logic. He would have taken any learnings and systematically applied them to the situation at hand. Using his method, I went over what I knew. The corner had been an outside edge sandwiched between north and west walls. The whole of the north wall in my aunt's office was a solid, non-ornate, birch bookcase filled to the brim with books. I moved closer to inspect the area near the west wall. The bookcase came within a foot of the corner window.

I scanned the books on the shelves. They seemed to be a collection of encyclopedias and other reference books. Being impatient, I tried pulling out a few books at random to see if they triggered any response. Nothing. I needed to be more logical, given my time constraints.

I tried the encyclopedia, beginning with the letter A. The volume seemed more worn than the others next to it and also had the first initial of my aunt's name. The book was heavier than I expected. It fell to the floor with a thud. I picked it up and tried to reinsert it in the shelf. The task proved more difficult than it looked.

It took me a moment to realize that all of the large books were inserted at a slight angle. The bookcase was shallower than its distance from the wall. I was definitely on the right track. There *was* space behind the bookcase!

After another ten minutes of pulling out more high-potential books, I surmised two things. First, the hidden space ran the entire length of the bookcase. Second, the books were not the triggers to opening the entrance. They were just books.

Out of sheer frustration, I went to flop into my aunt's desk chair. I had known my search would be difficult, but I hadn't counted on the extent of the time it was taking. I needed the book about Dormants. There was no way around it. Without the book, I would not know how to help Elin convert, and without her awakening, it would be very dangerous to present her to the Clan Council.

My periodic progress reports regarding my hunting mission were relatively thin already. I was not sure how long I could continue without getting reprimanded for lack of progress. I had never had a reprimand. It would look very bad for my first reprimand to be on my first solo mission.

I put my forehead down on my aunt's desk. The desk had no clutter. The space before me was wide and clear of any papers. The only item that rested on the surface was a neatly placed leather folio, which I guessed enclosed my aunt's SRT—Self Reporting Tool. The SRT was mandated to every clan member as a way to report on their own productivity as well as the productivity of those around them. The Clan Council encouraged members to report on family, friends, co-workers, or anyone else that they witnessed involved with unproductive activity. This way, the Clan Council could act in addressing any concerns before there were larger repercussions. The SRT was also the way that I filed my progress reports from the field.

I banged my head a few times against the center of the cherry desk's surface, the last time with a little more force, hoping the pain would ease my frustration. I heard a small click and then a *whoosh*.

I lifted my head from the desk and looked around. A small box had slid down and out from underneath the desk. Inside was a metal lever. I could barely contain my excitement. Was this it? The way to open the door? What if it was not? What if it did something completely different? What if it was a trap? The library was of extreme importance to *Stór-menni* worldwide. Could it be this simple?

It was 5:30pm. I had thirty minutes before my aunt came home. My fingers hovered above the lever. I had to decide whether to take the risk. All of my discoveries pointed to this being *the* lever. I knew that there was a hidden space behind the bookcase. I knew my aunt would want the most efficient way to access the library. What could be more efficient than a lever in her desk that opened an entrance in her office? I pulled the lever. I had to use my *megin* strength to get it all the way up, but as soon as I did, the bookcase furthest from the west wall came forward in the room and slid on top of the adjacent bookcase. It left a large opening in its wake.

I quickly stood up from the desk and with *megin* speed rushed to the entrance. The sudden disturbance rocked the chair that had been behind me. Luckily, it stayed upright.

Behind the other bookcase was a passage that continued to the right. I could see the light fixture that was emanating the warm glow I had seen from the basement. It was a simple bulb hanging by a wire over a similar spiraling staircase, which was used to access the basement.

Overcome by excitement, I rushed through the passage and to the staircase. Even with the help of the light, I could not see the bottom of the stairs. I judged that I had about fifteen minutes to explore before I needed to be back up in my aunt's office closing the lever.

Looking down into the darkness, I hesitated. I was not sure what kind of security measures my aunt would have in place, given that Clan devices would not be available to her. Well, I had come this far—and I was not about to stop now.

At first, I started down the spiraling staircase with *megin* speed, but the vibration grew to such a strength that I had to slow down. I was not sure how much strain the staircase could take. I counted three, then four spirals...I was just past the basement floor. On the eighth turn, I could finally see an earthen floor. I stepped off the last metal stair to inspect my surroundings.

The walls around me seemed to be made from large stones, almost like those from an old fortress. There was a tunnel in front of me that stretched so deep into the darkness that even with effort I was not able to pierce its secrets. Behind me, there was nothing except the metal spiraling staircase and the lonely light bulb at the top, which I could no longer see. The only choice was forward.

The tunnel gently sloped downward. I walked at a slow pace, ready for any security obstacle that might present itself in the darkness. Gaining more confidence when none appeared, I picked up my pace, eventually running at top speed.

I must have been running for two miles when in the distance I saw the glow of a small red dot in the darkness. I slowed down, unsure of what it might be. After a few more moments at a light jog, I arrived at a massive metal wall. The light of the red dot was next to what looked like an oddly shaped keyhole. The silhouette resembled the symbol for Mjölnir, Thor's hammer. It had a long stem that widened into an anchor profile at the bottom with a small notch in the middle.

There were no other dial pads or door handles. Just a metal wall covering the tunnel path, and the keyhole next to it. I placed my hand against the cool metal in front of me, realizing for the first time how cold and damp my surroundings were. The metal shimmered a little under my touch. I quickly dropped my hand.

This was no ordinary metal. It was a Clan-produced substance known as Caelum. How had my aunt managed to get it out of Falinvik? It had many properties, including incredible strength. Nothing could pierce or melt it. It was impenetrable. A far more unusual property was its ability to absorb and retain imprints from people or things that touched it. Depending on how often my aunt used the Caelum's scanning device, she would soon know I had been here. I had just started another clock on myself! I cursed silently.

There was no passing this barrier. It explained the lack of other security measures. There was nothing more I could do until I was able to get my hands on the key to the door. And I knew exactly where that key was. The challenge would be getting it off my aunt's keyring!

THIRTEEN

A revelation

ELIN

The last few weeks had fallen into a routine. Nothing too peculiar had happened since the car ride with Aedan and my dad. The school did have a major pipe burst in the cafeteria from the cold weather and ancientness of the plumbing. Now, to accommodate all students in the reduced circumstances, the school had instituted staggered lunches. The freshman and juniors had lunch from eleven to twelve. The senior class now shared a twelve-to-one lunch with the sophomores.

This meant that I could no longer look forward to lunch with Tristan. He had, however, remained very attentive before school and during the breaks between classes. For the first couple of weeks, while the stitches in my knee healed, he insisted on carrying my bookbag whenever possible. It had led to some awkward moments with other students gawking as Tristan helped settle me into my different class seats. He seemed oblivious to their stares and continued with the task whenever the opportunity presented itself.

I wasn't really sure what it all meant. Were we just friends, or did he want something more? I really couldn't imagine it being the latter.

I'd yet to give him an answer on the school dance, which was the following week. He hadn't brought it up again. I'd convinced myself that he'd changed his mind. He was, after all, the hot new senior guy. Why on earth would he choose to go with an unremarkable junior girl with no social standing in the high school hierarchy? Surely it had just been a first-day folly on his part.

I'd talked it over with Mia on FaceTime, trying to determine the right course of action. Should I bring it up or just ignore his earlier question? She'd been more encouraging in her assessment— although her mother, who held the intentions of men in a different light, had thrown Hindi interjections advising caution from the background.

Mia had been visiting her parents for the weekend to celebrate the Hindu holiday of Dussehra, so inevitably the message of good triumphing over evil had crept into our conversation. Mia's parents had immigrated to the island from the Indian state of Telangana when Mia was just four years old. They'd been able to maintain their culture and language even while adapting to their new surroundings. Sharing their heritage with the rest of Mia's friends had brought not only new delicious foods but also the celebration of new festivals into our circle.

With Mia's family's holiday preoccupation, we hadn't been able to see each other even though she was on Auor Island. FaceTime had been our consolation for the missed opportunity. She'd comforted me during our conversation by insisting that she was certain that Tristan would approach the subject again and all would work out. And if not, she had promised to join me for the dance instead. This, in her view, resolved the issue so that whatever the result, good would triumph.

I closed my locker door, smiling to myself over Mia's infectious optimism and her stubbornness. As I was shoving my history book into my backpack, Tristan appeared next to me, leaning against the lockers.

"Hi! Can I help you with that?" He extended his hand toward my bookbag while brushing his sandy hair back with the other.

"Hi! Sure, thanks." I'd learned that it was more effort to refuse Tristan's help than to accept it. He leaned over and grasped the handle of my bag once I finish zipping it.

"Where you headed?" he asked, smiling at me and slinging my bag over his shoulder as if it weighed nothing.

"History. Mr. Hutchinson's class," I answered as we started to walk side by side down the hallway.

Tristan was wearing a green long-sleeved merino wool sweater with a small V-neck collar, dark faded jeans, and motorcycle boots. He looked good. Like a casual olive-skinned James Dean from one of my mom's favorite classic movies. He carried his black motorcycle jacket tucked under his left arm. Around his neck, I spied a silver chain with large links. "What's that?"

"What's what?" he asked, looking at me.

"The chain around your neck?"

"Do you want to see it?" Tristan stopped walking and faced me.

"Sure," I said.

Given that Tristan's hands were occupied with his jacket and my bookbag, he responded by leaning closer to me and saying, "Go ahead and pull it out."

A little shiver of excitement went up my spine at being so close to Tristan. I carefully reached up to slip my finger around the silver chain. My finger caressed his neck and the familiar electricity ignited as my finger traveled along his dark olive skin. I could feel the redness of a blush blossoming on my cheeks.

A silver medallion emerged once I had the entire chain pulled out. Carved into the medallion was a strange symbol with eight arms radiating from the center of a circle. They almost looked like spiked tridents with three lines running across the stems of the spear. Around the main symbol were four smaller carved lines at the top, bottom, and sides. It reminded me of something, but I couldn't quite put my finger on it.

"Cool," I said, admiring the medallion as I turned it over in my hands. It tingled in my palm but in an entirely different way from what I felt when I touched Tristan's skin. "Does the symbol have any meaning?"

"Yeah, it does actually. It's called The Helm of Awe. It's supposed to protect me while creating fear and awe in my enemies. It is something that's given to all the members of my...um, family," he explained. He turned to keep walking and the medallion slipped from my fingers, landing back on top of his sweater.

"That's interesting. So, all your family has one?" I asked.

"Yup," Tristan answered as we reached my history classroom.

By this time, most of the other students were used to seeing Tristan escort me to class. No one gave us a second look as I slid into my seat. Tristan leaned over to place my bag on the floor. His medallion dangled between us as he leaned even closer to whisper, "Can I see you after school today? I have something to show you." His light-green eyes shimmered in excitement.

"Um...sure," I whispered back, slightly intoxicated by how close Tristan was to me.

As Tristan straightened back up into a standing position, Aedan's face appeared in my line of sight with a terrified look upon it. He quickly turned away, burying his face in his book, but something was definitely wrong.

"Okay, then. I'll see you later," Tristan said, smiling, as he turned to make his exit.

I turned my profile more fully towards Aedan, who was only a few seats away, trying to catch his eye. Upon finally succeeding, I mouthed, "Are you okay?" He gave me a nod, but it wasn't a very reassuring one. I'd have to remember to ask him at lunch.

With the history project having thrown us together and the new school lunch schedule, I'd been spending more and more time with Aedan, which also meant with Joel. While it was a rather odd grouping, lunch had actually started becoming one of my favorite parts of the school day. Both boys were witty and kept me laughing through most of the hour.

I could have never imagined hanging out with Joel before this year. Our social groups had not intersected, and I realized that I'd written him off as just another alternative wannabe without trying to get to know him. It had been easy to make assumptions and be closed off when my best friends were around to fill the social void.

In addition, I might never have been paired with Aedan for the history project if they'd been there. Even though I missed them a lot, their absence had given me a different perspective. My original boiling nervousness around Aedan had been reduced to a simmer. I attributed this to two things. First, Aedan was kind and easy to be around—although something still remained unexplained about him. Second, Tristan's attentions had siphoned most of my jittery feelings in his direction.

I waited by the side walkway for Tristan to arrive. I'd texted my dad earlier in the day to let him know that I wouldn't need a ride home from school.

I'd tried to ask Aedan during lunch if everything was okay given his reaction in class, but he'd brushed off the conversation. I knew I hadn't imagined the expression I'd seen, but I just didn't know what it was about. He'd remained preoccupied for the rest of the day, making me wonder if I'd done something wrong.

Aedan was definitely a little peculiar. During the deer

incident on the road, my senses had gone haywire. At first, I thought it was a reaction to being scared out of my mind, but my goosebumps and the feeling of electricity in the air had been just so overwhelming that I knew something else was happening. I'd thought back to all the other incidents, and except for the beach, Aedan had always either been there or arrived shortly thereafter.

I chuckled out loud. What was I thinking? It was absurd. What could *he* possibly have to do with it? I really must be having one of those hormonal imbalances that caused temporary sensory issues that I'd read about online.

The breeze lifted strands of my red hair and blew them into my face. I turned my head towards the wind and saw Tristan walking towards me. His black leather jacket was zipped, his boots buckled, and he carried two black helmets, one in each hand. Oh, my mom was not going to like this! But she wasn't here to comment on it, either.

I watched Tristan's good-looking figure as he lifted and waved one of the helmets at me. Butterflies took flight in my stomach. A few senior girls in the schoolyard raised their eyebrows when they saw who Tristan had waved at.

I still couldn't quite believe that he was interested in spending time with me. More so, what could he possibly want to show me? Perhaps Mia was right—maybe this was Tristan's way of asking me to the dance again. I felt the familiar warmth creep into my cheeks. Slightly self-conscious, I waved back and started to walk towards him.

"Hi!" I greeted him as we got closer.

"Hi there. You ready?" he asked.

"For what?"

"The beginning of an adventure. Do you trust me, Elin?" he answered, smiling.

"Um...I guess. Why?" I responded.

"Well, you are going to need to if you climb onto my bike. And more importantly, for what I'm about to show you." He gently placed the helmet over my head.

"What are you showing me?" I asked as I adjusted my hair out of my face inside the helmet.

He smirked. "You'll see." He put on his helmet and swung his leg over the motorcycle seat, holding out his hand to help me climb on.

"Keeping me in suspense, I see," I replied, slightly muffled by the helmet as I settled into the seat behind him.

Instead of verbally responding, Tristan started the motorcycle with a roar. That caught the attention of a few more students who were still milling around the schoolyard, including Aedan. He looked concerned.

I was adjusting my backpack when the motorcycle moved. I instinctively grabbed onto Tristan's waist. We were off before I could give a reassuring wave to Aedan.

We sped along the main road for about twenty minutes. I wasn't used to the movement of the motorcycle, so I was caught somewhere between exhilaration and terror every time there was a curve in the road. Feeling like I was going to fall off, I clung even more tightly to Tristan's waist. I was fairly certain this wasn't the cool-girl image he was hoping for, but in the moment the alternative seemed deadlier.

After we passed another curve on the road, Tristan slowed down to take a dirt road to the right. I knew this road. It led to the old lighthouse ruins, which were part of a designated island park system. You could still see the stone walls of the cottage and the remains of the tower that had once accommodated the keeper of the flame and the flame itself. We'd explored the ruins as young children, scrambling over the moss-covered stones and imagining what life must have been like for the lighthouse keeper.

Dark clouds were gathering on the horizon by the time we made it to the end of the road. We pulled into the empty dirt parking spot in front of the main walkway, adjacent to a large clearing. The dense evergreen forest came right up to the large granite peninsula where the buildings stood. The structures hadn't changed much since I'd last been here a year or so ago. The only new item looked to be a wooden fence the park service had added to keep visitors away from the ruins. I guessed it was there to keep more vandals from carving their initials into the stone buildings. There were already plenty of alphabet letters in various combinations marring the old stones.

The park was on the north side of the island in the shadow of Mount Hamar. When tourist season subsided, only a handful of locals enjoyed the coastal walking trails, and mostly on the weekends. Currently, there was no one but us. With the overcast skies and gathering dark clouds, the place had an eerie feel. I dismounted the motorcycle and removed my backpack, dropping it by the wheel. My legs felt slightly wobbly from clutching the bike so hard. I had pulled off my helmet and was taking in the view when Tristan came up behind me.

"Here, I can take that," he said, extending his hand towards the helmet.

"Oh, thanks." I handed it to him. "We use to come here as kids. My parents loved the coastal trails. Especially the part where my brother, sister, and I used all of our energy running back and forth to see what was around the next bend."

"Huh...what an interesting use of everyone's time. Didn't you have chores you should have been doing at home?" Tristan remarked as he busied himself with balancing the helmets just so on the handlebars.

I didn't know quite how to respond, so I started to walk towards the wooden fence. Of course, we'd had chores. But the trips had been a fun family excursion and a fond memory for me. I made it to the fence and leaned on the top bar, looking out to the darkened sea. Before I could glance back to see where Tristan was, he was by my side.

"Oh, hi. That was fast," I greeted him, surprised.

"You have no idea. Come on," he said with a smirk as he climbed over the wooden fence.

"Oh, I don't think we're really supposed to go—" I started to object.

"Don't worry. The thing I have to show you is just on the other side of that wall," Tristan interrupted.

He held out his hand to help me climb over the fence. I hesitated for a moment, but not wanting to seem unadventurous, I took his hand and put my foot on the first slat. The wooden rails shook a little in protest as I mounted them, but they held. Soon I was on the other side. Tristan kept ahold of my hand and a small electric current ran all the way up my arm, raising the little arm hairs under my sweater.

He led me through the broken door of the keeper's house. The inside stood completely bare to the elements, as the fourth wall facing the sea lay in large stone pieces. The remaining three walls were still erect, hiding us from any potential passersby. He brought me to a large boulder.

"Here. Have a seat." He pointed to the boulder.

"Tristan, I've seen the inside of this cottage before. Why are we here?" I asked, shuddering a bit from the cold wind that was picking up.

"Just have a seat. I'm about to show you," he replied as he took a few steps away from me.

I sat down on the cold rock, facing him. Tristan still wore his black leather jacket zipped to the collar. In the surroundings, the contrast between his dark olive skin, sandy hair, green eyes, and his black jacket gave him a slightly unnatural look.

As soon as I took a seat, Tristan rubbed his hands together and held out his palms faceup. Goosebumps materialized on my arms.

A strange feeling of electricity in the air crackled vibrantly around me. Tristan had a look of concentration and effort on his face, and a light began to glow from his palms. Before long the light had grown into a full flame. The orange-and-white tips danced upwards from Tristan's palms. Startled, I slid back a little too far on my sitting stone and fell backward onto the floor behind it.

"Ouch," I mumbled as I hit my head on the stone wall behind me. Before I could take my next breath, Tristan was beside me, trying to help me up from my awkward landing.

"Are you okay?" he asked, concerned, as his hands wrapped around my arm.

Instinctively, I looked down at his hands on my arm. The flames were gone but a more distant feeling of electricity remained in the air.

"Yeah, um...I'm okay. Just bumped my head," I replied, a little embarrassed, rubbing the sore spot on my head. Tristan helped me back to my feet. "What was that, Tristan? Is it some sort of magic trick? Like a fake flame emitter or something?"

"No, Elin. It's quite real." He opened his left hand and a flame burst forth again on his palm. This time it disengaged from Tristan's hand and floated into the space between us. I could feel the heat as it came closer to me.

"I don't understand," I said, shaking my head. "How are you doing that? It's impossible. One doesn't just grow a flame from the human body."

"Clearly it's not impossible, since I just did," Tristan responded with a slight edge of frustration in his voice. Suddenly a few more flaming balls jumped out of his palm and started to encircle me.

A nervous tension gathered in my stomach. I was alone in the middle of an empty park with a boy who could do something highly unusual—and potentially dangerous. And now there was a pearl of fiery flames dancing around me. Coming here was starting to feel like a big mistake.

"Um...yes. Okay...you are definitely doing it. I see that now," I said, trying to be soothing. "How are you doing it?" Perhaps changing the focus of the conversation would stop the flames from multiplying.

"I was born with the ability. All the members of my clan have an ability," Tristan stated.

My change of topic seemed to be working. The flames stopped jumping out of his hand. My shoulders relaxed a little. Now there were only six flames dancing around me. Yet there was still something unfocused—detached—about Tristan.

"I see. So, you have a clan. How big is your clan?" I asked, trying to buy time and draw as far as possible from the flickering flames around me.

Thunder erupted in the distance. I felt the first raindrop on my head. Subsequently, there were small hissing sounds all around me as the raindrops hit the fireballs. I felt like I could breathe again.

"My clan is about a hundred thousand strong. We are the most advanced civilization on earth," Tristan answered, becoming more engaged as the flames sizzled. The rain was becoming steadier. My fabric jacket wasn't going to hold out for long. "You should see the technology and advanced systems we have. Everyone has a clean and orderly home with the latest machines integrated for food and water. We have the best medicines to combat illnesses *Smá-menn* do not even understand yet. There is no hunger or poverty—and everyone has a job in our society. And it's all based on the merit of their ability...instead of the color of their skin, which seems to be a *Smá-menn* obsession."

"Wow...sounds impressive. Who are *sma-man?*" I asked. I wasn't really sure I comprehended what Tristan was telling me. I'd never before heard any mention, anywhere, of the utopia that Tristan was describing. Although, was it *truly* a utopia if you were still being evaluated on something? I shook the thought from my head. It hardly seemed like the best moment to debate the topic.

If it hadn't been for the flaming balls that I'd just witnessed, I would have thought Tristan had lost it. But then again, who was I to judge, given that I was conducting an internal philosophical debate in the middle of a supernatural revelation.

The rain was starting to come down harder and sideways now that the wind was picking up. The last of Tristan's flames were extinguished.

"*Smá-menn* is the name we use for regular people. People outside our clan. People without any gifts," he said.

"Oh...so, like me." I wasn't sure if it was safe yet to tell Tristan we should leave. I could feel the water seeping through my coat.

"Oh, no, Elin. You are something much...much more interesting. You are a Dormant Descendant," Tristan said as his eyes lit up and focused on me again.

"I'm a...what now?" I responded, surprised.

"A Dormant Descendant. You can become like us...have an ability of your own. You carry our gene, the Clan gene...which means you can join us!" Tristan said, grabbing my hand. His excited pale-green eyes looked into my eyes as if he'd just given me the best present in the world.

"Oh, wow...I really don't know what to say," I answered.

Maybe Tristan was off his rocker after all. The word *mistake* kept echoing in my head. I felt really stupid for having thought this outing was going to be a romantic gesture about the Harvest Dance. A flash of lightning split the dark sky and a crack of thunder roared, closer than before. I was getting soaked.

"Tristan, I think we should go home now. I'm getting wet and cold."

"Elin, this is important! I do not think you heard me. You are a Dormant. Do you know how rare that is?" Tristan exclaimed, getting frustrated again and dropping my hands.

"I heard you! But I don't think I can join anything if I'm sick and in bed from catching pneumonia out here!" I was getting angry now. "I let you bring me out here thinking you were going to ask me to the dance again. Instead, I got flaming balls, an unbelievable story of Utopia, and something about being a Dormant Descendant. And I don't even know what that means! What I do know is that I'm cold, wet, hungry, and my head is spinning from everything you just told me!" Rain was pelting me in the face as Tristan looked taken aback by my outburst.

After a few moments of digesting my words, a chided Tristan responded, "I thought we had already agreed to go the dance."

"Well...apparently that wasn't clear to one of us," I answered in a huff as I started to walk past Tristan. I'd had my fill. I no longer cared what he thought—or did—in that moment.

I'd barely made it outside the ruined cottage when Tristan was in front of me. "How...how did you—? Oh, never mind...you'll just tell me you have super speed or something."

"Well, that is true...but Elin, don't be angry. I just got excited in there. I will take you home right now," Tristan said. Without asking permission, he scooped me up and heaved me like a log over his shoulder, leaped over the fence, and had us by his motorcycle in a matter of seconds.

Still a little dizzy from the experience, I said, "Don't ever, I mean *ever*, do that again!" My anger had just started simmering down, but being unceremoniously hoisted into the air and bumped around like a sack of potatoes had made it resurface. I took a wobbly step forward. Tristan grabbed my arm to steady me.

"I'm sorry, Elin. I was just trying to get us here as quickly as possible," Tristan said. He demurely helped me onto the motorcycle, handed me my backpack, and climbed on only after he was sure I was safely tucked into my helmet.

The ride back home seemed to take forever. The rain pelted us from every angle the wind could hurl it. A small saving grace was my waterproof backpack. It protected my back from most of the onslaught. My arms and legs down to the toes in my Converse sneakers were completely soaked.

Island weather could change on a dime. It had been sunny and clear-skied for most of the day until the dark clouds had swiftly moved in. For which, I supposed, I should be grateful, given that they'd extinguished the fiery flame balls.

As we pulled up to the front stairs, Anders came out to greet us, having heard the noise of the motorcycle. I swung my leg off the bike and proceeded to remove my helmet. I turned to hand the helmet back to Tristan. He grabbed it but held onto my hand a moment longer.

"Elin, sorry about today. It was not how I wanted it to go." He paused as he searched for the right words. "But I do—I do I need your help with something. Can I come by tomorrow after school?"

My anger had subsided on the drive home. Now I was mainly wet, tired, and ready for a hot shower.

"Sure, but no promises on the help." I tugged my hand back and headed for the front door, where Anders waited, holding a towel. The motorcycle roared back to life behind me as Tristan drove off.

I felt oddly conflicted about the last few hours. My curiosity about what Tristan had shown me was strong. However, at the same time, it was very hard to believe that supernatural powers were real—or that I possessed a magical gene. I mean, given my lack of an apparent talent—what could my abilities possibly be? I laughed to myself.

The only thing that remotely pointed to a magical power was that I actually had a date to the Harvest Dance. My mom and sister would definitely believe that to be a miracle—although now I wasn't entirely sure whether I really wanted to go with Tristan. It had been a bewildering afternoon of revelations.

FOURTEEN

Hunter's medallion

AEDAN

With U2's "Fire" playing through my earbuds, I paced on the sidewalk, waiting for Edvin. I had to talk to my family as soon as possible. This was bad—really bad!

My parents had only described one to me. I'd been too little to remember seeing one in person before we left. However, I was pretty sure that what I'd seen dangling around Tristan's neck was a Hunter's medallion.

I'd texted my parents that we needed to talk right after school but hadn't conveyed the details. Who knew if the Clan monitored digital communications—regular humans certainly did— so it wasn't worth the risk.

The roar of the motorcycle brought me out of my thoughts. I saw Elin clinging to Tristan's waist as they sped out of the school parking lot. Oh, this *really* was bad! If Tristan was a Hunter, then the Clan had gotten to Elin first.

A Hunter wouldn't waste his time enrolling in high school and courting a regular girl. Tristan must know she was a Dormant. Who knew what twisted things he was telling Elin to persuade her to their side? The only question was, why hadn't he spirited her away already? What was he waiting for? I felt my neck and jaw muscles tighten at the thought of Elin holding onto Tristan's waist.

My father's Land Rover pulled up by the sidewalk in front of me. Through the passenger-side window, I could see both of my parents inside the car. I opened the back door and climbed in.

"Hi, Mom and Dad. I wasn't expecting you guys," I said, surprised, as I settled into my seat and took out my earbuds.

"Well, you can't send a message like that in the middle of the school day and not expect the cavalry to show up," my father responded, turning to look at me.

"It was urgent...because...well, there's a Hunter...in my school...he's got Elin...we need to help her," I blurted out all at once. Both my parents had turned around to face me in the car.

"What!" my mother exclaimed.

"Son, slow down. What do you mean, there's a Hunter? How do you know?" my father asked, trying to calm both my mother and me down.

"I saw his medallion. Tristan...he had the medallion around his neck. He's been hanging around Elin—a lot. Which—I mean, she's a good-looking girl...but he's a senior and she's a junior...and Candice is totally into him...so it doesn't make any sense. High school just doesn't work like that." I paused for breath. "And now he just sped away with her. Who knows where and for what purpose? We have to help her! Can you imagine what the Clan will do when they get ahold of her?" Both of my parents were trying to take in the stream of information spewing from my mouth.

"What kind of medallion, Aedan?" my mother asked, trying to focus on the pertinent part.

"I'm pretty sure it was a Helm of Awe. It's just like you guys said—the eight tridents coming from the middle of the circle..." I described it, drawing an image in the air. Both of my parents' mouths tightened into thin lines as I finished my description.

"Oh, Liam! Do you think they've found us again so soon?" my mother asked, looking at my father anxiously.

"Dara, there's no need to panic yet. We've had no indication that anyone has been tracking us—or is even interested in us. According to Aedan, Tristan is much more preoccupied with Elin. She may have inadvertently provided a great distraction," my father said, musing on the last part.

"Well? What are we going to do to help her?" I asked, impatient to get the process underway.

"Son, what would you have us do? If we ride to her rescue, we'll expose ourselves. The Clan will then in short order know where to find us. We would have to start packing right now to be able to escape before their reinforcements arrived. Plus, we don't know that she's in any immediate danger. We have to weigh the pros and cons here," my father concluded.

"But, Dad! She might be. Shouldn't we at least find out? What if she converts and ends up helping the Clan? It wouldn't be too long before she figures out about us," I argued back, desperate to get the car moving and spring into action.

"Liam, Aedan does have a point. With the 'do nothing' approach, we may end up in just as precarious a position, given that there's now a Hunter involved," my mother said as she laid her hand on my father's arm.

My father relented as he gave me a pointed look. "All right, then...we'll go see what the situation is. But we do not engage unless there's imminent danger. Understood?" I nodded. "Okay, Aedan, which way did they go?"

"They turned right out of the school driveway, heading north," I replied as my father put the car into gear.

We came to the first intersection after about five minutes of driving on the curvy island road.

"Dara, anything?" my father asked.

A look of deep concentration appeared on my mother's face as she tapped into her *megin*. My mother could not only sense emotions and amplify abilities but had also honed her skill over many years, so she could tell how many individuals were in the surroundings. If she centered on the number of emotions or *megins* she felt, she could figure out how many people there were.

"Nothing. They didn't go down this way," my mother answered. The Land Rover continued through the intersection.

"We should be only a few minutes behind them. They'd just left the school when you arrived," I added.

I rolled down the car window, thinking I could perhaps hear Tristan's very loud motorcycle. However, the only thing I could hear was the rotation of the Land Rover's tires against the asphalt. Leaning out the window, I could see dark clouds starting to gather above the treetops.

After about another five minutes of driving, we came to a dirt road on the right. There was a sign that read, "Light House Regional Island Park."

"Turn here," my mother announced, suddenly breaking the silence.

Luckily, my father had slowed down at the intersection and was able to make the turn. We continued down the dirt road for another few minutes.

"Stop, Liam! Stop!" my mother exclaimed. "We're getting close. They should be just ahead."

My father brought the car to an abrupt stop. In the distance, I could see the outline of a tower. We were still too far away to see Elin and Tristan. Our black Land Rover, however, would be very discernible in the middle of the dirt road.

My father spotted a trailhead pull-off a few paces up the road. It was a small U-shaped lane created by vehicles wanting to park close to the trail. A few trees grew in the middle of the U. My father brought the car to a stop directly in the center so we'd be somewhat concealed from the main road.

My father turned to look at my mother. "Okay, Dara. What do you sense?"

"I'm getting anticipation and excitement. Hold on...I'm trying to isolate between the two," my mother said as she closed her eyes. The lines on her face deepened further. "Now I'm getting hesitation and still excitement with an ounce of annoyance. Gotcha! Hesitation is Elin. I can now focus on just her pattern."

My mother continued her announcements of Elin's emotions: hesitation, curiosity, annoyance, surprise, apprehension...pain. At the last statement, my father unbuckled himself and opened the car door.

"You two stay here. Aedan, I'll call you on your cell phone for updates from your mom. I'm going closer in case we are needed." He hurriedly grabbed his cell phone from the console.

"But, Dad, I should come too! You might need help. We don't know what Tristan's ability is or what he's doing to Elin," I replied, concerned that something bad was already happening.

"No, Aedan. You stay here with your mom. If I need you, I'll let you know," my father said as he closed the car door. My mother and I were left staring through the window as my father disappeared into the forest with *megin* speed.

"Mom, anything new?" I asked, placing my hand on her arm to refocus her attention from the forest to the task at hand.

She closed her eyes to concentrate. Our *megin* was still regaining strength after the prior week's new moon, so harnessing our abilities required more effort.

"I'm getting embarrassment and curiosity. Now it is turning into apprehension—" My mother was interrupted by the ring of my cell phone.

"Hi, Dad. What do you see? Okay, hang on," I said as I switched the phone to the speaker setting.

My father's voice boomed through the speaker. "Dara, can you hear me?"

I turned the volume down a little. My parents hadn't quite learned that you didn't need to shout into cell phones for the other person to hear you. Their perception of the regular world's technology was that it was vastly outdated and required mitigation to be useful.

"I hear you, Liam," my mother responded, equally loudly.

"I'm on the edge of the forest clearing. I see a motorcycle in the parking lot and an old stone structure and tower. There is no sign of Tristan and Elin, so I'm guessing they're somewhere inside," my father reported. "What's the latest on your end?"

"Elin seems to be okay. Pain seems to have dissipated into embarrassment, but I'm getting apprehension again. There's definitely something unusual going on out there," my mother answered, leaning towards the cell phone in my hand to be sure my father could hear her. She then closed her eyes and dropped into her concentration again. "I'm getting fear now...and cold."

At those words, I quickly put my phone on the console, opened the car door, and started running at top speed before my mother could say anything. The branches of the trees tore at my jacket as I ran through the dense forest. There was a flash of lightning in the distance and thunder boomed. Rain fell through the trees as I ran.

Elin was clearly in danger! She needed help. I couldn't just stay on the sidelines and not try to do something. I could see the clearing for the parking lot ahead. I was getting close.

Whoosh! I was off my feet, circling through the air with my father's arms wrapped around me. We landed a few feet away in the meadow that sat beside the parking lot, and I rolled to a stop with my father on top of me. Thunder roared nearby.

"What in the Niflheim do you think you are doing, son?" my father exclaimed. "I told you I'd let you know if I needed help."

My father continued to pin me to the ground. It had started to rain at a good clip. The raindrops bouncing off his shoulder were splattering into my face.

"We have to help her, Dad! Mom said she was afraid and cold. Clearly, something bad is going on in there," I replied, struggling under my father's grip to get off the ground.

At the same moment, I heard Elin's angry voice in the distance. I stopped moving. My father dropped lower into the tall hay grass around us.

Suddenly, Elin's voice was a great deal closer, in the parking lot next to us. My father lowered himself beside me in an effort to further conceal our presence. I was now fully exposed to the hard-falling rain.

I could hear Elin chastising Tristan, telling him to never do something again. Tristan mumbled an apology. A feeling of deep satisfaction started to warm my insides.

We lay as still as possible until we heard the motorcycle roar into life and drive past us. Once we were certain that they'd left, my father and I stood up, soaked to the bone from rain. The wind blew the rain sideways and a low rumble of thunder echoed in the distance.

"Um...I'm...um, sorry, Dad," I apologized, feeling contrite about the false alarm but also relieved. Elin was okay—at least for now.

"We'll talk about it when we get home," my father replied, still upset over my disobedience.

"Are you...two...all...right?" My mother's voice crackled softly from my father's jacket. My father fished around in his pocket until he found his cell phone.

"Fine, Dara. We'll be back in a second." My father ended the call. "Okay, Aedan. Let's go get cleaned up."

In addition to being wet from the rain, both my father and I had large sections of our clothing and hair covered in mud and hay from the hard landing we'd taken in the meadow. I would definitely feel sore and bruised from the experience later. My father turned towards the forest and began running at a relaxed speed back to the Land Rover. I followed, my soaked sneakers squeaking.

~

After hot showers and fresh clothes, my parents sat me down to tell me I was grounded for the next week. I'd disobeyed my father's direction and could have potentially put us all at risk.

I understood their reasons. I still didn't like it—especially given that the Harvest Dance was the following week. I hadn't actually asked any girl to go, but the plan had been to join forces with Joel. The reason I wanted to attend was to keep an eye on Elin.

Given the attention Tristan had been paying her, I was pretty sure he'd asked her to go. He wasn't going to let his prize out of his sight. But the dance might be another opportunity to somehow disrupt his plans.

I'd spread a large orange towel on the wet front porch stairs. I had come to cool off after the drill-down my parents had given me. Being outdoors always helped to center me.

The rain had finally stopped, and the air had an earthy smell. Small patches of sun played on the grass between the breaks in the clouds. I took in a deep breath.

I had my earbuds in and Alabama Shakes was in the middle of "Hold On" when I heard the front door open and close behind me. My mother came and sat down next to me on the towel. She put her hand on my arm. I took out my earbuds and pressed "pause."

"Hi, honey," my mother said as she settled next to me. "I wanted to see if you were okay."

"I'm fine, Mom. I just needed some space," I responded, slightly annoyed that she was taking that away from me.

"Aedan, do you know why your dad takes this so seriously?" She looked at me.

"Yes, I know. He wants to make sure we're all safe and protected from the Clan," I answered in a rote manner.

"That's right, but there's more to it. You know, I have a love-hate relationship with that stupid Hunter's medallion. It used to be a symbol of great reverence for all of us. Your dad even has one —now hidden away somewhere," my mother recounted.

"What? He was a Hunter?" I asked, genuinely surprised.

"They weren't called Hunters back then. It was the symbol for our Protective Services or PS. Their mission was to keep us hidden from the regular world. It was a noble job. PS history has its origins in Clan formation when the god Máni blessed our people with his gifts. Some members received the abilities of great warriors. They were the ones who were on the frontlines during Ragnarök. Throughout our history, those with protective abilities have been called to the PS. Your father was one of them. It used to be a choice and a great honor," my mother related.

"Oh, wow! I'd no idea."

"That was, of course, before everything changed. You know the history of the Four Clans and how Falinvik's isolated northern location saved us from the same fate as the Sudri, Austri, and Vestri Clans. After their collapse, Chairman Arild disseminated his program of productivity through fear and further isolation. Many things were altered. He started to use the word Stór-menni, or 'men of greatness,' to describe our Clan instead of our original name of Nordri. He also designated Mannlegurs as Smá-menn... or, 'men of insignificance.' Our borders were closed and security became paramount. The PS became Hunters or Interrogators. They were there to keep our people under control rather than to protect them. The Chairman wanted your father to command a whole division of Interrogators. It required them to do terrible things to members who were just trying to survive or reunite with family members. It was a horrible time."

My mother involuntarily shuddered, gazing into the yard as she remembered. "Your dad refused to participate in what was happening. We became more afraid every day, not only for him but for you kids. We daily saw children ripped from families to be placed into mentorship programs. Frantic parents were carted off by the PS to be interrogated for noncompliance and under-productivity. It wasn't until we escaped that I slept through an entire night." My mom paused, looking at me. "Your dad isn't just afraid that we wouldn't see you kids ever again if we were caught...but that you'd be forced to do things...horrible things... with your abilities."

I threw my arms around my mom. I could see the toll of what my parents had lived through written on her face. I'd been a toddler when my parents had escaped, so my memories of Falinvik were very limited, mostly images that I wasn't sure weren't just old photographs. My parents had told us many stories about Falinvik, but I'd never heard the part about my father being a Protective Services member or how it had been the Clan Chairman who'd changed the Clan's identity from Nordri to *Stór-menni* so many years ago.

"I'm so sorry, Mom. I didn't know. It sounds awful," I mumbled into the soft black waves of my mom's hair.

The idea that anyone would or could force you to use your ability in a way you didn't want made me shudder. It also made me more determined than ever to get Elin out of Tristan's clutches.

FIFTEEN

An apology

TRISTAN

I did not understand *Smá-menn*. Not that Elin was exactly a *Smá-menn*, but she had grown up in their society. I had conveyed to her the incredible opportunity the Clan presented and how rare it was for her to have a chance to join. The result was not what I expected at all. There was no appreciation—just an urgent need to go home. I suppose she had been wet and cold, but that paled in comparison to the honor of becoming a Clan member.

I watched as another fireball grew from my palm. Once it was sufficiently large, I hurled it at a wet tree stump at the border of my aunt's backyard. The fireball left another satisfying black scar as it fizzled on the stump.

Aunt Adis's backyard was manicured to perfection. It had a well-trimmed grass path sloping down to an inlet, where it met a small jetty. The curving path was framed by various green bushes, some of which were in bloom with different-colored flowers. All of the yard was hedged by an evergreen forest. It was another testament to my aunt's productivity and mastery.

The serenity of my surroundings did not match my mood. I

could not abandon my plan at this point. I was too far into it. I needed Elin. I needed her in order to not only succeed at my main goal but also to get my aunt's library key. I would have to change something in my approach with Elin—but what? What more could she possibly want?

Part of graduating from the Clan mentorship program was to be recognized as truly self-sufficient. It is how I had gained the privilege of my first solo hunting mission. However, the irony now was that I was completely reliant on another person for my mission's success. The unfamiliarity of the circumstances was leaving me at a loss as to how to proceed.

"Tristan!" My aunt's voice boomed from the back porch. "Come here, please."

The sudden interruption of my thoughts and my aunt's demeanor made me swallow hard. Had she scanned the Caelum door? Had I been caught? My *megin* was only at half strength. The moon was not full until the end of the following week. I would not have a fighting chance against my aunt. I eyed the rim of the forest.

"Tristan, NOW!" my aunt exclaimed, clearly annoyed by my apparent delay.

"Coming, Aunt!" I answered as I started towards the house.

I had no choice. There was no escape. As I reached the back porch, my aunt took her time inspecting my appearance.

"Tristan, what on earth are you up to?" she asked. My mind raced for an answer. "Why are you expending all your *megin* on that tree stump? And your appearance—you are soaked from head to toe. Where have you been? Isn't your mission going well?"

I let out a small breath. She did not know yet.

"Sorry, Aunt. Just a minor setback in my hunt. I needed to relieve some energy before I changed clothes," I answered.

It was the truth without the details. I had had a setback and had not had a chance to change my clothes after my excursion with Elin.

"I will go shower and change right now." I turned to enter the back door.

"Not so fast, Tristan. I do not want those muddy boots in the house. Brush them off on the scraper and remove them before entering," she instructed. She grabbed my arm as I was about to walk towards the scraper. "Tristan, one more thing...have you been in my office?"

There it was—the skilled interrogator's strike. Their subject was lulled into complacency, and then the actual question was put forth.

"Yes, Aunt. I needed a pen for a homework assignment," I lied, keeping my voice steady. Better to admit to something innocent than get caught red-handed. "I hope you do not mind. I had to look through your desk drawers to find one."

"I see." She intently inspected my face. "Next time I would prefer if you asked first."

She dropped my arm and brushed past me into the house. I had no idea whether she believed me, but it was clearly a warning, one way or another. I would have to be even more careful.

The next day was a blur of classrooms and hallways. I had not seen Elin all day, and I did not seek her out. I needed time to come up with a plan.

No Hunter training had been provided for this sort of situation. Nor could I remember any words of advice from Henric on how to convince another person to help you. I felt at a loss. The school day was about to end—and I had nothing.

In addition, Candice had been acting very strange. One minute she would be flirtatious and the next moment irritated. I had given up on trying to appease her. I had wasted enough time and evenings with her. It was starting to feel like *Smá-menn* girls were a bigger mystery than I had bargained for.

The school bell rang, signaling the end of the day. I got up from my desk and headed for the classroom door.

The hallway was busy with students filing out of classrooms and accessing their lockers to find the right items to take home. The walls were plastered with homemade posters and streamers advertising the school dance the following week.

A *Smá-menn* girl with golden ringlets emitted squeals of delight as a hockey player from the school team handed her a rose and a small package. After opening the present, she lifted up a small necklace with a heart-shaped pendant and announced that they were going to the Harvest Dance together. The hockey player stood by her side proudly, grinning in a self-satisfied way.

The more time I spent with these *Smá-menn,* the less I understood them. What an overindulgence...to spend time thinking of ways to ask a girl to a dance instead of just doing it. However, in this instance, it had given me an idea. It meant I would have to swing by my aunt's house on my way to Elin's, but hopefully, it would be worth the effort to re-establish a more solid footing with Elin.

I arrived at Elin's pale-yellow house about half an hour later than I had originally planned. The sun was out, making it feel warmer than was typical. Elin sat in a roofed dual garden glider by the house, gently swinging and reading a textbook. She closed the book as I approached. I gripped the small parcel in my hand a little more tightly.

"Hi!" I called out as I got closer.

Elin set the textbook beside her on the bench seat. "Hi, Tristan."

"Can I join you?" I asked, standing by the glider.

Elin gestured toward the bench opposite her. "Sure, come aboard." She sounded friendly. I breathed a little easier.

I stepped into the glider as the opening between the benches came close to me. At first, the back-and-forth movement caught me by surprise. However, as I sat down on the bench facing Elin, the gentle rocking helped to ease some of the uncomfortable energy that had taken root as I drove up to the house.

"So...first, I just wanted to say sorry again," I started. "Yesterday was not quite how I had intended things to go. I probably just got a little too excited about sharing...you know...with you."

"I get it, Tristan. It was just...a lot...all at once," Elin responded.

"I probably did not do the best job in explaining what exactly —what the situation is. You must have questions about what I told you," I said. Since yesterday's Plan A had failed and I had not been able to come up with a concrete Plan B, I had decided the best way was to let Elin guide me.

"I do have some questions. Anders helped me think of a few, yesterday." Elin drew a slip of paper from her textbook.

"What?" I exclaimed, nearly falling out of the glider, I stood up so quickly. "You told Anders! Who is Anders?"

"Anders is my brother," Elin said, looking up at me, her lips drawn into a thin line.

Looking at her disapproving face, I had to remember why I was here. Remain calm, I reminded myself. I drew a deep breath and forced myself to take a seat on the bench.

"I might not have mentioned it yesterday, but we do not share our existence with anyone outside the Clan," I tried to say as evenly as possible.

If this ever got back to the Clan, I would be thrown into Ginnungagap for sure—and Anders would be joining me there, or worse. I felt like screaming at Elin. How could she be so careless!

Instead I asked, "Did you share yesterday's news with anyone else?"

"No, I didn't share it with anyone else. And Anders doesn't even believe me. He thinks it's just an elaborate hoax of some kind," Elin responded crossing her arms.

I breathed out a small sigh of relief. At least it was a contained problem. I would need to figure out how to deal with Anders later.

"Great! Well, let's just let him think that," I said, trying to keep my voice measured. "There can be serious repercussions for people who expose the Clan...or for those *Smá-menn* who inadvertently become aware of us. Sharing my ability with you yesterday was really meant just for you. No one else. That is why I took you to the lighthouse—to make sure no one saw us."

"But why doesn't the Clan want anyone to know about them? If they've got this wonderful utopia, why wouldn't they want to share it with the rest of the world?" Elin was still clutching the slip of paper in her hand. "More importantly—what can happen to Anders?"

"Nothing will happen to Anders. No one will find anything out. We just need to let him think that it is all just a trick. You understand?" I was getting a little frustrated again. I reminded myself that I needed Elin. "It is about keeping everyone safe. The Clan has always been a secret, since its inception. Can you imagine the *Smá-menns'* reaction if they were to learn about us? It would be chaos. Their illusion of being the apex predator on earth would be shattered. Never mind all the demands for help—supernatural and otherwise. No, it would never work." I laughed a little at the thought. Elin seemed to be contemplating my words.

"Huh," was all she uttered for a moment. "What exactly is the Clan's role in the world, then?"

"Well, we are here to protect everyone when Ragnarök comes, of course. Just like the god Odin chooses his Einherjar from fallen warriors to prepare for the great battle, the moon god Máni creates his own secret army here on Earth. That is why it is so important to make sure that all our Clan members are gathered together and united as one. According to Chairman Arild, blessed be his name, we will need everyone when the time comes... especially now that the Nordri clan is all that is left of the Four Clans. That is why I'm here in the *Smá-menn* world, tracking down lost members. It is how I stumbled upon you, Elin," I explained, excitedly reaching across the gap between the benches to grab her hand. I had forgotten how little Elin knew about the Clan or its history.

"Who are the Four Clans? And what's Ragnarök?" Elin asked, letting me hold her hand. The small, familiar electric current passed between us.

"The Four Clans, Nordri, Sudri, Austri, and Vestri, were the original chosen people. Long ago, the moon god secretly bestowed four societies from the north, south, east, and west with special abilities to help fight alongside the gods when the time comes. Amongst our clan, the great battle is known as Ragnarök. It is the pinnacle of the conflict between the gods and giants...and the end of this world and the beginning of the next—as long as the gods win. We are here to ensure they do and that humanity survives." I tried to keep my explanation simple. The details were complicated and best left to those who could convey them in the right way.

"Huh...I sort of remember hearing about something like that, but I thought it was all just mythological," Elin said.

"Trust me. It is quite real. I would not exist if it was not," I answered.

"So, what are Dormants, then? How do they fit in?" Elin was clearly becoming more curious. I took it as a good sign.

"Dormants...well, they are rare. Not a lot is known about them.

What we do know is that they have a dormant Clan gene and can change...convert...to become like us," I answered.

"How do you know that I might be one of them, then?" Elin asked.

"Because of this." I lifted our entwined hands from her lap. "I'm sure you feel that tingling...that electric current that flows between us when we touch. Clan members are especially trained to know the signs if we come across them. That is how much the Chairman values Dormants...values you."

Elin was intently staring at our hands. She looked up for a moment as if she was about to say something but instead looked back at our hands again.

"I know. It is a lot to take in. But you have a potential gift, Elin...a rare gift. Wouldn't you like to find out what it is?"

"How sure are you, Tristan, that the electricity is a marker? What if I'm just a...what do you call it...a sma-man?" Elin asked.

"A *Smá-menn*. No, Elin... you are definitely not a *Smá-menn*. I'm positive you are a Dormant Descendant, but there is an easy way to prove it." I dangled the lure to see if she would bite. "My aunt has a book, an ancient book of awakening, that spells everything out in more detail. If we get it, we can prove you are a Dormant."

"Well, if it's that easy...then why didn't you bring it?" Elin asked, piercing the heart of the matter.

"It is locked up in the Clan library...and my aunt has the only key." I paused for effect. "And I can't tell her about you because we need to prove you are a Dormant first. It is for your protection. The fewer the people who know about you, the better—for now, at least."

It was mostly true. I did not want to lose my prize. The discovery of a Dormant Descendant was a valuable commodity in Clan society. You could gain great favor with the Chairman—and that opened many doors. Plus, I had invested so much already. The fewer people who knew, the better my chances.

"So how do we get the book, then?" Elin asked.

"We steal the key," I answered, grinning.

"Um...I don't know, Tristan. Why can't we just ask your aunt?" Elin responded, frowning apprehensively.

"My aunt—my aunt is not a very understanding person. If she knew I had shared with you not only my ability but also information about the Clan, I would be in a lot of trouble...and you would not be safe. No...no, our only option is to steal the key and try to keep you hidden for as long as possible."

"Tristan, how do I even know there's a library? Or that anything you've told me is real? It just seems so unbelievable." Elin's mood seemed to have shifted suddenly. "I know...I've seen what you can do...I feel the literal electricity between us, but it's all just so surreal."

"I will take you," I interrupted before she could layer on any more doubts. "I will take you to the door of the Clan library."

It was my last option. The one I had prepared for. I reached beside myself for the small parcel. I had seen it in a catch-all box in my aunt's basement and hoped it might help me convince Elin.

"Here. This is for you." I handed the parcel to her.

"What is it?" Elin asked.

"Open it and you'll see."

She carefully unwrapped the brown paper I had hastily taped around the small box. She set the paper aside and opened the lid of the box. Inside on a small square of fluffy cotton lay a Trollkors ring. The setting of the ring had a silver loop with curled ends that met at the bottom. In the middle of the knot lay a large, clear crystal.

"It's beautiful," Elin said.

"It is a Trollkors ring. The crystal in the center has been engineered to create powerful illumination in dark places. The light reveals things that otherwise might not be seen," I explained. "The metal around the crystal forms a Troll Cross. It is a symbol of protection."

Elin carefully picked up the ring and held it to the light. The crystal caught the light and small rainbows danced around the glider from the refraction.

"Put it on. You will need it, where we are going."

SIXTEEN

The Trollkors ring

ELIN

I t hadn't been easy, explaining to Anders why I was choosing to go with the same weird guy from school again. I'd seen Anders surveilling us through the dining-room window while I was speaking with Tristan on the glider. Anders' big-brother protective instincts had kicked into high alert after I'd shared with him the previous day's adventures. Whether he believed everything I told him to be real didn't actually matter to him. All he saw was a strange boy trying to convince his sister of who knew what, for who knew what purpose.

"Elli, I don't like it," Anders had said sternly to me—and he was rarely stern with me. "What do you know about this boy other than that he likes to play tricks on unsuspecting girls? And now you want to go where with him? To the library to study...really? There's just something not right with him."

I'd opted for half-truths instead of full lies to help pacify Anders. I'd explained to him that Tristan had come to apologize for the previous day. That Tristan had admitted to the unusual demonstration being an elaborate illusion. A misguided way of asking me to the Harvest Dance. To make up for it, Tristan wanted to help me study for an upcoming exam.

If what Tristan had said was true and *Smá-menn* were punished just for knowing about the Clan, I didn't want to take any chances with my elder brother. There was still a lot to learn about this new world I was being introduced to.

"Andee, don't worry. What could possibly happen to me at the library?" I'd responded, thinking that Tristan would be taking me to the town library. That, of course, now seemed like a silly assumption as I stood outside Tristan's aunt's house.

It was finally Maria who'd inadvertently helped me convince Anders to let me go with Tristan. She'd walked into the dining room where Anders and I were speaking and asked, "Elli, who's that yummy-looking boy on the motorcycle? Do you finally have a date?"

"Sort of," I'd responded, shifting uncomfortably. Situations with the opposite sex that came naturally to my sister were awkward for me. We didn't share a mutual language when it came to boys. Anders was aware of the tension.

"What do you mean? There's no 'sort of' in dating—you either are or you aren't. And if you aren't, then I'm getting on the back of that bike," she'd said smirking. We both knew she wouldn't, given that she was dating Eric. It was just her way of taking a jab at me.

Coming to my defense and, more specifically, not wanting to let a golden opportunity to flummox my sister pass, Anders had jumped in. "Actually, Elli and Tristan were just about to go on a study date together. Right, Elli?" He smiled but then added more pointedly, "Don't forget to call me when you're ready to come home or if anything else occurs."

So, it was through this convergence of sibling rivalries that I found myself holding Ms. Haugen's porch door open and watching as Tristan unlocked the side door. The door opened, to reveal a house full of shadows. It was twilight already, and no lights were on inside. Tristan strode confidently into the gray hallway after pausing to clean his boots by the door.

"Come on, Elin. This way." He beckoned as I hesitated on the porch steps. "Just be sure to brush off the dirt from your shoes on the scraper." Tristan pointed to the bristled brushes by the door.

A growing bluish-white light was beginning to illuminate the hallway where Tristan stood. Looking down at my hand, I realized that the Trollkors ring was working. I quickly did as he commanded, cleaning my shoes, and then I walked inside.

It was a very tidy home. Immaculate shoes were lined up perfectly on a small rack by the side door. The framed pictures on the walls were in precise alignment. The rugs on the floor were exactly in the middle of the hallway and measured to fit the space neatly. It almost made one afraid to touch anything for fear of disturbing the space.

Tristan led the way further into the house. He wasn't bothering to turn on any of the lights. I followed him, guided by the light from the Trollkors ring. Towards the end of the hallway, Tristan opened a door on the right and entered a room. A few paces behind him, I caught up with him as he was bringing his fist down with a thud in the middle of an antique-looking writing desk. There was a small *whoosh*, and a small box appeared next to Tristan. He reached inside and, clearly with effort, pulled on something.

To my surprise, the bookcase on the opposite wall slid out and over the adjoining one on the right. There appeared to be a passage behind the bookcases. Tristan confidently strode around the desk and said, "This way, Elin."

He smiled at the astonished look on my face and grabbed my left hand to lead me into the dark space. The passage was narrow but not comfortable. With the Trollkors light, I could make out some sort of metal spiral staircase at the opposite end.

Tristan pressed a red button inserted into the back of the

bookcase. With the ease of a well-oiled machine, the bookcase slid back into its position. The only place left to go was toward the staircase.

Something about being in total darkness, except for the blue light from the Trollkors ring, left me with little to say. It felt like we were sneaking around and had to remain quiet. It was a comical instinct given that Tristan and I were the only ones in the passage. I suppressed a nervous giggle.

Tristan gave my arm a small tug as he moved towards the stairs. He entered the spiral first, disappearing into the darkness as he rounded the first turn. Carefully I stepped on the first metal stair and felt the vibration of Tristan's movement.

I aimed the Trollkors ring downward, looking for the bottom. The only thing the light captured was the top of Tristan's sandy hair. He was already a few spirals beneath me. I hesitated, uncomfortable with the vibration and swaying motion that both Tristan's and my movements were causing. Slowly, I continued down the stairs.

"Hurry up, Elin! We do not have all day," Tristan's voice said from the darkness below.

It was all the encouragement I received as I continued my progress down the swaying spirals. Somewhere on the fourth turn, I pulled out my phone to check my reception. The display showed zero bars. In fact, as I stared at the screen, the words "No service" appeared, replacing the signal bar. There'd be no calling Anders for help from down here. I tucked the phone safely into my back pocket and cautiously proceeded to the next step.

I hadn't thought that it could possibly get darker, but as I rounded the final spiral and stepped onto the dirt floor, my surroundings seemed to swallow me. The only light was from the Trollkors ring, which illuminated Tristan's annoyed face.

"Well, that took you long enough," he said as a welcome.

"The staircase was shaking pretty badly! And slow is better

than falling—especially with no cell service down here," I replied, equally annoyed. He could have waited for me and helped if time was such a concern. "Besides, apparently I don't see quite as well in the dark as you do. Any other abilities you'd like to share?"

"No, I think you know them all now," he responded with a haughty expression.

"So, let's see...night vision, fireballs, speed...what else...oh, right, strength." I listed out his abilities, feeling irritated at being judged, especially given my very apparent disadvantage. "Do all your kind share these?"

Tristan, apparently getting the memo that I wasn't pleased, changed his tone. "Not the fireballs, but yes, most do share the others," he acquiesced. Changing the subject, he continued, "It is 5:30pm now. We do not have that much time left before my aunt gets back home. I think I had better carry you the rest of the way."

"Like before?" I asked. "No way...I don't think so. I'd rather proceed on my own two feet." The idea of being hoisted like a bag of potatoes over his shoulder again made me queasy.

"Elin, it is at least two or more miles to the door. It would take too long," Tristan answered, exasperated.

"Oh... how about piggyback then?" I conceded, thwarted.

As an answer, Tristan came closer to me and presented his back, reaching his arms towards me. I placed my hands on his shoulders and felt the muscles ripple underneath my touch. The butterflies in my stomach flapped their wings.

"On the count of three, jump. Okay?" Tristan instructed.

We counted to three together, and then I jumped towards Tristan's back, using my hands on his shoulders as leverage. His arms wrapped around my legs and closed the last space between us. I carefully positioned my hands and arms across his shoulders to avoid choking him. It reminded me of the numerous piggyback rides I'd received as a child from both my dad and Anders.

Before I could think another thought, Tristan was off. His

speed made me feel like I was riding some sort of wild animal. The swaying movement and apparent wind loosened strands of hair from my ponytail. I shuddered a little from the cold, as my light hoodie was no match for my surroundings or Tristan's speed. The light from the Trollkors ring bounced wildly off the side walls. The walls seemed to be made of large cut stones or granite boulders, reminding me of medieval castles that I'd visited.

In the distance, a faint red light appeared. I bounced around on Tristan's back for a few more moments before he came to a stop. His arms loosened their grip on my legs. I was able to slide down to the dirt ground. Tristan stretched the cramps out of his arms as I rounded to his side.

In front of me stood a large metal wall. The red light I'd seen from the distance was beside an odd-looking keyhole. I raised my hand to feel the cool metal under my fingers. As soon as I did, Tristan's hand closed around them.

"Do *not* touch it," he said with measured calmness as if I'd just been reaching for a hot stove. "It is a Caelum metal door. It will memorize your imprint."

"My imprint...like my fingerprints?" I asked, startled.

"Sort of, but it will take much more information than just that. Like your DNA...from which it will be able to reconstruct what you look like, whether you a *Smá-menn* or *Stór-menni*, etcetera," Tristan explained.

"Wow! Okay. I've never heard of anything like that before," I said, amazed.

"You would not have. It is a Clan invention," Tristan conveyed, proudly straightening himself. "Now for the very interesting part. Point the Trollkors light toward the door."

I did as Tristan asked. The Caelum metal began to shimmer, becoming almost translucent under the direct beam. After a few moments, the area directly under the Trollkors light began to reveal what was on the other side.

At first, we could see only a dirt path. I angled the light upwards and let it perform its magic. After a minute or two, the blue light exposed a short passage to an octagonal room. The height of the room seemed to stretch way beyond the ceiling of the passage. The details were difficult to make out since the further the light had to travel, the dimmer the room became. What could be made out was that the walls held staggeringly tall bookcases filled with books of various heights and sizes. In the middle of the room was a large, round stone table with a wooden book pedestal.

"Oh, that's so cool!" I declared almost under my breath as I took in the view and processed what the Trollkors ring could do. "Will the ring do that with everything?"

"Only certain materials...usually ones the Clan has engineered. It *is* pretty cool, though," Tristan agreed.

After a few more moments of pointing the light around the edges of the room, a sensation of heat began to burn into my finger from the Trollkors ring. As it grew more intense, I yelped in pain. I quickly drew my hand away from the door and the ring off my finger. Immediately the blue light disappeared. We were plunged into darkness except for the small red indicator light on the door.

"What? What happened?" Tristan asked, concerned.

"It burned me." I rubbed my finger.

I could feel a hot indentation where the ring had been a few moments ago. I slipped the ring into my pocket as Tristan drew my hand towards him for closer inspection.

"It did, didn't it?" he said, stating the obvious. "Are you okay?"

"Yeah...I think so. It was just so...so unexpected."

"I have never heard of it doing that before... but then I'm no expert on the interaction between Caelum metal and Trollkors light. Maybe there is some sort of protection mechanism," Tristan speculated before letting go of my hand. *"Odin's beard!"*

"What? What now?" I asked.

"It is 5:55pm! We have only five minutes to get back and out of the passage, and get you out of the house before my aunt comes home," Tristan exclaimed, clearly distressed by the lack of time. "On my back, Elin. We have to go now!"

I had only the guidance of the little red light to try to find Tristan's back and jump on it. Tristan was muttering frustrations under his breath over my lack of progress. Piggyback success was finally achieved after the third try. Tristan immediately took off, running as fast as he could.

For some reason, the way back in the pitch-dark passage seemed longer. Perhaps because I didn't have the comforting blue light of the Trollkors ring, or maybe it was the anxiety over getting out before we were discovered. We both seemed to draw a sigh of relief as the metal staircase came into view...wait, I thought, why could I see the metal staircase?

There was faint light...and it was coming from somewhere above the staircase. Tristan quickly released me and I slid to the ground. He placed his hand on the metal railing of the staircase. He clearly felt a vibration. He put a single finger in front of his mouth, motioning me to stay quiet.

This was bad! There were only two ways to go—back where we'd come from or up the stairs. Neither were good options. Tristan seemed to be contemplating the same thing as he came close to me. He looked back toward the way we'd come and then up the stairs.

Suddenly he pulled on my hand, tugging me towards the staircase. However, instead of starting upward, he led me to the back of the last spiral. He motioned me to drop to the ground and crawl underneath the stairs. I did as he asked, crawling along the damp dirt floor until I reached the stone wall. Tristan was instantly beside me. I could feel the heat from his body as it hugged closer.

The shaking of the stairs intensified. I could hear a faint female voice above us. The voice grew louder as it approached. It sounded as if it was having a conversation with someone, but the responding voice was absent.

"Yes, of course, sir...I understand completely...I am on my way to check the register as we speak...No, sir. I have not seen any sign of the Resistance assembling on the island...No, sir. I took your call on SRT. I should hear you fine all the way...Yes, sir, that is correct. The *Smá-menn* have not developed unimpeded cell coverage yet." The voice paused.

I recognized the figure of Ms. Haugen, the librarian and Tristan's aunt, as she stood at the bottom of the staircase within reaching distance. She seemed to hesitate for a moment as if sensing our presence.

All she'd have to do was turn around. With her night vision, Tristan and I huddling underneath the stairs would be clear as day. I could tell that Tristan was holding his breath as well. Together we watched as she started to slowly turn her body towards us. We both shrank down, trying to get as small as possible.

"Yes, still here, sir...on my way," Ms. Haugen said, snapping her small, wiry figure back toward the tunnel and disappearing into the darkness. I didn't dare move lest she was still within hearing distance.

After a few moments, Tristan was the first to move. He removed his arm, which he'd wrapped around me as we'd waited, listening to his aunt. He crawled out from underneath the stairs and beckoned me to join him. I inched out and stood up, trying to shake the sand from the damp spots on my jeans. Tristan grabbed my hand, and we quickly proceeded up the stairs.

The friendly glow of the light above guided our progress out of the darkness. We reached the passage at the top to find the bookcase door wide open. We hurried out of the passage, the office, and the house.

We ran to Tristan's motorcycle, which he'd left at the top of the neighbor's driveway. I slid the helmet onto my head and climbed on the back of Tristan's bike. He didn't wait for a second but drove off the moment my arms wrapped around his waist.

I finally took in a deep breath as Tristan pulled to a stop in front of my house. He turned off the ignition and helped me off the bike. He too got off, removed his helmet, and came to stand beside me. There was something both scary and thrilling about our slim escape. It created a nervous, excited air between us.

"Well, that was close," he said, looking at me.

"Yeah, I'd say," I agreed. "Who do you think she was talking to?"

"Not sure. Definitely someone on the Clan Council. She would never be that demure with anyone else."

"Well, whoever it was, I think we owe them a thank-you note," I joked, looking at Tristan.

He smiled. "For sure." Then he paused, hesitating for a moment before meeting my eyes. "Elin, what do you think? Will you help me get that key?"

My curiosity was definitely piqued...a hidden library with a ton of secret, ancient manuscripts and books. One of them holding the answers to who I really was. I'd begun to accept the fact that, as far-fetched as Tristan's revelations had been, there might be some truth to them.

I looked up into Tristan's green eyes. "Yes, I'll help you."

"Really? That is great!" Tristan grabbed my hand and twirled me into his strong arms.

Before I could think another thought, Tristan dipped me, leaned in, and kissed me. I was slightly off-balance from the dip and caught so completely off guard that I nearly fell to the ground. Tristan's arms caught me, and he managed to hold me up to some degree.

My mind felt jumbled. I wasn't sure what to make of the

embrace. It had been my first kiss, but all I really felt was relief, once Tristan set me back upright. Shouldn't have there been more?

He was the hot, mysterious guy at school with supernatural abilities whom I'd been daydreaming about, hoping he'd sweep me off my feet. Here he was, literally doing that. I should count myself lucky that he was interested in me. What more could I want?

"Okay, so I will see you Monday at school. We can start figuring out the details then," Tristan said, smiling at me as he put his helmet back on.

"Sure, sounds great," I replied, smiling back.

I watched as he got back on the bike. He waved as he drove off. As I turned to the house, I could see my mom and sister staring from the dining room window, excitedly clapping, smiling, and giving me thumbs-ups.

SEVENTEEN

The librarian

AEDAN

Tristan and Elin were clearly planning something. They'd been huddled together every spare moment over the last week. It was definitely more than plans for Saturday's dance.

I'd also caught Elin staring at me with a funny look on her face multiple times in class recently. She always dropped her eyes and turned away before I could ask her what was up. I could feel something had changed in her demeanor towards me, but I just didn't know what or why. Our camaraderie over lunch, our classes, and the history project was still the same, but there was a new dimension in our interaction that I was not privy to.

I'd witnessed Elin and Tristan leaving school together and heading towards town the past two days. I'd decided to follow them. It was definitely risky, given that Tristan was a Clan Hunter, but I didn't feel like I had a choice. Somebody had to look out for Elin.

I'd ridden my bike to school in preparation, giving Edvin a rest from his chauffeur duties. There was no way I could keep up with Tristan's motorcycle, at least not without using my *megin*, but I figured I'd be able to catch up with them in town.

I grimaced a little as I watched Elin climb onto Tristan's motorcycle, wrapping her arms around his waist. I was about to mount my own significantly less-advanced two-wheeler when I received a swift, light punch in the arm.

"Hey, man! Where you heading?" Joel asked, smirking at me. He followed my gaze towards Elin and Tristan. "You'll never keep up with that"—leaving it vague as to whether he meant the motorcycle or Tristan.

"What do you mean?" I answered, rubbing my arm and trying to inject a tone of naivety into my voice.

Joel looked at me incredulously. "Come on, man. You're about to follow them." I was about to ride off in mock indignation when Joel continued, "I can give you a ride. I finally got my truck running." Joel smiled proudly, pointing to a grey 1950s Chevy pickup truck that was still in need of a paint job. He'd been regaling me with stories of his progress in fixing the old truck since I'd met him. It was an accomplishment worth celebrating, given the numerous tales I'd heard regarding engine trouble.

"Wow, Joel! You finally did it, huh? Congrats," I exclaimed, smiling sincerely. "A ride would be great."

Joel's smile widened, and he nodded in thanks. I swung my leg off my bike, and we headed towards the truck. I lifted the bike into the truck's flatbed and opened the passenger door.

The inside had a new bench with lively springs that responded to my weight as I settled into my seat. Joel had done an amazing job of restoring the cabin. The chrome glovebox and air vents gleamed brightly from their fresh polish—and even the seat belts had been neatly tucked into the bench, waiting for their passengers.

After a few false starts where Joel muttered curses under his breath and reassurances towards me, the truck finally roared to life. We were only a few minutes behind Elin and Tristan. They'd already left the school parking lot, but I knew the direction they had headed. I directed Joel towards town.

We bounced along the road with good speed. Conversation, however, was impossible. There was a loud roar from the rear of the truck every time Joel pressed the gas, indicating a possible puncture in the muffler. Nonetheless, the two of us had large grins on our faces as we enjoyed our newfound freedom.

After a few minutes, we could see a motorcycle driving ahead at a leisurely pace. Getting Joel's attention, I motioned with my hands for him to slow down. I didn't want to get too close. The point was to observe, not to *be* observed—which might be difficult given the loud syncopated noise the rear of the truck was emitting.

As we entered the town, the motorcycle turned away from the harbor, heading towards the center. Eventually, it came to a stop in the library parking lot.

I pointed to an empty parking space in front of Auor Hardware. Joel obliged me and pulled into the space. The truck sputtered to a stop. We both turned around in our seats, peering from the truck's back window as Elin and Tristan dismounted. They took off their helmets, ascended the library stairs, and disappeared through the entrance.

"Joel, you've got to follow them and let me know when the coast is clear," I directed. I didn't want to accidentally bump into Elin in the lobby, since it would defeat my purpose. I could hardly discreetly observe what they were up to if I was having a conversation with them.

"What do you mean, I've got to follow them? I didn't sign up for any spy games," Joel answered.

"Come on, man. Please! It'll be so much less odd if you go in first and clear the way," I pleaded.

"Oh, because I spend so much time at the library?" Joel responded. The sarcasm dripping from his words. He did have a point. Joel and the library seemed diametrically opposed—but "desperate times."

"Just do it, and I'll owe you a favor," I cajoled.

"I'm not going to get you out of my truck until I do, am I?" Joel said, only half-joking. I nodded my head vigorously. "Fine, but you're going to owe me big-time. I hate that library and the creepy old bat who runs it."

Joel turned the engine off, opened his door, and climbed out of the truck. He turned around to look at me with the door still open.

"Here," he said, begrudgingly tossing his truck keys to me. "Lock her up before you leave." With that, he closed the door, pulled up the back of his low-riding pants, adjusted his skewed baseball cap, and strode towards the library doors.

I smiled to myself at the image of a "determined" Joel. Despite my best efforts to remain distant from my new schoolmates, I was beginning to appreciate Joel's friendship more and more. Over the years in which I'd gone to numerous schools, it had grown more difficult to abandon attachments formed with *Mannlegurs* when we had to flee again. My solution had been not to develop any. But Joel was wearing down my resistance. He was generous and constant with his friendship—especially given that he himself had finally found a "comrade" at school.

After about five minutes, a text message pinged on my cell phone. It read:

JOEL LARSON:
COAST CLEARED. NO SIGN OF THEM OR THE OLD BAT.

The last bit made me wonder what Joel's problem was with the librarian. Granting his earlier request, I leaned over to the driver's side and punched the lock button down. Opening the passenger door, I slid to the ground. I closed and locked the truck door and headed to the library.

The building reminded me of an old bank. The front of the library had four white Roman Doric columns holding up a large pediment, which had the words "Auor Town Library" inscribed in the middle. Behind the columns were two weathered brass doors. I pulled on the matching handle on one of the doors. It opened without a squeak or much effort, which was surprising given its hefty appearance.

Walking inside, I was greeted by a short white hallway, at the end of which was a long wooden counter. On either end of the counter was a wooden swing door with the words "Entrance" and "Exit" painted in fading gold paint. A woman in her early twenties was stacking books in neat piles on the opposite and equally long counter that came into view as I approached.

"Can I help you?" she asked as I attempted to open the swing door marked with the word "Entrance."

"Oh, hi...I'm just coming to study," I answered, caught off guard.

She held out her hand. "Library card, please."

"Um...I don't have one," I responded. It hadn't occurred to me that I might need a card to just enter the library. "Do I need one if I don't plan on checking out any books?"

"I'm afraid you do. The librarian, Adis Haugen, runs a very tight ship here. She likes to know everyone who has come and gone from the library," she answered, frowning slightly. "However, it doesn't take long to fill out the application for the card. Then you'll be all set."

"Okay, I guess I'd like to fill out an application then," I replied, hoping it was a short form. I'd already missed the last ten minutes of whatever Elin and Tristan were up to. And where was Joel? He wasn't anywhere that I could see from where I was standing.

The clerk handed me an application. It asked for the basics: name, address, email, etc. I quickly filled it out and handed it back to her. She tore off the small rectangle with a bar code at the top of the page and handed it to me.

"Welcome to the Auor Town Library. That is your temporary library card. You will receive the real one in the mail soon," she said in a friendly manner. I thanked her and quickly entered through the swing door.

The inside of the library was much larger than it appeared from the outside. In the center of the room was a great domed ceiling with a large oculus that let a stream of sunlight filter onto the dark wooden tables below. The tables were arranged in three rows, with three tables per row. There were two green desk lamps and four chairs at each table. The walls of the circular room had two rows of bookcases filled with books of various shapes and sizes. Across from me, there seemed to be an additional higher floor, although I'd yet to locate the staircase. I made a mental note of potential exits, including windows, as I took in the library.

Joel suddenly appeared beside me. "Hey! What took you so long?"

"Had to get a library card," I explained. "So, where are they?"

"They're on the second floor in the stacks. They seem to be following the old bat around, which was my cue to leave."

"Okay, lead the way," I said, anxious to get back on track.

"I'm not going back up there to be fed to that she-devil," Joel said, shaking his head.

"What is it with you and the librarian?" Now I was really curious.

"We...we've just got some history. Okay?" Joel replied, giving me defensive look.

"Okay, okay. But I'll never find them without your help. I don't even know how to get to the second floor," I replied, relenting and pleading in the same instant. "You've come this far, Joel. Don't let her win now. Take back the library!" I ended with a flourish and a mock fist-raise, hoping to humor Joel out of his sour mood. Joel frowned at my attempt but seemed to be weighing his options.

"Fine, I'll take you. But then I'm out," he said.

"Thanks, Joel. You are a pillar of humanity, a beacon of hope..." I continued to jokingly praise him as he walked away, raising a single middle finger at me.

I followed him towards the back of the room, where there was a wide gap between two bookcases. As we went through, a hallway appeared on the other side, leading away from the circular room. On one side, there were doors and signs for both the men's and ladies' restrooms. On the other side was an opening revealing a staircase.

Joel led the way up the staircase to the second floor. The first room on the right was a large rectangle with rows of bookcases running throughout the space. Through the gaps between the bookcases, I could see a long, narrow bar-height table running below the windows on one side of the rectangle. Stools were precisely spaced along it for readers to sit at a comfortable distance.

High on the opposite wall was a narrow gallery that ran the length of the wall and down the adjacent one. Bookcases lined the side, and a wide catwalk separated them from a black metal railing that prevented an occupant from falling to the floor below. I could see the top of a black metal spiral staircase that connected the two floors in the far corner. How did such a small town have such a grand library?

Without a word, Joel shoved me into a nearby passageway between bookcases. He put a finger to his lips, motioning for me to be quiet. From between the books in the bookshelf, I could see a lean middle-aged woman walking down the neighboring passageway with a few books cradled in her arms. She was wearing a long-sleeved dress with buttons all the way up the turtleneck collar. Her ensemble was tied together with a narrow belt that had a key ring dangling from the side. She stopped a few strides down from us, clearly searching for something.

Given Joel's reaction, I assumed that this was the dreaded librarian. Recalling what he'd also said earlier about Elin and Tristan following her, I quickly proceeded down our aisle for a closer look. I was nearly at the end of the section when Joel caught up to me and grabbed my arm to gain my attention. With some very expressive arm- and hand-waving, he was clearly trying to convey to me that he was out of there. At that moment, Ms. Haugen rounded the corner and came upon us.

"Mr. Larson," she drawled, emphasizing Joel's last name. "I see that you are visiting the library again...and this time you brought a friend. Are your siblings ill?" Joel shrank at the sound of her authoritative voice.

"Um...no, Ms. Haugen. My siblings are fine," Joel answered, demurely bowing his head.

Ms. Haugen continued berating him. "I thought we had agreed that your library-visiting days were over until you had gained in wisdom what you have in years."

I was about to jump into the conversation in his defense when Elin appeared on the other side of Ms. Haugen. As discreetly as she could, Elin was reaching for the keyring dangling from Ms. Haugen's belt. The clasp holding the ring to the belt was already open, but the sway from Ms. Haugen's hips was proving to be a challenge.

The undulating voice of Ms. Haugen seemed to be gaining steam. She was emphatically pointing for Joel and me to move back in the direction we'd come. In an effort to encourage us to obey, she moved closer to us, apparently unaware of Elin behind her.

It was a split-second decision, but then I didn't much care for how Ms. Haugen was treating Joel, and Elin seemed quite desperate to get the keys. I tapped into my *megin*, carefully raised one finger, and motioned for Ms. Haugen's keys to slide off the clasp.

For a moment Elin's eyes opened up a little more widely as she witnessed the keys magically tumbling out of the clasp. Then, reacting quickly, she reached for the keys, obviously hoping to catch them before they fell to the floor. Instead, she succeeded in nudging the keys sideways, loosening one small key that tumbled to the floor at my feet.

Suddenly, a hand appeared with *megin* speed from the other side of the bookcase by Elin. It snatched the remaining keys from the air before they could hit the floor. Tristan! He must have been waiting on the other side.

I could only pray that he had not observed my contribution to the matter. Elin met my eyes, mouthed "Thank you," and quickly withdrew the way she'd come.

It felt like my heart had stopped. My limbs were paralyzed. She knew about me.

Meanwhile, the one-way discussion between Ms. Haugen and Joel was reaching a climax. Shaking myself out of my stupor, I quickly bent down to get the tiny key before anyone else could realize it had been lost. Then I straightened, grabbed Joel's arm, and moved between him and Ms. Haugen.

"Ma'am, I don't know what the history here is, but currently we're doing nothing wrong by being in the library. As far as I know, it's a public space, and we have library cards," I interjected. "We'll respectfully leave so that you'll stop hollering and disrupting the other occupants."

With that, I quickly turned around and tugged Joel back towards the stairwell before Ms. Haugen could say another word. Her stunned silence and the small key in my pocket gave me a warm glow of satisfaction on the way out.

"Thanks, man! She has always had it in for my family. Plus, I don't think she likes kids," Joel explained on the way out. "My four brothers and I used to come to the library for the after-school program while my mom finished work. The last time, there was an incident with my younger brother and his pet toad. Clearly, she's never quite forgiven us for the surprise in her coffee mug."

I looked at Joel. Both of us erupted into laughter, getting a fierce "Shush!" from the clerk behind the front counter as we made our exit.

EIGHTEEN

The key

TRISTAN

I could not believe I had it! Nothing had gone according to plan, but that did not matter now. I had Aunt Adis's keyring.

I had not had a chance to inspect it yet, but there was time. The remaining parts of the plan were for me to hurry back to the house, get the book from the secret library, and then later place the keyring in Aunt Adis's car so she would assume it had fallen out there.

It all had to be done with great speed, so I had left Elin at the library to find her own way home. I would pick her up the next day for the school dance, so there would be plenty of time to go over the particulars later.

I leaned into the curve to drive the motorcycle faster. I wanted to get to the house before my aunt could notice that anything was wrong.

What luck that those two junior classmen had come along! A perfect distraction. Aunt Adis had been so caught up in admonishing them that she had not even noticed Elin behind her.

It had been hard to see anything from between the books, but thankfully, I had been able to catch the keys before they clattered to the floor. Aunt Adis would have definitely heard the noise. Elin really should have been more careful in dislodging the keys. Well, there would be time to teach her agility and prudence after her awakening. The Clan had mandated classes for those, after all.

The excitement I felt was beyond my normal rush from driving at high speeds. I was so close to the book and, in turn, the adulation of the Clan Council for bringing in a Dormant. I could almost feel the pats on my back. Surely, I would be promoted as well—perhaps captain in the Hunter squad of the PS. I would probably be the youngest captain, but when was the last time someone had brought in a Dormant? I smiled to myself as I pushed the motorcycle harder.

I finally pulled into the shed at my aunt's house. Quickly but measuredly, I covered my motorcycle with the tarp, dusting off any debris that had collected on the drive. I ran to the side door, brushing my boots on the scraper before I entered the house.

Once inside, I headed directly to my aunt's office. Pausing for a moment by the desk, I pulled the keyring out of my pocket. There was a mixture of oddly-shaped and -sized keys on the ring. I knew exactly what I was looking for—Mjölnir in smaller form.

I slid the keys around on the ring, looking for anything that resembled a hammer. I went through them once, then twice, but nothing. Desperation began to grow in my stomach. I went through the keys again, this time one by one, looking for anything that might resemble the opening on the Caelum door.

There were several antique skeleton keys, a few modern house and office keys, a funny-looking key with tiny punctures all over the stem, and a few other oddly shaped keys—but nothing in the shape of a hammer. I ran my hand over my face. A key must exist, that was clear...but it was not on the key ring.

All that wasted time and effort. How could it not be there? My aunt carried this keyring everywhere. Its presence was a constant on her side. Where else could it be?

Elin—she must have taken it. I had shared too much with her.

I thought back to the library, running through the events one by one in my head. I had caught the keys in midair. Elin had never touched the keys. Had I dropped it? No, I had been much too careful.

I heard the screen door bang shut on the side door, along with steps and my aunt muttering to herself. I glanced at my watch. It was only 4:30pm. She must have noticed that her keys were gone.

I swallowed hard. I was in her office with the evidence in my hand. I felt frozen. There was nowhere for me to hide. If she came directly to the office, I would be caught by her again. Looking for a pen was not going to be enough of an excuse this time.

As quietly as I could, I eased the key ring back into my pocket. I did not have to advertise all my misdeeds at once. As with most old houses, the floorboards creaked, especially in her office. I had not had to concern myself with that before, but now I did not dare move.

With my heart pounding, I listened to my aunt pacing the hallway, talking to herself. I caught a few fragments of, "Where could they be...I know I didn't leave...must be in the house." A sudden exclamation of, "Changed clothes!" almost had me jump out of my skin. I heard the *whoosh* as my aunt ran up the stairs towards her bedroom.

This was my moment. I had to act now. Similar to my aunt, I rushed out of the house, using my *megin* for extra speed.

Her electric compact car was not in its usual space in the shed. Instead, it had been haphazardly left in the driveway with its lights still on and the driver-side door wide open. If I had not known the cause, I would have been really concerned about my aunt's mental state.

With a quick backward glance at the house, I hurried to the vehicle. I had no choice. It was now or never. Not that much more could be gained from the keyring, but it felt like an early defeat, tossing the keys to the driver's-side floor.

I had backed only a few paces from the car when my aunt emerged from the house in quite a state. A few hairs had loosened from her normally smooth, low, tight bun. Severe anxiety was etched across her face. It almost made me feel a little sorry for her.

"Tristan! What are you doing?" she screeched as she hurried towards her car. I had not backed away fast enough and was still much too close to the vehicle.

"Nothing, Aunt. I just noticed your car lights were on. I was going to turn them off," I answered as steadily as I could.

"No need," she replied. "I'm just leaving."

"Didn't you just arrive?" I asked, trying to appear nonchalant.

"Yes, but I left something at my office," my aunt responded, looking at me suspiciously.

She had reached the driver's side. She was about to sit down in the seat when she exclaimed with significant relief, "Thank Freyja!"

She quickly bent down to grab the keys that lay on the floor mat. Then, as if nothing extraordinary had happened, she sat down in the driver's seat, closed the door, and pulled the car into the shed beside my motorcycle.

A few moments later, she emerged from the car with her hair smoothly adjusted back into a tight bun. With her usual precision and efficiency, she hooked the charging cable to the car. She closed the shed doors and reappeared from the shed's side entrance, staring at me while making her way to the house. She did not say another word.

The rest of the previous evening had been uneventful. My aunt had left me to my own devices for dinner and had vanished entirely later in the evening. I presumed she had gone to check on the secret library. But given that the Mjölnir key was not on the ring, the library had not ever really been compromised. I had racked my brain to figure out where my aunt might be keeping the key, but nothing had come to me...yet.

My disappointment was equaled only by my apprehension about what my aunt might have concluded from all the events. In addition, reviewing my routine SRT reports was becoming increasingly uncomfortable, with the initial warnings for lack of productivity starting to appear on the screen. I needed to come up with a new plan, and fast.

This evening, however, the focus was the Harvest Dance. I had to keep Elin engaged. I could not afford to lose her.

I turned my attention to the task in front of me, which was choosing my suit for the Harvest Dance. I had researched options on my SRT to see what was customary for formal *Smá-menn* events. Even though the SRT's capabilities were severely limited in the *Smá-menn* world, it still had basic tools available, such as searching the *Stór-menni's* extensive knowledge bank.

I had had some doubts about whether the knowledge bank would include such a simple *Smá-menn* fact, but I should not have questioned the superiority of the system. After finding several references to what was typical, I had ventured to the mainland, given the limited store options on the island.

No *Smá-menn* apparel, of course, equaled how the Clan members dressed for formal occasions. The embroidered detail of men's tunics and cloaks was something to behold. Any gathering hall sparkled with radiance from the exquisite silversmithing that produced the jewelry and belt buckles Clan members proudly displayed during celebrations. Not to mention the ceremonial seaxes, swords, and daggers that showed off the precious stones embedded in their handles. The only thing that marred the pageantry was the awkward meetings between parents and children. It was only during these few yearly public events that one might bump into a family member or two.

I shook myself out of dark thoughts and refocused on the task in front of me. I had been unusually indecisive regarding my choices for clothing, so I had bought two options. I stared at them on my bed and tried to consider which best presented the image I had crafted at the high school.

The SRT had told me that for formal occasions, something called a Tuxedo was appropriate. However, the lady at the store had been convinced that a nice suit would be sufficient for the occasion. She had shown me two options: a two-piece and a three-piece suit. I had one in navy and one in grey herringbone laid out on my bed. I smoothed out the suits, picking a piece of fuzz off the navy one.

I tried both on with a crisp white button-down shirt. The navy highlighted my eyes nicely, but I couldn't figure out how to fit the suit jacket under my motorcycle jacket. I opted for the three-piece suit without the jacket.

I put on the pants, vest, and skinny tie—after consulting the SRT on how to tie one. My motorcycle boots were thin enough to fit under the pants once buckled tightly. I smiled at myself in the mirror. Not bad. A few strokes with the brush and some hair ointment, and I would be off to collect Elin.

When I came down the stairs, I noticed a note with my name on the hall table. Beside it lay two clear plastic boxes with small flower arrangements inside. I unfolded the note. It read:

Tristan - I don't know why you are bothering with this Smá-menn tradition, but since you are, you will need these to blend in.
Aunt Adis

Given my excursion to the mainland, I had not seen my aunt

all day. I took it as a hopeful sign that she was looking out for my supposed mission.

I inspected the boxes, turning them upside down and right-side up. There was a smaller arrangement with a single white rose, some greens, and a pearled needle stuck perpendicularly into the wrapped bottom. The second held a more elaborate display with three white roses, some greens, and a circular white cloth elastic on the bottom that attached to the flowers. I had no idea what they were for, but trusting my aunt to know the customs, I tucked them into my motorcycle bag. I grabbed my jacket and headed out the door.

I made good time to Elin's house. However, I was not expecting the spectacle that awaited me there. It seemed like her entire family was outside on the front lawn, participating in a photoshoot.

Elin was posing in front of a maple tree vibrant in its autumn colors. She was wearing a dress in a mustardy shade of yellow. The upper half was made from lace that came to her waist. A silk sash separated the lace from the layered tulle below.

At her mom's request, Elin turned her back to the camera and looked back towards it, revealing the V-line opening in the back of the dress. Her auburn hair was partially pulled up, with the rest spiraling in curls down her back. She looked great and so different from her usual jeans and sweater.

I dismounted from my motorcycle, smiling broadly. I grabbed my aunt's provisions from the saddlebag and headed towards Elin's family. They had initially turned at the sound of my motorcycle approaching, and now Mrs. Bodil was eagerly waving me closer.

"Come, come, Tristan," Mrs. Bodil encouraged, smiling. "We want some pictures with the two of you." Upon seeing the two clear boxes in my hand, she continued, "How sweet! You thought of the corsage and boutonnière. Here, hand them to me. Then Elin and you can help each other with them. Leif! Where are you, Leif? Oh, who knows where he got to! Anders, you take the pictures of them exchanging the flowers." Anders seemed rather reluctant about the task, but Mrs. Bodil's insistence soon had him playing cameraman.

In between shots, Elin and I were able to exchange a few words. After we finished flower pictures, Elin whispered, "Did you find the book?"

We posed for a photo. I replied, "The key was not on the ring." Elin looked surprised but quickly changed her features into a smile as her mother chastised her.

"What do you mean?" she said through her teeth, smiling as the flash from the camera blinded us momentarily.

"There was no key, so no book," I whispered in a momentary reprieve. "We are back to square one. Do not worry, we will think of something else."

I needed Elin to stay optimistic. She could not give up. I was well past the point of no return in my efforts and investment.

After several more poses, the necessary pictures seemed to have finally been taken. Mr. Bodil had emerged from the house to participate in some of the festivities. We now stood in a circular arrangement as Mrs. Bodil and Maria continued to fuss over Elin.

"Oh, don't you think she'll need a wrap? It might get cold later," Mrs. Bodil said as she did a final inspection of Elin. "Maria, run upstairs and grab the white shawl off my bureau."

"*Mom*, I don't think I'll need one. We'll be inside most of the time," Elin protested, squirming under the constant attention.

"No, no, I insist. You never know when you might get chilled," Mrs. Bodil responded. Then as if having an epiphany, she looked around the yard as if something was missing. "How exactly do you plan on getting to the dance? Is someone else coming to pick you up? I can't imagine that you'll be going on that. Elin can't possibly ride on it with her dress." She offhandedly pointed at my motorcycle as if it was a ludicrous thought. It had not even occurred to me that my motorcycle would be insufficient for the task. I swallowed hard, not having a ready answer.

"Mom," Elin said in a drawn-out way as if embarrassed. When no one seemed to be offering her the reassurances she sought, Mrs. Bodil called over Anders, who had been keeping his distance.

"Andee, I think your services are needed. Elin and Tristan need a ride to the dance," she commanded. At first, Anders appeared to hesitate, but then a sly smile appeared on his face as he scrutinized me.

"Yes...yes, I think that's a fine idea, Mom. I'll just go pull the Volvo out," Anders said as he seemed to warm up to the idea more. Before I could protest, Anders turned and headed for the garage.

"Well, you kids have a good time," Mr. Bodil said, breaking his silence except for the occasional "Hmm" and "Yes, dear" of previous remarks. "Please have Elin home by midnight, Tristan. I suppose you'll need to coordinate with Anders to pick you up again, but we're extending your curfew for the special occasion, Elin. I want you home and in bed by then."

"Okay, Dad," Elin replied, seeming pleased by the additional time.

"Yes, sir. Thank you, sir," I added for good measure.

Mr. Bodil smiled contentedly, seeming to appreciate my response. Anders pulled up the Volvo, scattering the group to either side of the vehicle. Elin and I ended up on opposite sides. I opened the back door and climbed into the car.

Elin had ended up by the front passenger seat, but instead of opening that door, she walked to the back door and climbed in next to me. I could see Anders frowning in the back mirror, but he made no comment as the vehicle moved forward, past Elin's waving parents and sister.

NINETEEN

The dance

AEDAN

I was very lucky that the maple tree's branch had grown directly outside my window. It nearly touched the slope of the roof, making for an easy climb down. It also helped that I was currently feeling fairly invincible.

We were two days past the full moon, and my *megin* was nearing full charge. I'd gone for a good long run in the morning with the powerful sounds of Creedence Clearwater Revival's "Fortunate Son" setting the pace through my earbuds. I'd needed to burn some energy since I couldn't afford any unexpected incidents this evening.

I dropped to the ground from the lowest maple tree branch. Standing up from my landing, I straightened my jacket and dusted off my pants. My apparel for the dance was a bit last-minute. I was supposed to be grounded, so I had to make do with what I could scavenge at our house. I'd found an old pair of red suspenders and a bow tie in the back of my dad's closet. These were complemented by my cream button-down shirt, grey slacks, and red converse sneakers. I wore my navy, insulated windbreaker to help stave off the cold and camouflage me in the darkness as I snuck out of the house.

I could count on one hand the times I'd ventured out of previous homes at night. It'd only ever been in the company of my older siblings. The prior adventures had been fun, prompted by the rebellious urges of the twins...but this was for something much more important.

I hadn't seen Elin since the library incident the previous day. She'd disappeared from the library so quickly that there'd been no opportunity to talk with her. What she and Tristan needed with Ms. Haugen's keys was beyond me. Plus, it seemed like recently Tristan had usurped all of Elin's time and was keeping her to himself. He was barely letting her out of his sight.

The trouble was, I really needed to talk with her—and soon. It was clear from her behavior that she knew about me. I wasn't sure if she'd fitted all the pieces together regarding the rest of my family, but in any case, it was really important that she not tell Tristan. I now had to save not only Elin but potentially my entire family from him.

Text or phone were not options. Who knew who'd be listening —and, frankly, it was too important a matter. I needed to see her in person, away from Tristan, for a few moments. And tonight's dance would be the perfect cover.

I jogged across the grass parallel to our driveway. Once I reached the edge of the woods, I crossed onto the dirt road, quickly disappearing into the forest. At the top of the road, Joel's truck was, thankfully, quietly idling. Joel was my willing conspirator and had offered to pick me up for the dance. He assumed that romance was the reason I wanted to attend and for once I didn't correct him.

"Hey, man! You made it," Joel greeted me as I climbed into the truck. I glanced in amazement at the Joel before me. Gone was his usual skewed baseball cap. His normally unruly hair was slicked back, reminding me of Al Pacino's in The Godfather movies. He wore a blue button-down shirt, which I was surprised he owned, given his propensity for t-shirts, and baggy black dress slacks. It was the most cleaned-up I'd ever seen him—and probably ever would.

"Hi! You look good," I responded. "Sorry, it took me a little longer to slip out of the house."

"No worries. I knew you'd make it," Joel said, smirking. "Love is in the air, after all."

I rolled my eyes in response and said, "Let's go, man! I don't want to wait here until my parents catch us."

"Aye aye, captain." Joel put the truck in neutral, slowly letting it roll down the small slope to the main road.

Once there, he switched gears and pressed the gas. The muffler responded with its usual roar. We both grimaced and crossed our fingers that my parents would assume it was just a passing car on the main road.

The Harvest Dance was being held at the Old Boat Clubhouse, where the members-only dining room had been cleared for the special occasion. The school student council, headed by Candice, had proudly given daily updates on progress and preparations over the past week while trying to recruit additional students for assistance.

When we arrived at the clubhouse parking lot, the security attendant seemed disgruntled by the noise from Joel's truck. However, Joel, pretending that he heard no such noise, calmly discussed where to park his precious automobile.

After being directed to the back of the lot, Joel steered us through the throng of students making their way to the clubhouse entrance. Once we found the designated spot, Joel pulled in and turned off the engine. We climbed out, and Joel locked the doors.

"Oh, man!" I said, slightly annoyed. "I forgot to take my jacket off."

"Just toss it in the back." Joel motioned to the flatbed. "No one will be able to tell it's even there in the dark." I removed my windbreaker and did as he suggested. "Looking snazzy there, Mr. Grady!" Joel said as he took in my bowtie and suspenders.

"Thanks, Joel! Best I could do given the circumstances." We started walking toward the clubhouse.

We merged into the sea of autumn-colored dresses and button-down shirts that were streaming towards the front entrance. We recognized a few other students along the way and greeted them, exchanging the occasional compliment.

"Aedan, isn't that your sister?" Joel asked as we neared.

Indeed, there was Claire mounting the clubhouse steps, accompanied by Mr. Tibadeau. I recognized her emerald-green silk jumpsuit underneath her green wool overcoat, fluttering in the breeze. I quickly ducked behind a small tree, surveilling the scene from between the branches. *Leynasking* was obviously not a choice given the public situation. Plus, Claire would've seen me anyway, since she always wore her shield-knot ring.

"Yeah, that's her," I answered as Joel joined me.

The lower half of our limbs were visible but not distinguishable from those of the other students. Claire and Mr. Tibadeau seemed to pause by the doors to take in the view of the students entering.

"What are they doing here? I mentioned to Claire that you'd seen her at the coffee shop with Mr. Tibadeau. But she brushed it off as a chance meeting and nothing more," I continued, half annoyed and half curious.

Joel concurred. "Once might be a coincidence, but twice...that makes you wonder. Plus, when they left the coffee shop, it sounded like they had plans. Hard to do if it's just a chance meeting. You don't think they're dating, do you?" Joel turned to me with slight concern on his face.

I responded by giving him a look that said, "Really?" We

continued to peer at them through the branches while trying to look nonchalant to the rest of the students streaming past us. Finally, Claire and her companion entered the clubhouse. It was risky to go in, but I'd come this far.

"Hey, Joel. Can you go ahead and spot for Claire?" I asked. "I really can't bump into her. She'll march me right back home."

Joel sighed bemusedly. "Seriously? You want me to enter the school dance alone? You know that clearing the way for you is becoming a habit, right?"

"Come on, Joel! I promise to join you as soon as you say the coast is clear," I pleaded.

"Fine, man...but only because it's Claire. And, by the way, the favors you owe me are starting to stack up," Joel said, grinning as he strolled past me.

As I stood there waiting for the all-clear, I heard Elin's laughter. She'd just exited her parents' Volvo, where Anders was in the driver's seat. She looked amazing in a yellow dress with her auburn hair half pinned up and curled.

I was about to approach her when the Volvo pulled away, revealing Tristan on the other side. He walked to Elin, grabbing her hand as they turned toward the clubhouse entrance. A few of the senior girls outside stared at the pair and started to whisper amongst themselves as they passed.

I tried to blend into the tree as much as possible. Tristin and Elin walked past me without noticing. Elin was smiling broadly and looked happy to be entering the dance.

At the same moment, I received a text from Joel. All it contained was an arrow and a door emoji. I let another minute pass before I rounded the tree and proceeded up the entrance stairs.

The clubhouse doors opened into a wide hallway that ran sideways. It had glass cases displaying various sailing trophies to the right and fishing awards to the left. There was a photo backdrop set up on the right that had drawn a crowd of students posing for their dance photos. On the left, students were milling around talking, taking selfies, and sharing the photos they'd just taken with a novelty Polaroid camera that had been left on a close-by table.

The dining room entrance was directly in front of me. It was a half-moon-shaped room with large windows along the sea-facing side, which made for plenty of emergency exits. The rest of the room was decorated with an abundance of autumn-colored streamers and paper flowers. A net high above the middle of the dance floor held similarly colored balloons. I assumed they were to be dropped at the announcement of the chosen Harvest King and Queen.

I walked further into the room just in time to see Candice stomp up to Tristan and Elin on the dance floor. At first, I couldn't hear what she was screaming at them. The pop music coming from the deejay was drowning out her words, but then as if on cue, the music stopped. One of Candice's followers seemed to be talking to the deejay, distracting him from playing the next song.

Candice's voice boomed over the dining room and many of the students stopped what they were doing to witness the event. This only encouraged her further. Most of her yelling seemed to be directed at Tristan, with an occasional insult thrown at Elin. Elin looked shell-shocked.

"...You two-timing jerk! After everything I've done for you, you have the nerve to show up here with her! I can't believe you didn't ask me to the dance. I'm senior-class president and probable Harvest Queen. And you chose her! What is she but a junior classman without any friends?" Candice bellowed, her anger only growing. She turned to Elin with a scathing look. "And you, did you know all along? You think someone like him could really be interested in a tiny red mouse like *you?*"

"Tristan, what's she talking about?" Elin had turned to Tristan, awkwardly asking for an explanation.

"Elin, I can explain. I just needed her help with the school assignments. There is nothing else going on," Tristan pleaded, trying to grasp Elin's hand.

"What? Nothing else going on! What about all those days and nights at my house? You call that *nothing*, Tristan?" Candice interrupted.

"So, you just used her...or led her on?" Elin asked. "Are you just using me?"

"Of course he is! I thought you were supposed to be one of the smart ones, Elin." Candice laughed sarcastically.

"No, Elin...no, it was for you. All of it," Tristan said, trying to sound convincing. Elin had an incredulous look on her face. She ripped off her corsage, threw it at Tristan, turned on her heel, and ran right past me, dropping her white wrap.

I couldn't help the small sense of satisfaction that seeing Elin run from Tristan brought. However, my gut twisted for her. She'd looked devastated as she ran past me. It ignited a quiet burning in my chest, making me want to punch Tristan.

He was about to follow her, but with a flick of my wrist, I released the catch on the balloon net. All the balloons came pouring out on top of Tristan and Candice, causing further chaos in the room. I snatched Elin's white wrap from the floor and ran after her.

I found her wandering around the parking lot, looking for a place to hide. I ran up to her, offering her the white wrap. She turned away from me, clearly trying to conceal the tears that were streaming down her face.

"Elin, I'm so sorry! He's...he's a jerk...and some other choice words. And Candice...well...you know how she loves the spotlight. But you...you did nothing wrong. In fact, you were pretty amazing in there," I said, trying to comfort her. "You're just caught in the middle of something...bigger. Don't be embarrassed...I'm a big fan of crying." I tried a joke to see if it might help. All I got was a hiccup for a response, but at least she glanced at me. And there seemed to be a pause in the tears.

"Aedan, can you...get me out of here?" Elin asked through another couple of hiccups and sniffles. "I can't stand...to be here. And I don't...don't want to see Tristan!"

"Sure. Of course, I can," I said, reassuring her.

Meanwhile, I was racking my brain to figure out how to achieve her wish. Joel had driven me. I had no vehicle of my own, and I couldn't call my parents for a ride.

Then I remembered noticing stairs by Joel's truck that led away from the parking lot. They had seemed to descend onto the gated docks.

Without thinking, I offered my hand to Elin. She accepted and placed her hand in mine. A strong electric current started to pulsate between us. Elin saw me hesitate for a moment, and she clasped my hand tighter.

"Don't worry. I know," she sniffled, with another hiccup. I nodded and squeezed her hand.

"Does he...know?" I asked. She looked at me as if she understood my meaning and shook her head to say no. "I think we have a lot to talk about. Come on. I think I know where we can go."

I led the way towards Joel's truck, holding Elin's hand. It felt nice—even with the strange, pulsating current. It was almost as if the electricity created an invisible bubble around us.

I stopped briefly to grab my jacket, recalling a packet of tissues in its pocket. I handed the package to Elin.

"For emergencies," I said, shrugging.

"Thank you." Elin opened the flap to take out a tissue for her sniffly, stuffy nose.

"This way." I pointed down the stairs. Elin looked surprised that we were leaving the truck but then followed me.

"You know there's a locked gate at the bottom, right? The gate leads to all of the boat docks in the clubhouse marina," she said before she took the first step.

"I guessed, but that's no problem as long as I can see the handle on the other side of the gate," I answered.

"If I remember correctly, it's a chain-link gate, so you should be able to see the lock. Although there's a wide steel plate so you can't reach around to open it," Elin informed me.

"Not a problem," I answered.

"Do you have a boat in mind to go to?" Elin asked.

"Um...no, but I'm sure we can find—" I started to respond.

"I do! I have the perfect one," Elin interrupted, smiling slyly. It was good to see a smile even if it was brief. We could now hear Tristan somewhere close to the clubhouse calling Elin's name. Her smile disappeared as quickly as it had come.

"Shall we?" I asked, offering my hand to her.

"Yes, please!" Elin answered, quickly taking my hand and starting down the stairs before I could lead the way.

We silently descended the remaining stairs to the locked gate. I peered through the chain link to the other side, where I could see the top of the door handle. I carefully raised my hand, and then, as if opening the handle, I pushed down while pulling the gate door open with my other hand. My *megin* pulsed in my veins, and the door opened with a click.

"After you," I said to Elin, who gave me a genuine smile of amazement and walked through the opening. I quickly followed her, closing the gate as quietly as possible. Elin had already walked down the ramp to the docks and was standing by the first intersecting dock.

"This way," she whispered as she took the dock to the left.

I followed Elin for a few more turns, after which she stopped at a berth on the left-hand side. She then proceeded to climb into the old thirty-foot sailboat that was secured there.

"Come on. It's my Uncle Bertie's boat. He won't mind us sitting in the cabin, especially since he rarely visits the island," she said, encouraging me to board. "Plus, I know where the key is." She opened the lid to a small grille that was secured to the back railing of the boat. She turned it upside down and found a small magnetic key holder.

At that same moment, there were voices from the dock parallel to ours. We could see the lights of an incoming boat as it drew closer to the people waiting at the end of the dock. As the large trawler arrived, its lights illuminated the waiting party. The same emerald-green silk that I'd seen earlier that night flapped in the wind. It was Claire and Mr. Tibadeau.

They climbed aboard, to be warmly welcomed by the occupants. How did Claire know this many people on the island already? And what was she doing with them? I'd have to talk with her later. Something was definitely up.

As the trawler departed, I used the railing to draw Uncle Bertie's boat closer to the dock and stepped aboard. Elin was already unlocking the cabin doors and sliding them open so that we could enter.

In the light of the moon, she was able to locate an old camping lantern and matches. Her auburn curls danced around her as she struck a match and lit the lantern, placing it on the main table in the cabin. Its flickering flame cast a friendly glow, making the cabin feel cozy.

The cabin smelled a little musty from disuse. We both opened the side windows to let the fresh sea air drive out the staleness. Then Elin rummaged around in the galley cabinet, emerging with two cans of Coca-Cola a moment later. I scooted onto the bench seat that surrounded the main table. Elin joined me, sitting kitty-corner to me. Her amber eyes met my eyes, and a nervous energy started to build inside me.

She placed one can of Coke in front of me and dropped her gaze to inspect her own. Not knowing what else to do, I opened the can and took a sip. Neither one of us seemed to know how to start the conversation. So we sat there for a while, watching the flame dance in the lantern and sipping our lukewarm beverages.

I wasn't sure if Elin wanted to talk more about what had happened with Tristan, or if we could discuss the other elephant in the room—her knowing about the Clan. What I did know was that having her evening ruined by Candice and Tristan probably hadn't put Elin in the best frame of mind. And I wasn't sure how I could make it better. I was at a loss for words—but at the same time, a tingle of excitement ran through me as I sat across from her.

As I was stealing a glance, Elin broke the silence. "So you're telekinetic."

Caught by surprise and not sure if it was a statement or a question, I answered, "Yes, telekinesis is my ability, but not who I am."

"Oh, no. Of course, I didn't mean to imply…" Elin trailed off, clearly embarrassed.

"I didn't think you meant it in a negative way. My parents are always just so adamant that our abilities don't define us. They're just a part of us," I answered as an explanation. "How did you figure it out? I mean about me having an ability."

"It's that funny electricity that happens when we touch," she responded. "Tristan said that was how he knew I was a Dormant Descendant. He said the Clan had trained them to recognize the feeling of electricity. I guess it's a rare thing, but it seemed to be happening to me everywhere…although not quite as strong as with you." She said the last part a little more quietly, looking back down at her Coke while a little bit of color rose into her cheeks.

"Why didn't you tell Tristan that you'd experienced it elsewhere?" I asked.

"Umm...I don't know...umm...I guess I just felt like it wasn't his business. It was happening to me, not him. Plus, he never asked," Elin answered, looking back up at me.

"Well, I'm really glad you didn't," I said with significant relief. "Elin, I'm not sure what Tristan told you, but his job is to hunt people like me and my family."

"What do you mean, 'hunt'? He told me he was searching for lost Clan members so he could reunite them," Elin asked, bewildered.

"Well, that'd be a VERY gentle way of putting what the true experience is like. They're called Hunters for a reason. It's their job to track families that have escaped and drag them back to the Clan. Once they reach Clan territory, the families are separated. Depending on the members' age, they're either sent to Ginnungagap for what the Clan calls 'reformation' or placed in a mentorship. If you're caught, you might never see your parents or siblings again." I conveyed the information in a straightforward manner. Elin needed the unvarnished truth. Tristan had been clearly spinning a story for her.

"*What*? I don't understand! Tristan made it sound like a utopia where everyone's taken care of and there's a solution for every problem. There was nothing about dragging off and separating families. Why would they do that?" Elin said, stunned.

"Some aspects of Clan life are good. Everyone does have their basic needs met...nutrition, a place to live, healthcare. Until about twenty years ago, it might've been considered a utopia, but it all changed. There was a reshuffling in the Clan Council, and Chairman Arild took the reins. He promoted a new model for Clan society, which slowly evolved into a machine of productivity and efficiency. Anyone who stands in its way gets removed. Children are considered a distraction for their parents. They reduce the productivity of their mothers and fathers. But of course, they're future productive Clan members, so they can't just be disposed of. So, the leadership came up with the concept of mentorship programs. Elder members who match a child's ability are given the children to bring up and mentor into the roles that they once held."

"It didn't sound horrible until it was put into practice. Small children were ripped from their loving families. Parents weren't informed of where or with whom their children were placed. Visitation or efforts to retrieve a child were strictly prohibited. It's one of the many reasons my parents escaped with me and my siblings," I explained.

"That sounds awful!" Elin said, looking at me with wide eyes. "Why did the leadership change and the focus become productivity?"

"I don't have the best grasp on Clan politics, but essentially it was an ideological shift. The council started to propagate the belief that something called Ragnarök hadn't happened yet," I responded.

"Oh, right...Tristan mentioned Ragnarök," Elin commented.

"If it was true that Ragnarök hadn't happened, then the Clan would have a moral imperative to prepare for it. The legend goes that a long time ago, the moon gods or goddesses of four clans from the North, South, East, and West gave special powers to their worshippers to help prevent the end of the world...or Ragnarök. The Nordri Clan's moon god Máni gave my ancestors their powers so we'd be warriors alongside the gods during the battle," I explained further.

"Yeah, Tristan said something about the moon god and the four clans...and something about Odin and his warriors in Valhalla," Elin interjected. "But why four clans from the compass points?"

"Well...as far as I remember, the myth says that each clan had sacred beings... dwarves, animals, earth elements, or sons of gods... that guarded the cardinal points. I guess the belief was that these beings would add layers of power and protection for each chosen clan," I said, taking a sip of Coke.

"What do you believe, then?" Elin asked, looking me in the eye.

"I'm not sure...clearly my powers came from somewhere. And our Clan has survived," I answered. "Most members who now live on the periphery or are fugitives, like my parents, believe that Ragnarök happened thousands of years ago and that we're living in the new world born from that chaos. They believe that we should continue to work discreetly to protect and help all of humanity. But single-mindedly preparing for a war that isn't coming doesn't make sense...and serves very few individuals."

"So, what happened to the other three clans? Tristan told me the Nordri were the only ones left." Elin's amber eyes stared at me intently. I fidgeted with the coke can trying to calm the waves of nervous energy her gaze ignited in me.

"I'm a little fuzzy on the details of what went down between the Clans. But what I do know is, even though over generations, the Four Clans intermingled developing multicultural pockets in their societies, there were still a lot of conflicts between them. The Nordri Clan was lucky in a way. Our isolated location in the northern fjords kept us well protected and out of most of the skirmishes... or so I've been told at least. Chairman Arild now touts his isolationist policies as the reason why the Nordri Clan has survived while Sudri, Austri, and Vestri Clans disintegrated. It's also given him another reason for establishing more protective and productivity measures. And apparently why he has a keen interest in locating and capturing Dormants."

"Argh...I feel like my head's spinning again." Elin put her head in her hands. "Why...why on earth would I want to convert into a Clan member right now?"

"I'll be the first to admit that the timing sucks, but you may not have a choice. Tristan knows about you. And given this evening's events, his patience for waiting until you convert and then taking you to Falinvik will not be the same. According to my parents, there are rumors about the Chairman's increasing obsession with Dormants and the Clan Council's plans for them," I said, commiserating.

"He doesn't have the book, so he doesn't know how," Elin mumbled from between her fingers.

"What do you mean? Who doesn't? What book?" I asked, taken aback.

"Tristan. He doesn't have the book of awakening. His aunt has it in the Clan library at her house," Elin said, raising her head again. "Wait, you don't know about the book?"

"Um, no...nothing. And Tristan has an aunt on the island? *And* there's a secret Clan library here?" I was completely stunned.

"You don't know that Ms. Haugen is Tristan's aunt?" Elin asked, surprised.

"Ms. Haugen, the librarian, is his *aunt?*" I exclaimed. The surprises kept coming. I swallowed hard, thinking back to how close I'd been to an active Clan member at the town library...and I'd used my *megin*. It was my turn to put my head in my hands. "I guess I never really thought about where he was living."

Elin went on to recount everything she'd learned over the last two weeks about the secret library, Tristan's pyrokinetic abilities, the underground tunnel with its Caelum metal door, the hammer-shaped key, and the book of awakening. She also told me how the mission to retrieve Ms. Haugen's keys had turned into a failure because the key wasn't on the ring.

"Wait...you knocked off a tiny key when you tried to grab them out of the air at the town library," I interrupted. "I took it, and I still have it at my house!"

"Was it hammer-shaped?" Elin asked, equally excited.

"No...I guess not," I replied frowning. "It looks more like a key to a lockbox or something." The conversation paused as we took in all the new information we'd shared.

"Aedan...what does the word *Smá-menn* mean?" Elin asked.

I grimaced. "It's a pejorative term for regular people. It means 'men of insignificance.' The Chairman came up with new names for Clan and *Mannlegurs*. He now calls our Clan *Stór-menni*, meaning 'men of greatness,' instead of Nordri."

Elin's eyes widened further as she took in the additional information. Then she asked, "Why did he change the names? And what does *Mannlegurs* and Nordri actually mean?"

"I'm not sure why...but I'm sure he has a reason. *Mannlegurs* means 'humans'' and Nordri means 'the one in the North.' We used to be known as the Northern Clan...just as the other three are the Southern, Eastern, and Western Clans. And '*Mannlegur*' just reflects the supernatural difference between regular people and us," I replied. I stifled a yawn and stretched my arms above my head.

"Huh...I wonder why he changed the names." Elin pondered, lost in thought momentarily. "Aedan, what time is it? I don't have my phone. Tristan was keeping it for me in his pocket."

I pulled out my phone from my pocket. There were several texts from Joel wondering where I was, with progressively unhappy emoji faces. I was sure that he'd heard or witnessed what had happened with Candice, but I felt a little guilty. I'd left him to fend for himself at the dance after promising to find him. Plus, now it looked like I'd ignored his texts. I'd definitely have to make it up to him and explain what had happened. The clock on my phone said 11:36pm.

"It's almost 11:40pm," I replied.

"Oh, shoot! I have to be home by 12am. Can I use your phone to call Anders?" Elin asked standing up.

"Sure. Here." I unlocked my phone and handed it to Elin. Our fingers touched as she took the phone, sending small sparks of electricity up my arm. She quickly dialed Anders' number.

"Hi. It's me...I know, it's Aedan's phone...it's a long story...can you pick us up?...Yeah, now," Elin said into the phone. "Okay, thanks. See you soon!"

We shut the cabin windows and tidied up after ourselves. Elin extinguished the lantern, and we climbed out of the cabin into the moonlight. The sea breeze caught Elin's hair, sending streaks of red across the full moon. I disembarked first, then helped Elin climb down. She led the way out of the dock maze and back to the parking lot.

The dance had officially ended at 10pm. The parking lot was empty. I wasn't surprised to see that Joel's truck was gone as well. I was thankful that Elin had asked Anders to pick both of us up—especially since I still needed to sneak back into the house.

While we waited for Anders, Elin and I talked about how to keep her safe. We both eventually agreed that the only way was to have her convert before the Clan forced her to. At least then she might retain some control and have some protection from whatever the Chairman's plans were.

The only hiccup in our plan was, like Tristan, we didn't know what the awakening ritual entailed. We needed that book. But neither of us had any idea how to get it. We agreed to keep thinking and discussing potential ideas and see if we sparked a moment of genius.

Our other issue was Tristan. How were we going to keep Tristan away from Elin? Obviously, the evening's falling-out between them gave Elin an excuse not to speak with him for a while. Then next week was exam week, followed by a week of vacation. Elin thought she had enough excuses to keep him at bay for a few weeks at least, but I could tell she was nervous. I put my hand on her arm and promised to help in any way I could.

With the moonlight spilling over her shoulders, she looked up at me with her amber eyes.

"Thanks, Aedan...especially for everything tonight," she said. I had a strong urge to touch her cheek to gently brush away the concern that had formed there. I could feel my fingers tingling in anticipation.

"Hi, guys. How was the dance? So good to see you, Aedan! Climb aboard, and we'll be on our way before Princess Elin turns into a pumpkin," Anders said, grinning. He'd come to a stop in front of us and lowered the Volvo's window. He seemed genuinely pleased to see me. I, on the other hand, felt an unexplained disappointment that he'd gotten here so quickly.

TWENTY

A symbol

ELIN

Besides my having to muddle through exams and weather Candice's further attempts at humiliating me, the past week had been less difficult at school than I expected. This was mostly thanks to Tristan's absence and Aedan's presence.

Once Anders and I had gotten home after the dance, I noticed that Tristan's motorcycle was gone and my phone was on the front porch step. Underneath it was a note tucked into an envelope. Not wanting to discuss anything more that night, I'd bundled both items into my white wrap so Anders wouldn't see, and left them encased until the following morning.

Sunday family breakfast had come with a side of endless questions. My overly excited mom and sister peppered me, wanting to know how my evening with Tristan had gone. I shrank at their questions, having no idea how to convey the ugly truth about what had happened. Or even approach explaining my time with Aedan. I couldn't very well tell them about the Clan or Aedan and his family. Tristan had made it very clear that bad things happened to those who knew and weren't members. Plus, I didn't want to jeopardize Aedan or his family any more than I already had.

So, I stuck to the basics. Tristan and I had a fight. Aedan had helped me leave. The lack of detail didn't exactly go over smoothly. Quite the opposite—it invited more questions. But eventually, my mom and sister had accepted that no new tidbits were forthcoming.

After enduring their third degree, I finally escaped to my room. The envelope was sitting on top of my previous night's wrap. I stared at it with the same hesitation that had marked my answers to my family's questions about the dance. I wasn't sure if I wanted to know what was written inside. Tristan had broken my trust in more ways than one. And I very much doubted that the contents of the envelope would put me in a better or more forgiving mood.

Given what had happened at the dance, I saw no reason to question what Aedan had told me regarding the Clan. If Tristan was willing to manipulate relationships to his advantage, then he'd probably be willing to do just about anything else for something he held as more important.

The only reason I reached for the small white envelope with my name was that it might hold a clue to Tristan's intentions. With a deep breath, I opened the flap and unfurled the note.

Elin,

Everything I have done is for you. I wish you had had the maturity to talk things through openly with me tonight instead of running away. What we are working towards is so important! The wild misunderstandings of one simple Smá-menn girl should not break us apart. We just need to move forward—together.

To prove how important that is, I wanted to warn you. After

you left, I discovered that my aunt had hidden a Clan listening device in the small flower arrangements we wore. She is probably now aware that we are looking for a book from the Clan library. I do not think she knows about you, but I cannot risk going back to her house...at least not yet. I am leaving the island to seek some advice and formulate a new plan.
I will be back for you soon,
Tristan

My shoulders tensed at the condescending tone of the letter. If I "had had the "maturity"...indeed..."to talk openly" with him. The gall—after what he'd done!

I could feel the embers of anger being stoked in my chest. I took a deep breath, trying to relax. It boggled my mind that he thought I could overlook his treatment of both Candice and myself. She may not have been my favorite person, but no one deserved to be misled like that.

Later at school, I told Aedan about the letter and the relevant bits of its content—Tristan leaving the island and his aunt knowing about our interest in a Clan book. Tristan's aunt, of course, didn't know why we wanted the book, or what book, to be exact. However, I was sure that it wouldn't be long before she could hazard a guess—especially given Tristan's attention to and keen interest in a *Smá-menn* girl.

Aedan had been relieved to hear that Tristan had left the island but was concerned about his aunt learning about me, the book, and perhaps even Aedan's family. I reminded him that I'd torn off the corsage at the dance before he and I had talked on the boat, a small saving grace amid the chaos. And before that, Tristan and I had only mentioned the key and book during our photo session, so hopefully, the damage was minimal. However, Aedan still insisted that either he or Joel accompany me everywhere at school.

Ironically, this was made easier with exams, since normal classroom schedules were interrupted to allow for extended testing periods. Aedan's and my exam schedules aligned to the point where there were only a handful of periods left where Joel had to keep guard.

Once Aedan apologized for leaving Joel hanging at the dance and provided a non-supernatural explanation of events, Joel accepted his apology without too many questions. We also convinced him that Tristan had made some threatening statements, which is why the escort was necessary. It was, after all, mostly true.

During the week, Aedan was as good as his word. We studied together at breaks, sat together during exams, and ate together at lunch. I don't think I would have made it through the week without him. Whether it was his intelligent coaching on exam subjects or his constant presence thwarting some of Candice's more public tantrums, Aedan refocused my energy where it needed to be.

With Tristan's absence, my embarrassment was Candice's only source of consolation. Any opening and she was sure to be there to twist the knife a little deeper. Through it all, Aedan distracted me with his ever-present iPod playlists and once in a while managed to squeeze a rare smile and laugh from my lips with a well-timed joke. And there was even an occasional flutter from the melancholy butterflies in my stomach when his sea-blue eyes met my eyes. Somewhere in my enthrallment with Tristan, I'd forgotten how good-looking Aedan was.

At home, after much prodding, Anders eventually got tear-filled details out of me regarding the fight with Tristan. He now knew about Tristan's non-supernatural two-timing ways and had become even more determined to keep him away from me. I tried to reassure Anders that Tristan had left the island, but his big-brother instincts kept him at my side.

I joked that I expected to wake up with a tracking chip embedded somewhere in my body any day now. To which Anders responded half-seriously that it wasn't a bad idea.

The other big event in the past week was Maria's departure preparations for college. She'd been like a whirlwind going through the house as she gathered boxes to take and organized boxes to be stored. A few scuffles had broken out between Anders, Maria, and me over who was the actual owner of items, but somehow we'd found a peaceful resolution—without the intervention of our parents. I chalked it up to a small blossoming of goodwill as one sibling was about to leave home.

Her impending departure had also been a considerable distraction for my parents. My mom trailed after Maria's tornado, trying to offer helpful suggestions, while my dad avoided the chaos by hiding in his office. Otherwise, I was pretty sure they would have noticed Anders' and my odd behavior.

My parents were leaving that afternoon to drive Maria to her new school. They'd also planned a small vacation on the mainland after dropping her off. Anders and I would be left to hold down the fort for the next few weeks.

It was good timing from my perspective. Exams were over, and vacation week had started. Plus, Mia, Sam, Betty, and Derek were coming back to the island for their week off. And I was eager to spend some uninterrupted quality time with them. We'd planned to meet up the next day for a leisurely picnic at Witner Hill and a rappel to the rocky beach below.

Before I knew it, my dad's Volvo was ready to go. The car sat in the driveway stuffed to the brim as the last maple leaves fell from the trees. The jigsaw puzzle of how to fit all of my sister's boxes plus my parents' vacation luggage in the car had taken most of the early afternoon. My dad, the chief orchestrator, had received a steady stream of "helpful" suggestions from my mom and Maria until he'd figured out a more productive task to occupy them.

Anders and I had steered clear of the drama, opting to observe from the safety of the front porch rockers as we sipped hot apple cider from our mugs. The hot drink was a perfect remedy to the increasingly chilly afternoon. The season was definitely starting to show signs of winter.

"Guess that does it," my dad said with satisfaction as he gave a final shove to close the trunk. The Volvo now only had room for the three passengers to squeeze inside. To say our goodbyes, Anders and I climbed down from our perch to join the rest of my family by the car.

"Are you sure you got everything, Leif? Is the little green suitcase aboard?" my mom twittered, peering worriedly into the car through the windows.

"Yes, dear. Everything is in the car." My dad calmly reassured her.

"Oh, I forgot one thing!" Maria exclaimed, raising her palm to her forehead.

"Maria, we really don't—" my dad began, but Maria was already up the porch steps and disappearing into the house. My dad shook his head and opened the side door, trying to find space for whatever Maria had forgotten.

My mom busied herself with tightly embracing Anders and me. She reminded us to take care of each other, and that there was plenty of food in the freezer and grocery money in the jar on the kitchen counter. Anders gave the necessary reassurances that all would be well and that he had everything under control. I, in turn, wished them a very good drive and a relaxing vacation.

"Found them!" Maria announced as she returned, carrying her forgotten items. "Here, Elin. Grandma's multi-striped scarf. I know how much you love it. And Anders, I didn't forget about you. Your lost three-volume edition of The Lord of the Rings. I found it cleaning out my closet." Maria smiled widely as she handed the items to us.

"Wow, are you sure, Maria? I know you like the scarf too," I responded as I accepted the present. It had been a coveted favorite—especially since it had been knitted by our grandmother.

"Yeah, I'm sure. Something to remember me by." Maria reached around me for a quick hug. She then turned to Anders for the same.

"Thanks, sis! I've been looking for this forever. Thought I'd lost it for good," Anders said as he returned my sister's hug. I was positive that Anders suspected, as I did, that there may have been a reason why his favorite book had been all too difficult to find. But all things seemed forgiven in the moment as we accepted our symbolic gifts.

My dad, relieved that no new items were entering the vehicle, came to give us big hugs and last pieces of house-care advice. Then, with at least two more hugs and promises of phone calls from my mom, the three of them piled into the car. They opened the windows and waved goodbye as the car moved down the driveway. My dad gave a few final honks of the horn as they rounded the bend. Once they'd disappeared, Anders and I looked at each other and raced inside the house for our pre-planned movie and pizza night.

I woke up the next morning with more energy than usual. I couldn't wait to see my friends. I'd been craving a normal, carefree day. With all the hoopla over the last few weeks, spending time with my oldest friends seemed like the perfect remedy for feeling more like myself.

Aedan and I had devoted hours to trying to come up with a

plan to get the book of awakening. No good strategy had yet emerged, but it certainly wasn't for lack of effort.

I'd told Aedan that my friends were coming this week but I'd be sure to find some time to continue our research. Today, however, I was planning on not thinking about how to get into a fortified library or worrying about what potential actions by the Clan the future might hold.

I quickly got dressed in skinny jeans, a t-shirt, and my warm green wool sweater. The sun was peeking through clouds, but I could see frost on the grass. It wouldn't be long now until the grass turned yellow-and-brown from the cold and the mountains would be covered in snow.

As I searched for my wool socks and light hiking boots, I heard a ping from my cell phone, indicating a new message. I grabbed it from my bed and glanced at the screen.

MIA ARYA:
MORNING ELLI! MEET AT THE TRAILHEAD AT 11 AM.
BRING A BACKPACK AND BLANKETS. BETTY AND I HAVE
FOOD. BOYS HAVE DRINKS AND RAPPELLING GEAR.
CAN'T WAIT! 😃🩶

I quickly responded by simply sending a thumbs-up and a heart emoji. Glancing at my watch, I saw that it read nearly 10am. I'd need at least a half-hour for the bike ride to the trailhead. That left me with thirty minutes to find all the necessary items and eat breakfast.

I resumed the hunt for my socks and boots with more vigor. After a few more minutes of diving toward the back of my cluttered closet, I emerged in triumph. As I kept telling my mom, we were all organized in our own ways.

I hurried downstairs to the kitchen. As I passed Anders' bedroom, I heard sounds of life, so I knew he was also awake. I'd talked over my plans with him the previous night. We'd agreed that as long as I didn't wander off from my friends and texted him a few times to let him know I was all right, he'd stay home.

I had just poured myself a bowl of my favorite cereal when a sleepy Anders walked into the kitchen, wearing just his pajama bottoms.

"Morning, Elli," he said, lazily pulling a stool up to the kitchen island and slid my bowl of cereal in front of himself. He then proceeded to pour some milk into it. "What a thoughtful sister, to make her brother breakfast."

I responded by sticking my tongue out at him and grabbing a fresh bowl from the dishwasher. As I jostled the box to loosen the cereal into my new bowl, I reminded Anders of the day's plan.

"So how are you getting to the trailhead?" Anders asked.

"I was going to bike," I replied as if it was obvious.

"Nope, I don't think so. Wasn't it Tristan who drove you off the road last time? 'But...but...' nothing, Elli." Anders interrupted my attempted protests. "We have an agreement. I'll drive you. Maybe Derek can drop you off or something?"

"Okay, fine. But you better hurry, because you're not driving me like that." I pointed at him. Anders just grinned and shoveled another spoonful of cereal into his mouth.

I rushed through the rest of breakfast, hurrying Anders along as his food seemed to be disappearing at a snail's pace. Once I finished, I rushed off to find my green and navy backpacks and the requested blankets. I piled everything as I found it into the front hallway.

After the last item was collected, I put on my white insulated puffy vest from the closet and waited for Anders to emerge from his upstairs bedroom. After two minutes of haplessly staring at the top of the stairs, I yelled, "Come on, Andee! If you are not down in a minute, I'm leaving on my bike."

I hoped this small encouragement would speed his descent.

Anders had never been a morning person. His definition of morning was whenever he decided to get out of bed, regardless of the actual hour.

"Hold on! I'm coming," Anders called out as he appeared at the top of the stairs wearing an outlandish, mismatched outfit. He was sporting Maria's ski hat with its pink pom-pom on his head, my dad's bright neon-green anorak from the eighties, and his favorite pair of ripped jeans. "Your chauffeur is ready!"

I couldn't help but laugh out loud as he mockingly sashayed down the stairs, the pink pom-pom dancing on his head. Anders had a history of ridiculousness when he thought I needed cheering up. Apparently, he still thought it necessary—even though today was the first real day that I was feeling better about things.

"What?" He feigned innocence as he pretended to search for what I was laughing at.

"Come on, you fool!" I said with endearment, still chuckling. "We need to get going so I'm not late."

Anders took the truck keys from the entry box, grabbed one of the backpacks, and opened the front door. I pressed the button on the remote that I was holding to open the garage. We hurried out to the truck and threw the packs into the cargo bed.

Anders had the truck down the driveway in no time. We were off. I opened the truck window, sticking my head out to get a deep, full breath of the crisp air.

Most of the leaves had fallen off the deciduous trees, leaving bare branches to frame the sky. The only green now was from the pine and fir trees, their dark-green branches a stark contrast to the backdrop. The sun played hide-and-seek with the clouds. It was going to be the perfect day for a picnic.

It took us about ten minutes to reach the trailhead for Witner Hill. I could see Derek's blue station wagon parked on the side of the road. At the thought of seeing my friends, warmth and eagerness enveloped me.

Anders brought the truck to a stop next to Derek's car. Mia, Sam, Betty, and Derek emerged from the woods, walking up the trail. They were smiling and waving. I jumped out of the truck and rushed over to give them big hugs. We all started talking at once with no one really paying attention but wanting to express the joy of seeing each other.

"Hey...hey, Elli!" Anders tried to interject above the noise. He'd stuck his head out the window, catching the pink pom-pom on the top so it folded over. I turned around to face him with a big smile. "Do you need me to pick you up or can Derek give you a ride? Great to see you all, by the way." He raised his hand in greeting to my friends and smiled.

"That's no problem," Derek replied before I could even answer. "I'm happy to give Elli a ride."

"Okay, great! Make sure she takes it," Anders said, making a point of it. "Elli, do you want to grab the backpacks?"

"Oh, right! Yeah." I ran back to the truck. Derek came up alongside me and reached for the bags before I could. "Thanks! I brought two just in case we needed an extra."

"Perfect. We needed one for the food," Mia piped up as she joined us.

"Okay, I'm off, Elli. Remember your promise. I'll see you later," Anders said as he put the truck in gear.

"Thanks for the ride. See you!" I called out as the truck started to roll away.

Mia and I started to organize the food into the spare backpack while Betty and the boys gathered up the other items. After a few minutes, we were ready to start up the trail. The boys had the heavier backpacks with the food, water, and rappelling equipment. Mia, Betty, and I would be trading off with the blanket backpack as we hiked. With a few more double-checks for missing items, we proceeded down to the trail from the road embankment.

The hike up to the top of Witner Hill took us about forty-five minutes. It was made more enjoyable with our friendship picking up right where it had left off. We joked, teased, and talked about old times, leaving the more significant catch-up items for the picnic. Breckhaven's strict "no cellphones during school hours" rule and my friends' busy weekend schedules of extra-curricular activities had made keeping up with each other's lives that much harder.

Derek made an effort to be by my side and gave me some lingering looks, but I chose to ignore the implications. There had just been too much drama recently to process any further romantic entanglements.

As the cover of the evergreen trees thinned, we reached the clearing at the top of the hill. We paused, taking in the view.

The large granite clearing ran straight towards the horizon and the undulating deep-blue water. There was a quick drop-off where the cliff began. Below it lay a rock beach. You could see a small granite island that was close to shore. It had the remains of an old guard tower built upon it. I'd lost count of the number of times we'd rappelled down the cliff to the beach and then at low tide used the large, exposed boulders to cross to the island.

There was a slight breeze that bent the tops of the tall grass that grew in the granite cracks. The air had a slightly salty tang to it, and the sun shone brightly, giving a false sense of a warmer day.

We looked at each other, happy to be reunited on our playground. We followed the granite towards the center, laying the blankets in a level section. Hungry after our physical exertion, we plopped down and dug into the sandwiches and drinks that appeared from the navy backpack.

After the sandwiches had vanished, Betty smiled mischievously and reached further into the backpack. She pulled out a Ziploc bag full of her famous chocolate chip-and-cinnamon cookies. There were exclamations of delight from the group as we took in her present. Betty had always been a great baker. She'd learned from a young age, sitting on a kitchen stool as she watched her mother mix ingredients into some amazing concoctions.

Content from our feast, we all found comfortable positions, lounging on the blankets and enjoying the sun and company. Not knowing where to start, I simply asked how they all liked their new school. From the few sporadic text messages that I'd received from Betty and Mia over the last few weeks, I'd gotten the impression that all was not smooth sailing. The responses and stories that they now shared confirmed that things were as different for them as they'd been for me.

Breckhaven was much bigger and, with their individual sports and activities, they'd ended up with very different class schedules. This meant that they had only a few opportunities a week to get together, with limited time to see each other. It also meant new friendships had been made with other students. It sounded like the last part had had the greatest impact on Sam and Betty's relationship. Betty tactfully changed the subject by asking me how my year had gone so far.

I let out a deep sigh and rolled onto my back, looking up at the sky. I shared with them the significant events of the past few months. I told them how different school was without them and how I'd become good friends with Aedan and Joel. I of course left out the supernatural bits and any mention of the Clan.

Mia and Betty knew the details about my short-lived romance with Tristan since I'd shared a few tidbits in real-time through text messages. However, Derek and Sam tended to be more squeamish about "talking boys" with us, so I didn't get into the gory details of the falling-out with Tristan while they were listening. Once Sam and Derek left to set up the rappelling equipment, I turned to look at Mia and Betty and related the events from the dance.

"You mean Candice Andersson? Miss Mean Girl herself?" Mia asked, bewildered by the revelations. "Hmm...I'm not entirely sure if I feel bad for her. She was never very welcoming to me...or to my family."

"I agree. She definitely does not win the congeniality award...but on the other hand, no one deserves to be cheated on," Betty chimed in. "But Tristan...he really messed up! What was he thinking, trying to date the two of you at the same time? What are you going to do, Elli, when he comes back?"

"Argh...I don't know! I'm clearly not looking forward to seeing him, but he's...um...very motivated to try to...make it work," I answered as I rolled onto my back again. I hated not being able to tell my closest friends the whole truth.

"You said he lives with his aunt, right? Wasn't she on Sparrowhawk Lane? At least that's not close to your house," Mia said, trying to find a silver lining.

"Nope, but it's close to here," Betty added without thinking, pointing towards the south. "Only a mile or two as the crow flies."

"Betty!" Mia exclaimed.

"What?" Betty replied, confused.

"Not helping," Mia said. Out of the corner of my eye, I saw her nodding towards me.

Betty tried to clarify, grimacing. "Oh, I'm so sorry...I was just thinking about the road, not who lives there."

"Don't worry about it," I replied, shrugging off the association. "Tristan isn't there right now anyway."

At that moment, Derek and Sam came running up to tell us that everything was ready for us to rappel down to the beach. We quickly stuffed the remains of lunch into the backpacks and cleaned up the blankets to minimize the temptation for the seagulls or ants.

Our parents had sent all of us to summer rock-climbing camp before our first year of high school. It had further cemented our trust in each other and confidence in ourselves. Now we only got to put our skills to use a few times a year, so we hurried down to the cliff edge where the boys had set up two rappel lines.

Betty, Mia, and I did a safety check of the boys' handiwork. Once we were satisfied that everything looked good, Mia and I put on our climbing harnesses and hooked up our rappelling equipment. The boys had chosen the easiest point on the cliff face, which was slanted and had many craggy stepping points that made for a simple rappel and climb-back-up. In addition, the boys would be acting as belayers for the girls as we descended. Sam, being the expert climber amongst us, would be the last one down.

Mia and I were ready to go after double-checking our personal lines. We slowly started our descent, walking backward down the cliff, using one hand to feed the line and the other as a stopper. It was a short distance to the beach, so I paused for a moment halfway down to take in the view.

I looked at the blue sea and the ruins of the guard tower, thinking about what life must have been like for the individuals who built it. Something nagged at the back of my mind about what Betty had said about Tristan's aunt living only a mile or two south of Witner Hill. I knew Betty hadn't intended anything bad by bringing up the fact, but something about it was bothering me.

"Hey, you coming, or are you gonna hang all day?" Mia called out from below.

"Just coming...stopped for the view," I replied as I continued to rappel down to the beach.

Once there, Mia and I called out our all-clears to the climbers at the top. It was low tide, and the boulders, which provided a route to the old ruin, were exposed. I turned to Mia, pointing towards the small island. "Should we go explore, just like old times?"

"Yeah, why not! But let's wait for the others first." Mia did a little hop of excitement and smiled widely.

The sun was warm and the waves lapped against the shoreline.

It was a perfect day. We took a seat on the rocky beach and watched as our friends made their descent.

Once they were safely on the beach, we suggested our next adventure. Everyone was game, so we made our way to the first boulder. The very tops of the boulders were dry from being exposed to the sun, but the waterline was still very close. All it would take was one wave and the boulder would be slippery or submerged again.

I quickly checked the tide calendar on my phone. Low tide was peaking in about thirty minutes. It gave us plenty of time to cross over, poke around for a while, and still make it back before the path disappeared again. I informed the others.

Betty went first with Sam on her heels. The rest of us followed them. There were a few wobbles and excited squeals, but eventually, we all made it safely across to the small island.

Sam and Betty sat down together on the far side, taking their shoes off to dip their toes in the chilly water. Mia and Derek wandered around the ruin, examining some markings on the stone.

Beckoned by the cut stones of the tower, I put my hand on the surface. They felt cool and rough under my hand. Something about them was familiar. I walked around the tower, coming to where Mia and Derek were now peering at something on the old doorframe.

"What are you guys looking at?" I asked as I joined them.

"There's a funny-looking symbol carved into the vertical stones on the doorway. I never noticed it before...see?" Mia answered, pointing. The moss or lichen that had previously covered the stone seemed to have been torn off by a recent storm.

"It almost looks like an anchor or something," Derek said as I leaned in for a closer look. I grew increasingly excited as I inspected the symbol, tracing the pattern with my finger.

"It's not an anchor, but a hammer...Thor's hammer, to be exact!" I answered enthusiastically.

My head was buzzing. Betty's comment about distance, the familiarity of the tower's cut stones, and now the Mjölnir symbol on the doorway...it could all be just happenstance. But I recalled how the Clan library had seemed to stretch upwards past the point that we could see from the other side of the Caelum door. I couldn't be sure, of course, but it seemed like a lot of coincidence.

I peered into the opening of the ruined tower. The room was large and circular. You could still make out the first stone steps of the tower stairs leading upward. The floor was covered in driftwood and seaweed, indicating that during storms, the island itself could become partially submerged.

The far corner adjacent to the tower stairs seemed to be a low point of some significance since the water from the recent storm had pooled there. It seemed odd. I entered the tower, stepping over the driftwood and seaweed clumps. The stone floor was slippery and still wet. I slowly inched my way over to the pool. It was dark in the corner. I reached for my phone's flashlight to illuminate the surroundings.

"What are you doing, Elli?" Mia called out from the doorway.

"Just checking something. I'll be out in a sec," I replied as I squatted for a closer look. Too much water had collected in the pool for me to see anything on the floor, but at the base of the wall I could make out the top of a symbol before it was submerged in the water. It was very similar to the top of the hammer I'd just examined on the doorway. A whole flight of butterflies took off in my stomach. Could the Clan library have another, more-secret entrance?

Derek poked his head into the tower. "Hey, Elli! We've got to go. The tide is rising."

"Okay, okay. I'm coming," I answered as I straightened from my position. My hands were wet from inspecting the damp walls and wet floor. Having no better alternative, I wiped them off on my jeans and stuffed my phone back into the safety of my vest pocket.

I wanted to text Aedan immediately, but it would have to wait until I was back at the beach. We couldn't afford to lose our window to get off the small island.

"So? What'd you find in there?" Mia asked when I got outside.

"I found another symbol similar to the one on the doorway," I said as the butterflies swirled inside me.

"How do you know it's a hammer? It was so worn down and hard to make out," Mia asked as we lined up to cross the boulders again.

"Um...Tristan. He's a big fan of Vikings and Old Norse-world stuff. He showed me something similar," I answered as smoothly as possible. Thankfully, Mia was up next to cross the boulders, so she couldn't ask any more questions for the moment.

"So, you really liked him, huh?" Derek asked when we were left alone.

"Um...yeah, at the beginning...before I knew who he really was," I answered distracted. My thoughts were occupied with all the implications of another entrance. We might actually have a way to get to the book of awakening—which meant I could convert. I'd finally know if I really was a Clan gene carrier. A small, tight lump seemed to establish itself in the middle of my chest. Would it hurt to get a supernatural ability? And what would mine even be? Flying could be pretty cool or controlling the weather. I smiled to myself. But what if the power came with something visible...like horns? I fidgeted uncomfortably.

"You're up," Derek repeated, jogging me out of my thoughts.

"Oh, right! Thanks." I started to cross the boulders. Once I made it to the beach, I grabbed my phone from my pocket. Mia had stopped to wait for me a little further up the beach.

"Just one sec...I have to text Anders," I called out to her, waving my phone.

I sent two texts. The first one was to Anders:

ELIN BODIL:
EVERYTHING GOOD HERE. HOPE YOU'RE HAVING A GOOD DAY! 😊

And the second one, to Aedan:

ELIN BODIL:
FOUND SOMETHING. 😀 COULD BE THE ANSWER TO 📖! CAN YOU COME OVER TONIGHT?

I remembered Aedan warning me not to put anything important or too meaningful in texts or phone calls, so I'd kept it short. His response was almost immediate.

AEDAN GRADY:
VERY CURIOUS. YES, CAN COME. WILL 8PM WORK?

TWENTY-ONE

Black Moon

AEDAN

E lin's text had been unexpected, as I knew she was spending the day with her friends from the mainland. However, what she shared with me later in person had been even more surprising.

After replying to her message, I rushed to find my parents and tell them about Elin's request. They'd been in their bedroom, packing overnight bags. At the sight of the luggage, I assumed that we'd been discovered and were in a rush to leave. A slight panic had invaded my heart. We rarely took trips or vacations—and never separately—so, seeing the bags, I'd drawn the usual conclusion.

My parents, however, quickly reassured me that this was not the case. They'd instead learned of some potentially valuable information regarding the Clan library. But to get more details, they'd have to go to the mainland's Historical Building and Land Surveys department. They expected to be gone a few nights, since requesting documentation took time. Since they were going to be on the mainland for a while, they planned to take care of a few other errands.

Edvin was going with them to help since they could cover

more ground with three people. Claire and I would be staying behind to keep watch on Elin and any other developments on the island.

My parents and I had reached a new understanding after the dance. They'd caught me climbing back through my bedroom window near midnight. I hadn't been that surprised to find them sitting on my bed—especially given my mother's routine of using her ability to do a bed check. She could always tell when one of us was missing. While they hadn't been happy about my sneaking out —especially since I'd been grounded—what I shared about Elin's and my conversation had seemed to sideline some of their reaction.

Whether it was the shock of learning that a Clan Librarian was living on the island or just how far Tristan was willing to go, the new information had also persuaded them to help Elin. They'd agreed to look into the Clan library and the book of awakening in particular. In addition, they'd even agreed to keep watch on Elin during exam week when I didn't share an exam period with her—a little extra backup for Joel, just in case.

Even Claire and Edvin had been brought up to speed on the events and had asked to join in the effort. In return, I'd agreed to loop my parents in on any future happenings. To my relief, we all now seemed to agree—keeping Elin safe was essential to keeping all of us safe.

By the time I got back from Elin's house that night, my parents and Edvin had already left to catch the last ferry to the mainland. The house was dark and shuttered for the night. Claire's bedroom door was closed, indicating that she must have gone to bed already. It left me with no one with whom to share the exciting news about Elin's discovery at Witner Hill. Calling my parents would have been pointless since I wouldn't have been able to tell them much of anything over the phone.

So, I did the only thing one does in such circumstances: I got a quick snack from the kitchen and headed to bed. I was feeling a little tired from the day's events anyway. Plus, we were only three days away from the second new moon in the same month, a rare occurrence known as a Black Moon. When it occurred, which happened every thirty-two months, the Black Moon always left us feeling more depleted than usual.

As I drifted off into sleep, my last thoughts were of Elin and our plan to go back to the tower the following day.

It was easy to sleep in the next morning. There was no thunderous snoring from Edvin's room or restless footsteps in the hall from other occupants. I finally rolled out of bed when my watch indicated a time close to ten.

I stumbled down to the kitchen in my pajamas, immediately missing the smells of my mother's home-cooked breakfasts. Claire was sitting on a stool at the kitchen island, nursing a coffee and reading a document. She was slumped over the counter, leaning on her palm as she flipped the pages. This was not someone who'd gone to bed on the earlier side.

"Morning, Claire," I greeted her as I entered. "Rough night?"

"Hi, Aedan," Claire mumbled in response. "There's cereal and toast for breakfast. Coffee too, if you feel like a cup."

She indicated the pot on the opposite counter. I walked over to the other side of the island. I took my iPod from my pocket and selected Wham's "Wake me up before you Go Go" from my Cheerful Morning playlist. I hit "play" and the song started to stream through the connected speaker in the kitchen.

My sister looked up from the document. "Really, Aedan?"

I shrugged, grinning, and rummaged through the pantry for my favorite cereal box while Wham serenaded us.

"So, what's that you're reading?" I asked Claire as I sat down next to her at the island counter and slid my bowl of cereal closer.

"Oh, just something a friend gave me to look over. Just boring paperwork stuff," she answered, brushing off the question and turning the document over so only the blank white side was visible.

"Your friend Mr. Tibadeau?" I asked between spoonfuls of cereal.

Claire's face remained serene as she replied, "Yes, in fact. Florent Tibadeau."

"Oh? How'd you get to know the school French teacher?" I asked as I reached for my glass of orange juice.

"We met in town when I was doing some errands." She took a sip of coffee.

Claire would have been a good spy. She'd remained completely composed—but I had one last card to play.

"What were you two doing at the marina on the night of the dance? And who were the other people on the boat?" I inquired, watching her carefully. She hesitated, clearly not expecting that question.

"Well...it was a night boat tour." She stopped short as she saw the look of incredulity on my face. "Okay, fine, Aedan. You caught me. But you can't tell Mom and Dad—or anyone else, for that matter. Promise?" I nodded. "They're part of an underground resistance movement. They help people fleeing from Falinvik and generally try to make things more difficult for the Clan in any way that they can. Most of them are fugitives like us or regular people who've somehow become involved."

I was stunned. I'd always suspected that there was some kind of a resistance movement against the Clan, but now that a member was literally sitting in our kitchen, it was somehow more astonishing. My mind was also blowing up from the irony that Elin and I had spent most of the fall semester researching and writing about such groups in other conflicts. I just never pictured finding a resistance group on this island—and, importantly, Claire being involved.

My dumbfounded silence must have unnerved Claire because the rhythmic clinking of her spoon against the side of her coffee cup had greatly increased. She looked at me expectantly. It was very apparent that she'd been wanting to tell someone in the family.

"Mom and Dad are going to kill you when they find out," I blurted. "I mean, I won't tell them or anything...but they'll eventually figure out that something's up."

"I know...I just couldn't sit by and do nothing anymore. So many of us have just disappeared...or worse, been taken to Ginnungagap," Claire said with passion. "More people are trying to escape every day, and they need help. We can't just leave them out there to fend for themselves...especially with the Hunters becoming more and more aggressive."

"I get it," I commiserated. We all felt a certain helplessness at being at the mercy of a much more powerful enemy. I'd seen the different coping mechanisms my family employed to combat the dark feelings and maintain a sense of control. I could hardly blame Claire for taking a more active stance. "Once things are more settled with Elin, I want to help."

Claire shook her head. "Aedan. I don't think that's a good idea. It's very risky. Just think of how Mom and Dad would react if they knew I'd gotten you involved. I'd probably end up chained in the basement or something." Claire gave a small laugh as she jokingly said the last part, but both of us knew my parents would be less than thrilled.

"Not a fan of the basement, huh? Well, I guess we can't have that, then. Besides, who else would keep Edvin in check?" I joked as I rose to clear my dishes. "Just be careful, Claire."

I knew not to push my involvement right then. I'd circle back later when I didn't have other pressing things on my mind—like the symbol Elin had found on the tower.

During our previous night's planning, Elin had recommended that I wear athletic clothing and sturdy shoes. She'd mentioned we would need to rappel down to the beach. I tensed up a little at the thought. I'd never done anything like that—especially given a childhood aversion to heights.

Omitting that small detail, I told Claire about Elin's discovery and our intended reconnaissance later that day. She made me promise to be careful and not to go in if there was another entrance. She insisted we'd need a comprehensive plan if that was the case. I assured her it was just a scouting trip to see if Elin's hunch was real.

The rest of the morning went by quickly as I gathered the various items that Elin and I had determined we needed based on her first visit: a flashlight, plastic containers to scoop out the water, a knife, and a small garden hand-rake for the seaweed. I also threw in a couple of granola bars and two bottles of water. To conserve my *megin,* I asked Claire to drop me off at the bottom of the trailhead where I was to meet Elin at 2pm.

Elin showed up right on time. I wasn't surprised to see Anders dropping her off in his truck. Elin had told me how protective he'd become after the incident with Tristan. It had made me like him even more.

He smiled and gave a small wave as he drove up. I raised my hand in acknowledgment. Elin got out of the truck and grabbed a heavy-looking navy backpack from the flatbed.

"Hi," she greeted me as Anders put the truck in gear and drove off. "You ready?"

"Yeah, ready to go," I replied as Elin tried hoisting her backpack off the ground. "Why don't you let me take that one with all the equipment? You can take this one." Elin hesitated, apparently contemplating my offer. "It's only fair, considering that you're setting up the rappel."

Elin acquiesced. "Okay, thanks. Here." She offered the heavy backpack to me. I took it and handed her my lighter one. Once the packs were settled on our backs, we began the climb to the top of the hill.

We both seemed to be lost in our thoughts on the way up the hill, so conversation was sparse. My mind was occupied with what Claire had told me earlier regarding the Resistance. I had about a bazillion questions zooming around in my head after having had time to absorb the information. I'd promised to keep silent about their existence, so I couldn't share my thoughts with Elin—at least not yet. Instead, I focused on putting one foot in front of the other, with Buffalo Springfield's lyrics to "For What It's Worth" playing silently in my head.

We made quick work of the hike and were at the top in about forty minutes. The light was already beginning to show signs of dimming. We had only about two hours before the sun would set. Elin headed straight for the edge of the cliff, veering toward the left. She seemed to be scanning the ground for something. I hurried after her.

"What are you looking for?" I asked as I caught up with her.

"I'm looking for the anchor bolts the boys permanently fixed to the ground," she answered as she suddenly stopped. "Here they are! Okay, I need the equipment from the backpack." I obediently dropped it at her feet.

"How can I help?" I asked as Elin began to pull various ropes and carabiners out of the bag.

"You can lay out the equipment on the ground so it's easy to see," Elin offered as she grabbed a few pieces of rope and began rigging the anchors in the ground.

Now that we were at the cliff's edge, the incline seemed less steep but still very much a cliff. I looked towards the horizon and took a deep breath to calm the flurry of activity in my stomach. I'd never been one for heights since a childhood accident. I tried to focus on something else.

There was a bite to the breeze even though it'd been a beautiful sunny fall day. The light played on the top of the undulating deep-blue waves, and a few seagulls curiously flew overhead. I took another breath of the salty air and then dropped down to sort through the various items that had been dumped from the backpack.

It took Elin about fifteen minutes to set up everything. She had a confident air about her as she made various knots and loops. She meticulously double-checked her work, especially the safety measures. After she had everything ready, she showed me how to climb into the second harness she'd brought along. Once it was secured, she plopped a helmet on my head.

Elin then proceeded to clip me into the rope lines and showed me how to use my hands to feed and stop the rope. We practiced a few times on the cliff edge before she said I was ready. She then informed me that she'd be staying at the top to help my descent by acting as a belayer.

I swallowed hard. I don't know why I'd thought we'd go down together somehow. Suddenly the cliff edge seemed a lot steeper. Given the phase of the moon, my *megin* was at a low point, so it wouldn't be of much help should anything happen. Elin put her hand on my arm and brought my focus to her.

"Aedan, you can do this," she said, looking straight into my eyes with her amber ones. "I'm going to help you. We'll talk throughout the rappel. Just don't look down and you'll be on the beach before you know it."

She smiled and gave me a reassuring squeeze with her hand. Sure, I'd be on the beach before I knew it...falling was a very quick way down. I took a big gulp of air.

My options at this point were limited. I'd come this far, and it was the only way to get to the tower. Plus, I wasn't going to let Elin down.

Taking yet another deep breath and letting it out, I told her I was ready to go. At the same time, I was desperately trying to stop the chorus from Tom Petty's song "Free Falling" from playing in my head.

Elin led me to the point on the edge where I'd start my descent. She told me to keep walking backward, holding the rope in my hands as she'd shown me. Holding my breath, I did as she told me and took my first step off the cliff edge.

It was about halfway down that I actually started to enjoy myself. The cliff didn't feel as steep as it had looked from the top. Plus, it was a totally different perspective, rappelling down the side where the only usual visitors were the birds.

Finally, on the beach, I congratulated myself on maintaining my bodily integrity. I unhooked myself, exhilarated by what I'd just done. I called out to Elin that I was free and clear. She yelled back that she'd be a few minutes as she had to change the rigging to a "solo top-roping setup"—whatever that was.

I looked around the rocky beach. A dark line at the base of the cliff disclosed how high the tide brought the water. I slipped off my harness and helmet and walked down to the boulder path to the tower island. I took a seat on the beach, wondering about the individuals who had built the tower. Had they been Clansmen or some other medieval soldiers looking to safeguard their stronghold?

When I noticed that Elin had started her descent, I walked back over to the rope lines to watch and wait for her. Being the more experienced climber, Elin had my backpack with our other provisions on her back. Before too long, she was stepping onto the beach with a large, confident smile on her face. She quickly took off her harness and helmet.

We hurried down to the boulders, not wanting to waste

another minute to cross to the island. It took some care to balance on the still-wet boulders, but somehow, we managed not to fall into the chilly water. Once we were on the island, Elin hurried to the tower entrance.

"See...it's right here," she said, pointing to the marking on the vertical stone. I leaned in for a closer look.

"You're right. It definitely looks like a Mjölnir symbol." I traced the outline with my finger. "Where's the other one?"

"This way," Elin said as she entered the tower.

The top of the tower had fallen many years ago, but the base seemed to have withstood the trials. Elin carefully made her way to the back corner by the remains of a staircase. She bent down next to a pool of water. She turned on the flashlight she had grabbed from the backpack. "See, the top is here. I'm sure once we get the water level down far enough, we'll see the rest of it."

I went to kneel next to her to examine the surface. When I leaned over to the symbol, I was so close to Elin that I could smell the sweet apple shampoo in her auburn hair. It was distracting. I tried to refocus on the symbol.

I reached over to trace the pattern with my left hand. My medallion cuff came close to the symbol as I did. A bluish light started to emanate from the outline.

"Wow! Did you see that?" I exclaimed, startling Elin, who seemed a bit preoccupied herself.

"See what?" she asked, bewildered.

"Watch," I said as I brought my cuff and medallion close to the symbol.

We couldn't see the bottom, but it was very clear that the top of the outline was emitting a blue light. We both turned to look at each other with large grins on our faces. As quickly as we could without falling on the slippery seaweed, we rushed outside to grab the plastic containers and other supplies from the backpack. I'd brought two small containers and one large one that could be filled and then dumped.

We carefully proceeded back into the tower and eagerly began our clean-up effort. Elin stopped for a moment to set an alarm on her watch to remind us when we needed to cross back over the boulders to avoid getting stranded.

It took us a good half hour before we'd managed to clear the water and other debris from the small section of floor in the back corner. Our labors revealed a large square stone slab that was similar to the others on the floor but different in size. The symbol on the base of the wall was clearly another Mjölnir.

I glanced at Elin and then leaned down to touch my medallion to the symbol. Aligning it with the middle of the symbol had an additional effect. Now not only was the symbol emitting blue light from its outlines, but the blue light was pulsing, almost like a button. Without thinking, I leaned over and pushed the symbol inward.

The ground underneath our feet began to shake. We could hear the button with its circular symbol slowly grinding through years of grit. It had clearly been some time since its last use. Once the button reached its depressed state, the ground began to shake more violently and produced some strange groans.

Elin and I grabbed hands to steady ourselves. Then, as if by magic, the slab beside the symbol began to sink, revealing a similar set of slabs that formed a staircase into the darkness.

Elin and I both drew an inward breath. I felt her body tense up beside me as we imagined the worst.

Suddenly we heard a loud, trilling alarm. I nearly knocked Elin over as I jumped backward.

I grabbed her waist to steady her and myself. It took us both a good minute to realize it was Elin's watch warning us about the tide. We both nervously laughed as our adrenaline spike eased. Elin shut off the alarm on her watch. She looked up at me.

"We have about ten minutes until we absolutely have to cross back over to the beach," Elin informed me as I awkwardly removed my hands from her waist.

A little color rose into her cheeks. She looked down, intently focused on resetting the alarm for a final warning.

"Okay. Then it's probably best not to enter until we have more time and a better plan," I said, thinking about my promise to Claire.

Elin nodded. I looked over at the symbol in the wall. The pulsating blue light was beginning to fade. I hoped we hadn't set off any alerts in opening the hidden staircase. Elin must have had the same thought since she kept throwing suspicious glances at the opening while we collected our strewn supplies. But neither of us heard any sounds from the darkness of the staircase or elsewhere. All seemed quiet around the tower island.

As Elin and I finished packing our supplies into my backpack, I noticed the symbol's blue light fade out completely. It was followed by ground shaking and the grinding noise of the staircase. Elin and I watched as the stairs folded themselves back into their original position. Apparently, it was on a timer. Elin and I shrugged at each other and bundled the remaining items into the bag.

As we exited the tower, I handed Elin a granola bar and a bottle of water. We sat down in a sunny spot on the granite island to enjoy the last few minutes.

We talked excitedly about the symbol, the blue light, and the potential of the library being below as we ate and drank. Then Elin fell silent as she ate the last few bites of her granola bar.

"Aedan," she said, clearly in mid-thought.

"Yeah," I mumbled through the granola in my mouth.

"What do you think will happen during the awakening ritual?" Elin asked, barely audible.

I turned to face her. Her forehead was crinkled in a worried way.

"I'm not sure, Elin. Um...I do know that there've been people who have gone through it and nothing bad happened to them," I replied, trying to be comforting.

"What do you think my ability will be?" she asked, turning to look at me.

I thought for a minute. "All the people I know were born with their ability already active. So...I'm not sure how the awakening will determine your unique power."

"Do any of them have..." She hesitated, looking uncomfortable. "Have horns or something?"

"What?" I'd just been about to take another bite of the granola bar, but my hand froze midway to my mouth.

"I mean... do any Clan people show *visible* signs of having an ability?" Elin tried to clarify, clearly a little anxious.

"Um...none that I've seen," I answered truthfully.

Elin paused for a moment. "Do you think the awakening process will hurt?"

"I don't think so...at least, I hope not," I replied, struggling to come up with something more reassuring to say. "Hopefully the book will answer a lot of questions. Regardless, it'll always be your choice whether or not you go through with it. We'll figure it out either way."

Not knowing quite what else to do to comfort her, I inched my fingers closer to where hers lay on the granite. Our hands came to rest side by side, just touching. The familiar electric current established itself between our fingers. She didn't draw her hand away.

We sat there looking out at the water with our hands resting next to each other, watching the sunset. We lingered until Elin's watch trilled its final alarm.

~

The following morning, I filled Claire in our progress at the tower. She'd come home late again the previous night but this time hadn't bothered to conceal the fact.

After stumbling out of the dark trail with only the flashlight and my night vision as guides, Elin and I had decided to meet up the following day at my house to plan. Of course, technically it was still a conjecture that the staircase path led to the library, but it would be good to be prepared. We wouldn't know for sure until we found the library entrance, but where else could the stairs lead?

While we were finishing breakfast, Claire's cell phone began to ring. She looked as surprised as I felt. I was generally the one member of our family that received outside phone calls. I was still in school and interacted the most with *Mannlegurs*. Claire reached for her phone and tentatively picked it up.

"Hello," she said. "Yes...I see...I'll come immediately." She hung up the phone. "Apparently something has happened. They wouldn't say on the phone. I have to go." We both knew the "they" meant the Resistance.

"Okay, no problem. Elin should be here any minute. We'll get started with the planning and fill you in when you get back."

My sister was already up and out of her chair, heading upstairs to change her clothes. I busied myself with cleaning up our breakfast items and loading the dishwasher. I wanted the place to look nice when Elin arrived.

A short while later Claire came rushing down the stairs. She grabbed her purse from the hall table and yelled out a "See you later" as she opened the front door.

"Oh, hi, Elin! I'm just heading out but will see you later, okay?" I heard my sister exclaim in surprise.

Elin must have arrived. Nervous energy blossomed in my stomach. I quickly wiped my hands on the kitchen towel and closed the dishwasher door. I walked to the front hall to see Elin standing in it.

"Sure, no problem," Elin responded to my sister, who was standing by the open front door.

"Hi," I said. She turned to face me.

"Hi," Elin replied, raising her hand for a short wave.

"Bye, Aedan. I'm off."

"Bye, Claire," I replied as my sister closed the front door behind her.

I turned to Elin, smiling. "Let's go into the living room. Do you want anything to drink? A glass of water, juice, or something?"

"Water, thanks," she answered as we walked toward the living room sofas.

I'd placed a few notepads and pens on the coffee table in preparation. I'd also jotted down a few items from Claire's and my conversation that morning.

"Make yourself comfortable. I'll just grab the waters," I said as I headed to the kitchen. When I returned, I found Elin reading my notes. "Those are just some suggestions Claire had on how to start planning. She said the easiest way was to make a list of all the risks we could think of and then figure out ways to address them."

"It's a good idea. I see you started with some already," Elin replied as she continued scanning the notes.

"Yeah, some thoughts came up as I was talking to Claire." I placed the two water glasses on the coffee table and sat down cross-legged next to Elin on the floor. She looked at me and smiled, offering me one of the notepads.

Getting right to work, we started to eagerly bounce further ideas off each other regarding potential risks. We wrote down the agreed-upon ones. After about an hour we'd formed a list with three columns: risk, mitigation, and disadvantage. We'd also starred the ones we were most concerned with and made them into a separate table.

Risk	Mitigation	Disadvantage
* Ms. Haugen's megin	Enter on the new moon; no megin	We won't have megin either
* Getting caught by Ms. Haugen	Enter in the middle of the night when she is asleep	We'll be tired so get extra sleep
* Entry Alert	Enter on the new moon; slows response time; Ms. Haugen's age makes for a slow runner	Conservative estimate gives us 45mins in library
* Booby traps	Trollkors ring; none in Ms. Haugen's tunnel; this one hasn't been used in a while	Don't know if the ring can reveal all
*High tide - especially high during the new moon	Go by small boat	Don't have a boat; maybe borrow Mia's
* Tristan	He's out of town; go while he's gone	None; don't know when he'll return

We both also learned unexpected facts during our conversation. Tristan had neglected to tell Elin about how the phases of the moon affected our *megin*. I'd assumed during our discussion on the night of the dance that she already knew, so it hadn't occurred to me to bring it up.

Elin surprised me by conveying that she had a Trollkors ring. She'd forgotten about it until that point. I'd only heard about them from my parents' stories and had never actually seen one. We were both intrigued by what the other shared and the effect it had on our plans for the library.

Once we were satisfied with our risk list, we started thinking about the equipment we might potentially need. As we were goofing around, thinking about silly items to bring, I heard my sister rush back through the front door.

"Aedan! Aedan, where are you?" she called out breathless.

"We're in the living room. Everything okay?" I yelled, still partially laughing at Elin's latest ludicrous suggestion. Claire hurried into the room and threw herself on the couch close to us.

"I'm afraid I've got some bad news," she said as she grabbed my water glass and drank thirstily.

"What?" I sat up a little straighter. Claire was usually the composed one.

"Tristan is on his way back," Claire announced, sucking the jovial mood right out of the room. I glanced at Elin, who'd gotten a little paler.

"How do you know?" Elin asked, trying to keep her voice steady.

"A few friends of mine spotted him about a day's ride from the ferry port on the mainland. The earliest ferry he'll be able to make is late tomorrow, so we have some time to prepare," Claire said with empathy. "Whatever timeline you're thinking about for the library excursion, we need to move it up. It won't be long before Tristan tries to renew his acquaintance with Elin."

"Here." I held out the notepad to Claire. She shifted around to remove her overcoat and accepted it. "That's our risk list. The top sheet is a condensed version of the main concerns. We'd been planning on going during a new moon to mitigate some of the risks. The next one is tomorrow."

I saw Elin get possibly even a little paler. I gave her hand a quick squeeze. She looked at me and gave me a weak smile.

"This is good...really good stuff," Claire said as she turned the pages, reading our notations. "Are you ready to go tomorrow night? Our parents won't be back, but I think the three of us can handle it. We'll just sneak in, take some photos of the relevant pages, and sneak out. No one will be the wiser." Claire smiled, trying to keep the plan simple-sounding—even if it wasn't. She looked encouragingly at Elin for an answer.

"Um...yeah, I guess I'm good to go. Better to get it over and done with," Elin replied, a little hesitant.

"I think we can do it, but if we find the library, we've got to stick to the forty-five-minute timeline. I don't think there's an alarm on the tower door, but there might be one somewhere else. Better safe than sorry," I agreed and then turned to Elin. "Remember, this is just to give you the choice. We're just gathering more information at this point."

Elin nodded. I gave her hand another gentle squeeze and was rewarded with another smile.

"Great! Let's get going on some of the logistics. Elin, can you drive Mia's boat?" Claire asked.

"Ah, no...I don't know how," she answered.

"No matter. I can drive, but it means that you two will have to enter the library. According to a few friends who know the waters, there's no place to moor the boat on the island or the beach close by...especially at high tide. Also, there's a strong current in that area, so I'll have to stay with the boat. Can you call Mia and see if we can borrow the boat?" Claire directed her last question to Elin.

"Sure," Elin responded as she rose to get her cell phone.

I assumed that Claire's knowledgeable "friends" were actually Resistance members. It looked like they were already coming in handy.

"Sorry this is happening so fast, but it might be our only shot at this. Given that Tristan is on his way back, it won't be long before he and his aunt get on the same page. Then the book might be lost to us," Claire explained.

I got the sense that the word *us,* in this case, meant more than just Elin and our family.

$\sim$

Was it Robert Burns who wrote, "The best-laid plans of mice and men often go awry"? I couldn't help but think of the quote the next night as we arrived at the marina to meet Mia, and Claire received another unexpected call. It was clear that it was some sort of emergency and that she'd have to leave us to fend for ourselves.

Since neither Elin nor I could drive the boat, and upon consulting Mia, found that she couldn't drive it in the dark either, I had to enact Plan B—Joel. We had no choice, given the time pressure we faced.

"Hello, fellow mischief-makers!" Joel greeted us as he arrived, slightly sleepy and disheveled given the late hour. "What is tonight's deviltry, Aedan? Am I *once more unto the breach* by myself?" he joked, quoting Shakespeare's *Henry V*.

The high school's drama club was putting on the Shakespeare play, and Joel had scored the title part. As it turned out, he was a surprisingly good actor.

"What *he* is 'plan B'?" Mia said with apprehension.

I ignored Mia's question and addressed Joel. "Hey man, thanks for coming! No, tonight Elin and I are doing the breaching... namely of Ms. Haugen's basement. You get to hang back and play boatman."

"Fantastic! Anything for a good cause," Joel replied with enthusiasm.

I wasn't sure which was more pleasing to him, that we were doing mischief to Ms. Haugen or that for once he didn't have to go in first.

"We found an old tunnel system. And one tunnel runs directly to Ms. Haugen's basement from the tower island. Tristan left something there that belongs to Elin. We're just getting it back," I explained.

"Oh, wow! Cool. Is that what you figured out on the island the other day, Elin?" Mia asked, surprised.

"Yeah, I suspected something. Aedan and I confirmed it yesterday." Elin was obviously trying to keep her explanation brief.

Now that everyone knew the basics, Mia insisted that she was coming along if Joel was— especially given that he was the Plan B driver. No amount of persuasion could bend Mia's decision. Her final declaration that it was her family's boat left us little option but to take her along as well.

We discussed the best route to the island, how to disembark once there, and how to call for a pickup once we were done. Joel was pretty sure there was a cove not too far away where he and Mia could safely wait so they didn't have to go all the way back to the marina.

During the discussion, Elin and I intentionally left out any details regarding our actual mission. Neither Joel nor Mia could know our real goal. We had to keep them safe from any Clan blowback in case things went wrong during our excursion.

I glanced at my watch as we boarded the boat—11:30pm. Joel estimated that it would take twenty to thirty minutes to reach the island, given the tides, currents, and lack of visibility. He established himself behind the wheel at the center of the boat. The girls took the seats behind him, and I went to sit at the bow of the boat to act as a lookout.

Once we left the marina lights, it was dark—very dark. There was no moonlight to aid in lighting the way tonight. Plus, without my *megin,* my night vision was the same as anyone else's. I couldn't help but think of CCR's song "Bad Moon Rising" as the boat navigated the black, moonless waters. The only lights were the red and green ones on the boat itself and the few yellow glows from the homes that dotted the shoreline.

Joel was relying mainly on his knowledge of the island waters and the navigational equipment on the console and his phone to guide the boat. I'd remembered Joel telling me fishing stories from his many boat trips with his dad and brothers, so he'd been a natural choice as a Plan B driver.

I shuddered in the cold wind that blew as Joel increased the speed of the boat. I glanced back at the girls. I could just make out the contours of Elin's wool hat and Mia's figure as she huddled closer to Elin to stay warm. Winter was definitely starting to make an appearance.

It took another fifteen minutes before Joel slowed the boat, battling the high tide currents to get us closer to the tower island. Once we made it around the last eddy, Joel called out to me to get ready to jump to the island with the lead rope that was attached to the bow of the boat.

Unsure of what rocks lay close to the island, Joel had to pull up the motor and use the oars to push the boat closer so we could disembark. Once we were near enough, I'd jump out first and then help by pulling with the rope to bring the boat in.

I swung the backpack with our supplies onto my back and stood balancing myself at the nose of the boat as it rose up and down with the waves formed by the high tide. Elin joined me at the bow, while Mia and Joel were using the oars like gondoliers to push the boat forward. Joel turned the boat lights on to help see the potential rocks and the island itself. Elin and I also turned on our headlights.

When the distance seemed short enough, I propelled myself off the bow, landing on the granite in a slight squat. I quickly turned around, pulling on the rope to bring the boat in a little closer. I could see Elin balancing on the nose now, waiting for a good opportunity to jump.

As she finally leaped, a wave hit, raising the bow and causing Elin's jump to fall lower than she intended. She landed with one foot slipping behind her into the chilly water.

Quickly, I leaned forward to grab her arm and pulled her further up on the granite. The slack in the rope caused by my movement sent the boat unexpectedly backward, where we heard the distinct scraping sound of the hull against a rock. I quickly rose again and tugged on the rope to bring the boat back in.

"Everything okay?" I yelled to Joel and Mia, who had also stumbled with the sudden movement. I saw Joel's head disappear for an instant as he leaned over the side to check the back hull. "You okay too, Elin?" Elin nodded as she inched her bottom a little higher on the granite.

"Looks cosmetic! I think we're okay," he yelled back over the noise of the waves hitting the rocks and boat.

Mia was next up on the bow. Her jump was better timed and she landed on the granite near where Elin was now sitting, wringing out her sock. Mia quickly sat down next to her. She removed her shoe and offered her dry sock to Elin.

"Here. It's better that your foot stays dry. Do you want to switch shoes as well?" Mia offered.

"No, I think my shoe is okay. It's Gore-Tex. I think my sock got the brunt of it. Are you sure about the sock?"

"Yup, I don't really need socks with these shoes. They have a nice fake-fur lining." Mia pulled back the side of her shoe to show the inside.

"Not to rush you ladies from your fashion, but we're on a bit of a clock with this thing," I said as I struggled to keep the boat steady with the rope.

"Almost done," Elin replied as she slipped her foot, now covered by the dry sock, back into her boot. Once she had the laces tied, she came to stand next to me.

"I think it'll take both of you to hold the rope while I go make sure I can open the hatch," I said.

Elin looked slightly disappointed but nodded as she and Mia grabbed the rope. I quickly headed inside the tower, my headlight bobbing around the dark walls. Luckily, the high tide hadn't reached high enough to erase our cleaning work from the previous day.

I continued to the back corner by the stairs and bent down to touch my medallion to the symbol. It immediately began to emit the pulsating blue light. I took a deep breath and pushed on the middle of the symbol. The familiar ground-shaking and grinding noises began. My insides began to feel jittery from anticipation. I left the hatch to open by itself and quickly ran outside to where Mia and Elin were grappling with the boat's rope.

"We're all set," I announced as I reached them.

I couldn't shake a nagging feeling in my gut, given all the things that seemed to be going wrong tonight. Hesitantly, I removed my cuff from my wrist. I handed it to Mia, pressing it with some weight into her hand. "You need to put that somewhere safe. If Elin and I aren't back in two hours, I need you to take it to my sister Claire and tell her what happened and that it's time for sailing. The last part is really important. Remember, 'it's time for sailing.'"

"Okay...but is there something else going on?" Mia looked a little worried now. She glanced down at the cuff and then back at me. "Shouldn't we go to the police if you don't return?"

"I'm sure everything will be fine," I answered, trying to reassure her. "It's just a precaution. And my sister will be in a better position to talk to the police if anything should happen. Just promise me you'll go to her first?" I looked Mia in the eye, trying to impress upon her the importance of following my instructions.

"Sure, okay...no problem. You want me to give her the cuff and tell her that it's time for sailing," she repeated back to me, looking a little perplexed.

"Yes, that's right. Time for sailing," I confirmed.

She didn't know just how precious and irreplaceable the cuff was. However, my face must have betrayed something, because Mia opened her coat and placed my cuff in the inside pocket.

It was the only thing I knew my sister or family would trust from a stranger with our code phrase. I hoped Elin and I wouldn't need my cuff again tonight, but I didn't see much choice about sending it with Mia. If something happened to us, I wanted to make sure my family would have time to escape.

I took the rope from Elin and pulled the boat in as much as possible so that Mia could climb aboard again. After a quick hug and reassuring words from Elin, Mia approached the boat. With Elin's help, she successfully hoisted herself back into the rocking boat. I then threw the line back onto the boat's bow, where Mia collected it as Joel used the oar to guide the boat into the darkness. We waved a quick goodbye as they disappeared. I turned to Elin.

"Shall we?" I extended my hand towards the tower with a mock bow. Elin nodded, and we hurried toward the hatch before it closed again.

TWENTY-TWO

A confrontation

TRISTAN

I had been practicing what to say to my aunt all the way back from my mentor Henric's house. After the dance and finding that my aunt had placed a listening device in the small flower arrangement, I had—well, frankly, panicked. The discovery of the listening device was the one consolation I had from the dance humiliation.

In a twist of irony, when Elin hurled her corsage at me, it had broken apart, revealing the small device amongst the flowers. Otherwise, I might have never known of its existence and in fact, might be sitting in Ginnungagap at this very moment.

I knew panicking was a very un-Clansman-like reaction, but I had never been placed in a situation where the threat was so imminent. My aunt was not only powerful in ability, but she could also be ruthless when she felt Clan directives were not being obeyed. And what I had done, or rather failed to do, with my actual mission could be considered a rogue act—let alone all the other infractions, like trying to gain unauthorized access to the Clan library, telling Elin about the Clan, and stealing my aunt's keys.

The only person I knew I could trust in the situation was Henric. He had raised me since I was five years old and taught me everything I knew about being a Hunter.

I had used my *megin* to run back to Elin's house for my motorcycle. Once there, I had scribbled a note with pen and paper from my saddlebag, tucked it into an envelope, and left it with her phone on the porch steps. I would come back for her when I had a plan. She was, after all, still valuable as a Dormant Descendant. I had then jumped on my motorcycle and headed to catch the next ferry to the mainland.

Getting to Falinvik by *Smá-menn* roads was a cumbersome process and took several days. The roads were purposefully unmarked and unpaved, looking almost abandoned. Once the snow fell they were impassable.

It was a rare Clansman that actually left Falinvik—let alone by road. Traditional roads were of little use to us. Our Outer Aerial Transport Carriers, or OATC, were made for moving official people like Hunters over Falinvik's outer perimeter, while our Intra-City Aerial Transit System—ICATS—and autonomous hover vehicles made individually owned vehicles unnecessary. The OATCs were well *leynasked* as they exited the city perimeter so no *Smá-menn* could witness their flight. It was how I had been initially dropped off for my mission.

As I had drawn closer to the city, there had been several checkpoints to cross, including the outer shield wall. However, the Clan guards had yielded quickly and without any questions, once they'd scanned my Hunter's medallion.

Luckily, Henric's house was on the outskirts of the city, so I did not have to enter the metropolitan area with my motorcycle, which might have drawn more scrutiny and stares. His house sat on the edge of the fjord in the cover of dense trees. It was a traditional Norse wood cottage. The green grass that grew from the dirt roof was highlighted by the house's dark wooden walls and red-trimmed windows. The intricately carved front-porch posts had always reminded me of Viking longboat figureheads. It was also the only home that I could remember.

When I had finally reached the house and found Henric chopping firewood in the backyard, he had been less than thrilled to see me upon learning of my failures. He had chastised me that he had raised a better Hunter than one who would go so far off his mission and then completely botch his side plan. I had grown up with his diatribes, so I knew to give him some time to cool off before asking for further advice.

Mentors and pupils were intrinsically tied together. Mentors knew that their students directly reflected upon their standing in the Clan. If a mentee failed in his or her task, it was viewed as a failure on the mentor's part as well. And failure of any kind was not looked favorably upon, since it was unproductive. It created a strange and unique bond between the mentors and their students.

As expected, Henric had eventually come to find me dangling my legs from the dock that stretched into the fjord. It was my usual refuge when I needed to give Henric space. He had eased himself onto the lone rocker. His long white beard had folded into the creases of his wool cloak, as he had wrapped it tightly around his large frame to abate the early winter chill. You could still tell from his figure that Henric came from a long line of Norse warriors. His red hair had long since faded into white, but his tall stature and well-muscled arms and legs made him an intimidating sight.

"Well, Tristan. There's no easy way out of this pickle," he had said unsympathetically. "As with most things, the only way is forward. And I think you already know what you have to do. Did you come all this way just to hear me say it?" He paused as his steel-blue eyes flashed in disapproval. I had bowed my head, acknowledging the truth in his words. "All right—if it helps, I'll say it. You have to confide in your aunt and hope to Odin that she's understanding." He had paused and then in a softer tone advised, "Play to her vanity. Adis always was a vain woman. Offer to share the glory of finding a Dormant Descendant. That should appeal to her ambition." We had sat on the dock a while longer, both deep in thought, until hunger had gotten the better of us.

I had stayed a few more days with Henric until I had worn his patience to a raw nerve. He knew I was hiding. I had not felt ready for the inevitable confrontation with my aunt—or the potential consequences. If it went badly, I would be heading to Ginnungagap for an undetermined amount of time. But Henric was right—the longer I waited, the worse I was making the situation.

I had left the following day to make the long trip back to the island. Somehow I would have to find the right words to convince my aunt. To accommodate the worst-case scenario, I was timing my arrival for the night of the Black Moon so I might have a fighting chance to flee...if needed. Without her ability, my aunt would just be a frail middle-aged woman.

I roared my motorcycle to life as the ferry finally pulled into port at Auor Island. As I drove by the town library, I thought of Elin for the first time since my hurried departure. She of course had come up in conversation during the past two weeks, but only as the Dormant. There had been no other need to discuss her.

I felt confident that she was still on the island, leading her simple life with her *Smá-menn* family. I was sure she would be excited to see me again after a few weeks' absence. Whatever prior misunderstandings we may have had at the dance would surely have been put aside by now. After all, she had an opportunity to become a Clanswoman and needed me in order to accomplish it.

After I peeled off the main road, which was lit by street lights, the roads were very dark without the moonlight. The only lights were from a few houses that peeked from among the woods and the circular headlight from my motorcycle.

I had taken the last ferry from the mainland, so it was close to eleven when I finally pulled into the shed at my aunt's home. As I lingered there, steeling myself, I saw light suddenly appear on the ground outside. My aunt had turned on the side porch light. Even though it meant that she was awake, it also reminded me that my aunt had no night vision—meaning her *megin* was dormant, just like mine.

I took another breath and forced my feet towards the side porch entrance. My aunt stood in her tightly wrapped blue night-robe and matching slippers, holding the porch door open. Her expression was blank. She did not say a word while I scraped the dirt off my shoes and passed by her into the house. I waited in the hallway as she came in after me. She closed the door and flipped the deadbolt into the locked position.

Her gaze coldly pierced me as she said, "Hello, Tristan. Would you like to explain yourself?"

Even though it was a question it came out as more of a threat, and I knew she meant more than my two-week absence. I involuntarily swallowed hard.

"Yes, Aunt. Very much," I answered, my brain on fire as I tried to figure out how to de-escalate the situation. "Should we go sit in the living room? It is a long story."

My aunt motioned for me to lead the way. I suddenly felt very hot under my sweater. Once in the living room, I forced my body to slowly ease itself down in one of the thinly padded Scandinavian armchairs. My aunt rounded the coffee table to sit on the upholstered gray couch, her icy eyes never leaving me.

It felt as if we were in one of those old *Smá-menn* Western movies where two gunslingers circled each other at sundown. And it was clear that I was the underdog in this fight.

"I'm listening," my aunt said as she calmly smoothed the creases out of her blue robe.

I took a breath and started to spin the story I had been practicing. I recounted how I had met Elin and come to suspect that she was a Dormant Descendant. I smoothed over the bumpy details in the story by not mentioning our efforts to enter the Clan library or steal my aunt's keys. I spun a more appealing story of my quest to find something to help me prove Elin was a Dormant. How my plan all along was to bring the information and girl to my aunt once I had solid proof. I had not wanted to interrupt her important work with a false lead, I explained.

My recent absence was because I had learned of a book about Dormants and had been chasing a lead to find it on the mainland. I tried to weave the story so it fit the timeline of events and any potential information she may have heard from the listening device. I could not tell whether my aunt believed my tales, but I continued with my concocted story, watching her stony face for any signs. As I concluded, silence descended upon us. She watched me fidget uneasily in the chair, which now felt slightly too small for me.

After an uncomfortably long time, she finally asked, with frightening calm, "Tristan, do you think me stupid?"

"No, Aunt. Of course not," I replied. This was not going in a good direction.

"Then why would you expect me to believe that cow dung of a story? I know what you have been up to. I checked the Caelum door. And it does not lie," she said with iciness.

In trying to remember all the details from the last few months, I had forgotten about my first visit to the Caelum door—and my imprint upon it. I internally cringed. My only choice now was to try to negotiate.

"You are right, Aunt. I did leave a few items out of my story, but they are immaterial to our current circumstance," I said with as much confidence as I could muster. It was almost imperceptible, but my aunt's eyes widened just a fraction in surprise.

"How is trying to break into the Clan library immaterial? As I'm sure you are aware, this could be interpreted as treason," she responded.

"It is simply not a part of the current equation," I stated. "I think we are both aware of how highly the Chairman desires Dormants. I'm sure a potential Dormant would be equally appealing. And in this equation, I have built the relationship with her." I paused for breath.

I knew I was traversing a very narrow tightrope, but it was my only chance to avoid Ginnungagap or becoming a fugitive. I continued before my aunt could interject. "I can get her to come willingly...which I am sure is the preferred method. I cannot imagine that an abduction would go unnoticed by the *Smá-menn* in such a small town as this. However, given my past indiscretions, I am willing to share the benefits of her discovery with you. The Chairman would surely look as kindly upon two as one."

Even though my aunt was silent, I had seen a glint in her eye as she considered my offer. Henric might have been right to advise me to appeal to her ambition. Perhaps there was some hope in this standoff.

Before my aunt had a chance to answer my proposition, her SRT, which was lying on the coffee table, began beeping wildly. My aunt looked stunned at the noise.

"Impossible...it can't be," she mumbled as she reached for the device, clearly recognizing the warning sound. "Tristan, who have you told about the library?"

"What?" I asked, caught off guard. "What do you mean?"

She ignored my questions as she focused on authenticating into the device in her hands. Upon success, she was finally able to quiet the warning sound.

"*How on earth...how did they get in?*" my aunt nearly screamed as she witnessed something on the SRT screen. She tossed the device into my lap as she rose in a state of panic. "Who are they, Tristan?"

"I don't understand...who is who?" I asked as I watched my aunt rush out of the living room and up the stairs towards her bedroom.

I glanced down at the screen in front of me. It showed a video feed of what appeared to be the Clan library, as far as I could tell. There in the center of the room by the circular stone table was Elin with a familiar-looking boy.

I nearly dropped the SRT as I rose quickly from the armchair. How had she gotten in? How dare she not wait for me! A deep burning sensation was building in my stomach. After all, I had done for her. I had risked being sent to Ginnungagap or being alienated from the Clan just so she could become a Clanswoman. This was how she was repaying me. Of all the underhanded things!

My aunt came rushing back down the stairs. She was no longer in her blue robe but had on a black turtleneck and loose black slacks. Around her neck on a golden chain hung her Clan medallion, and next to it dangled a metal Mjölnir. From a belt at her waist hung a large seax and a small electronic-looking remote. My eyes lingered on the hammer, as I judged it to be about the correct size for the missing key.

"Come on, Tristan! No time to lose. We have to stop these intruders," Aunt Adis commanded as she headed for her office.

She made a quick stop by the hall closet, where she pulled out something that resembled a car jack.

"Quit dawdling and come help me," she ordered.

I sprang into action, grabbing the car jack from her bony hand and following her into the office. She went straight to her desk and gave it a great thump in the middle, using all of her force.

When nothing happened, my aunt mumbled something that

sounded like curse words in Old Norse. She tried again, this time slamming her fists into the middle together. It seemed to register and the box emerged with a *whoosh*.

"Bring that carjack here, Tristan," my aunt commanded.

I quickly obeyed. With some maneuvering, she was able to insert the correct part under the lever. She then pulled a nearby stool over to support the bottom of the jack.

"Okay, Tristan. Start pumping," she directed, pointing me towards the carjack.

I rounded the stool and did as she commanded. At first, I was a bit perplexed at the antics as I started pumping. But when it required more effort than normal, I quickly remembered the Black Moon.

Opening the hidden bookcase door required *megin* strength to pull on the lever. We had no powers. I had forgotten all about it with Elin's surprise appearance. She had timed her intrusion well.

After a few minutes of effort on our part, the carjack was able to lift the lever high enough for the bookcase to slide open. Without a backward glance, my aunt hurried through the opening. I followed her. She paused just long enough to flip the light switch by the doorway to the "on" position. The single bulb at the end of the hidden tunnel flickered for a moment and then illuminated the stairs.

My aunt quickly approached the spiral staircase, stopping again to plug something into a previously unnoticed wall outlet. A long string of Christmas lights lit up along the wall falling into the darkness below. Not unexpectedly, she had thought of every detail.

Without my *megin*, I felt like we were moving at the speed of molasses. The spiral staircase seemed to stretch on forever and played havoc with our balance as both of us tried to descend as rapidly as possible.

It was starting to feel like possibly the slowest response to an intrusion in Clan history. It had already been somewhere between ten and fifteen minutes since the warning had gone off. We still had to reach the ground floor and then had a two-mile stretch of tunnel to cover at *Smá-menn* speed.

Elin had indeed planned well. What I didn't understand was how they had gotten into the library. My aunt and I would have noticed someone trying to enter through her office as we sat in the living room.

"I take it the girl is the Dormant Descendant," my aunt said, interrupting my thoughts.

"What—um...yes, it's Elin. I just don't understand how they got in," I responded, puzzled.

"Who is the boy with her?" my aunt asked, ignoring my bewilderment. She did not seem quite as perplexed by how they might have entered.

"It's just some *Smá-menn* boy from her class. No one of importance," I answered. I could not remember his name, but I was pretty sure I had seen him at the school or somewhere else.

"So now we have a *Smá-menn* in our Clan library," my aunt said with disgust. "Well, it leaves us little choice. We will have to deal with him as well."

Finally, we reached the ground level. I was about to start running when my aunt stopped me. She reached for the small remote at her waist and hit the button in the middle. Part of the stone wall next to the staircase slid open to reveal a single-rider hovercraft. Why was I not surprised that my aunt had access to yet another piece of Clan technology in the *Smá-menn* world?

The single-rider hovercraft had always reminded me of my motorcycle. This particular unit was gray and had T-bar steering, with a narrow bench seat that stretched towards the back.

There were no wheels. Once you turned on the craft, a gravity propulsion system lifted the vehicle to your desired height and sped you forward. Although it was meant for one person, you could fit two people, with some sacrifice to speed and achievable height.

I was about to climb onto the driver's seat when my aunt stopped me with two simple words: "I drive."

I gave way, and she climbed into the driver's seat. I mounted the bench behind her, determined to find a handhold other than her waist.

The narrow tunnel and height limitations restricted the hovercraft's speed. Even so, it was definitely saving us time. Yet we were still at a significant disadvantage. Depending on how quickly the pair was able to locate the book of awakening, we might miss them altogether. I consoled myself with the knowledge that we at least knew where Elin lived and could easily find her accomplice, the *Smá-menn* boy, with some research.

My aunt's lit Christmas lights continued onto the ceiling of the tunnel, stretching down the small incline into the darkness. They created a strange perception of a long landing strip as the hovercraft sped along.

I knew we were getting close when I spotted the tiny red light in the distance. My aunt was impatient to get to the door now that it was within sight. She pushed the hovercraft to go faster despite the flashing warning light on the console.

The hovercraft added an annoying beeping sound to the flashing red light as it warned of an impending obstacle ahead. My aunt did not slow down until the last second, bringing the hovercraft to an abrupt stop...making me lose my grip and crash into her backside.

After a few indignant huffs, my aunt was able to disentangle herself from between my arms and legs. Off-balance, I slid to the ground clumsily, landing on my side with a thud.

When I finally regained my footing, Aunt Adis was already at the door, inserting the Mjölnir key into the lock. I quickly moved to her side. With a small twist of her wrist, the key found its home. The Caelum door slid open.

There on the other side of the stone table in front of the book pedestal stood Elin. The boy beside her was frantically trying to gain her attention. Elin seemed to be lost in some sort of trance.

TWENTY-THREE

The library

ELIN

Aedan and I started down the steep staircase at the back of the tower. Our headlamps bopped up and down with our movement, illuminating the walls and stairs. The stone steps were slippery from dripping saltwater and seaweed that had found its way down with us. The walls of the circular staircase were made from the same stone as the tower above. It had clearly been built during the same era. As the staircase narrowed, the cold damp emanated more tangibly from the walls.

Not knowing what to expect around the next corner, Aedan and I moved as quietly as possible. We must have circled at least four or five times before Aedan's headlamp illuminated a dark, sandy bottom. He slowed his pace as he took the last step down.

We'd come to a T-intersection. There was a stone wall ahead of us and a tunnel that ran both left and right. I joined Aedan on the wet sand. We paused, trying to decide on the correct path.

"Which way do you think?" Aedan whispered to me, his headlamp swinging from left to right. I'd lost my sense of direction as we circled down the staircase.

"We want to go whichever way is south," I whispered back.

It was impossible to tell which was north and south after all the turns. Aedan shrugged, indicating he was at an equal loss. I dug out my phone from my pocket. I remembered a compass app that worked with the magnetometer and didn't require a cell signal. I pulled up the app to the forefront. It indicated that south was to the left.

"It's that way." I pointed.

"I wonder where the other direction goes," Aedan said as he turned left, letting the darkness swallow the right tunnel. At the same moment, there was rumbling and grinding behind me as the staircase started to fold itself back up.

"Well, it looks like we might have a chance to find out, given that our path out of here just disappeared!" I said with mild panic.

I used my headlamp to scan the walls, looking for a similar Mjölnir symbol as above. None was readily apparent. Then I remembered that it wouldn't have helped anyway, since Aedan had handed his cuff to Mia.

"Aedan, what are we going to do? We can't just go wandering around these tunnels aimlessly."

"There's got to be an opening mechanism. Whoever built this place would've wanted a way out," Aedan rationalized as he started sliding his hands over the stone walls, feeling for such a thing.

"What if it requires your cuff to open again?" I asked, voicing the worst case. "Why'd you give it to Mia, anyway?"

It hadn't made sense to me at the time, but I'd trusted Aedan to know what he was doing. He was after all much more familiar with this supernatural world. Now with us being potentially stuck in an underground tunnel system, it didn't seem like the best decision.

"I had to. It was the only way I could think of that Claire or my parents would trust an outsider with a message telling them to run," Aedan said, a bit defensive. "Our medallions are the most precious item we've got. They're specific to a person. They help regulate our ability and conceal us from outsiders when needed...and as I'm learning, have significant other properties," Aedan added as an afterthought. "No person with an ability would give theirs up without a very good reason. If something goes wrong tonight, my family will be in immediate danger. I just couldn't leave them to face whatever that is without a warning."

I understood Aedan's reasons but wasn't quite sure where that left us now.

"Okay, I get it, but how are *we* going to get out?" I replied.

"Well, we've got two hours before Mia will go to my house to find Claire. So...the way I see it, we've got two options," Aedan said. "We can either focus on finding a way out now or figure it out as we go along. Although we may not get another chance at the book if we leave now. What do you want to do, Elin?"

Aedan was right. This might be the only chance I had to learn about the awakening ritual—at least as my choice. Who knew what Tristan had planned for me?

"Okay, you've got a point," I admitted. "Plus, we don't even know for certain that we'll need the medallion, right?" I rationalized. "Worst case, we might be able to sneak out through Ms. Haugen's hidden staircase." I paused for a moment, making sure of my decision before announcing it. "We go forward and figure it out."

Aedan nodded in agreement and started down the dark tunnel. My dad always said, "No risk, no reward." I really hoped it was true in this case.

"Aedan, do you really think your family would leave without you?" I asked as we walked in cold, damp darkness. I pulled my wool hat a little further down on my head.

Aedan took a moment to answer. "Probably not. But one thing's for sure, they wouldn't stay at the house like sitting ducks. They'd go to our emergency meeting place."

"You've got an emergency meeting place?" I asked.

"Yeah, we have to. We've had a lot of hurried departures in the past—and most of the time, my family isn't in the same place. We have to assume the Hunters know where we've been staying, so we always select a secret meeting place." Aedan paused, hesitating for a moment. "You know the old boat landing at Arne Point? That's our spot here on the island. We've got an escape boat moored there. But, Elin, you've got to keep that to yourself. Otherwise, you could be placing my family in great danger."

"Why tell me?" I asked, surprised that he had.

"I don't know...something about tonight has me on edge a little...it's probably just the Black Moon," he answered. He meant the last bit to be comforting—but it only stirred the nervous butterflies in my stomach further.

We didn't have to travel far before we came across an arched doorway with an iron gate. It was chained to the wall with a very old padlock. The kind that took a skeleton key.

Aedan took off his backpack and rummaged around to find the bolt cutter. We'd anticipated encountering some obstacles in our path. The bolt cutter was one of the items that had made the final pack list.

"What do you think...the lock or chain?" Aedan asked as he weighed his options.

"I say try the lock arm first," I advised.

Aedan picked up one prong of the old lock's arm in the bolt cutter's teeth. It snapped on the first squeeze, the ancient, rusting metal being no match for the sturdy steel on the cutter. Aedan unhooked the chain from the lock, and it fell to the ground from the gate with a loud jangle.

I cringed, expecting someone or something to emerge from the darkness. But no one came. Aedan opened the gate, and we passed through it.

It was only a couple of paces more when we came to another

archway. This time there was a wall of stone in front of us. It was a dead end. There was nothing but wall around us, except for behind us. Aedan took off his headlamp and used it as a flashlight to examine the walls.

The tunnel had narrowed after the first arch, but there was still enough space for me to fit next to Aedan. I moved to go up next to him to help inspect the walls. But I didn't make it.

Suddenly, I was sailing through the air. My boot had caught the tip of a protruding stone slab. I landed on my knees with my hands splayed out.

"Are you okay?" Aedan asked, concerned, as he bent down to check on me.

"Yeah, I think so," I said as I put weight on my hands to push myself back up.

Two things happened as I did. I felt pain and wetness on my left knee, and my right hand seemed to sink significantly lower in the sand.

"Hey, there's something here!" I exclaimed, pointing to the spot.

"Where?" Aedan asked with excitement as he bent down again. He helped me brush the sand aside from where my right hand had been.

After a few minutes of clearing, a square stone slab was revealed underneath. It was definitely lower than the rest of the ground beside it. My instincts told me to push harder on the slab. I pushed with my palm. It felt like something shifted but nothing substantial happened.

"I think something moved," I said. "But it needs more weight. Help me push!"

Aedan grabbed my hand to pull me into an upright position. We were now so close our noses almost touched. For a moment our eyes met. I held my breath. Aedan hesitated and then let go of my hand. I quickly stepped to his side, hiding my flushed face.

Refocusing on the stone slab, we each managed to fit one foot on it. We counted to three and pushed. The square sank a little bit, while at the same time, the stone wall in front of us opened about one-third of the way.

We both curiously peeked around the wall. All we could see was wood paneling. The opening was still too small to fit through, so we put our feet back in the depression and pushed again. The wall opened to the halfway point. We could now fit, so I tried pushing on the wood wall. It did not budge.

"Maybe we have to open the stone wall all the way," I speculated.

The square hole was now too deep for both of us to press down on it further. Before I could stop him, Aedan looked at me, shrugged, and jumped into the hole with both feet. The force of Aedan's jump opened the stone wall all the way. I heard a faint click as if something else had unlocked as well.

Aedan had sunk waist-deep in the hole as the slab had descended even further from his effort. I held out my hand to help him up. He grabbed it and scrambled out. We stood in front of the wood wall, examining it.

"I think it could be the back of a bookcase, Elin," Aedan said giving me an excited look. "I think we might be close. We should start the forty-five-minute timer to be safe."

"You think that's all there's to it? It just seemed so easy," I said.

"I don't think this path is used very much. Clearly, the tower entrance hadn't been used in a long time. Plus, it could only be accessed by someone with a Clan medallion. I doubt there're too many regular folks who stumble in here. And we don't know what other obstacles might be down the other tunnel," Aedan speculated. "Are you ready?"

I set the timer on my watch for forty-five minutes and nodded. Together Aedan and I pushed as hard as we could on the wood wall. This time it swung open easily.

Neither one of us expected what followed. Luckily, my sense of balance and being on the hinge side of the door kept me from pitching straight into the dark void. Aedan wasn't so lucky.

He'd pushed harder and now was desperately clutching the bottom shelf of the bookcase we opened and the top of one that looked to be below it. He was stuck in a V with his legs dangling into the void and no ability to get a foothold.

I wasn't even sure how he'd managed to grab anything in the first place. I quickly bent down, clutching his closer arm with both my hands.

"Hang on, Aedan! Can you get your other hand on this shelf?" I asked, holding on to him tightly.

"I'm not sure," Aedan responded, clearly straining.

He was trying to sway his body so he could grab the top of the closer bookcase. His momentum was causing the open bookcase to sway further into the darkness. I tried to use my foot to stop it from the hinge side. It wasn't helping much, but I didn't dare let go of Aedan's arm.

On the fourth swing, Aedan let go of the open bookcase. I held on to his arm as firmly as I could. He managed to bring his other arm around and grab the top of the closer bookcase. I could hear his sneakers scraping against the bookcase below. I gripped his arm as tightly as I could.

"I think...I got a foothold...for one foot," Aedan said between breaths.

"Okay, on the count of three. You push and I'll pull," I replied. "You ready?"

"Yes!" Aedan responded, clearly ready to be back on solid ground.

"One, two, three!" I exclaimed as I pulled with all my might, leveraging my foot against the corner of the stone wall and leaning backward.

With our combined effort, Aedan was able to heave himself

up, coming to rest beside me on the sand floor. Both of us were breathing hard.

"Well, that was unexpected," Aedan said with a small, shaky laugh.

I nodded in agreement, still breathing heavily. I sat back up, pointing my headlamp into the dark void in front of us. We'd indeed entered the Clan library. We were just about three stories higher than where thought we were. I remembered thinking that the octagon-shaped room of the Clan library seemed to stretch upward, but I'd never imagined it to be quite so high.

"No wonder no one uses this path," I mused as I swung my headlamp around the room for a better look.

The bookcase we'd opened jutted out unnaturally into the empty space before us. A few books and papers dangled dangerously from its shelves, threatening to fall into the darkness below. The rest of the walls around and opposite us were bookcases as well. They were crammed with books of varying heights, ages, and colors. There were scrolls and pamphlets tucked between sections. As I turned the headlight upward, I could see that the bookcases continued upward even further. It was an amazing collection of knowledge in one incredible space.

Trying to refocus on the task at hand, I said, "Guess our fastest way is to rappel down."

I looked at Aedan. I knew I could do it given my rock-climbing experience, but I wasn't sure how comfortable Aedan was, especially after that near-fall. But we didn't have much choice, either. We were tight on time, and there was no apparent alternative.

Wanting to reassure him somehow, I awkwardly placed my hand on top of his and gave it a quick squeeze. I stood up quickly, not daring to look at his face.

"I'll set up the anchors and lines we need. We can use the

bookshelves as climbing walls to help get us down quickly and safely," I said as I stood up.

My climbing gear was another set of items that had made the pack list. I'd prepared as much of the ropes and equipment ahead of time as possible. I swooped down to grab the items I needed from the backpack and tossed Aedan a harness. His face gave away the discomfort he was feeling.

I gave him an encouraging smile and said, "You can do this, Aedan. It'll be similar to the rappelling we did off the cliff. I'll be right there with you this time."

I walked back into the tunnel and found six anchor points between the large stone slabs in the wall. I used them to create two climbing lines—one for me and one for Aedan. We didn't have the time to go down the same line.

I adjusted the lines to be self-equalizing so our movements wouldn't dislodge the anchors. I climbed into my harness and clipped it into the lines. I did the same for Aedan, who had put his harness on and wore a slightly apprehensive look on his face.

I reminded him how to feed the line and how to stop. I did the final checks with Aedan's help and then proceeded to the edge of the bookcase. I beckoned Aedan to join me and asked if he was ready. He nodded. Together we started down.

I'd never rappelled down a bookcase before, but it turned out it wasn't that different from a climbing wall. The lower part of the shelves made natural footholds when they weren't occupied by a protruding item. I paused to check in with Aedan a few times. After a while, I noticed that similar to when we were at Witner Hill, he became more comfortable as he went along.

I started to enjoy the challenge and made it down before Aedan. I looked up. He wasn't too far behind. As I waited for Aedan, I realized for the first time that my earlier fall had torn my pants at my knee and caused a small scrape. It didn't look too bad.

I glanced at my watch. We had thirty minutes left to find the book, take our pictures, and head back up the ropes. I unclipped from the ropes, wondering how on earth we'd find the book in this massive collection in less than thirty minutes. I'd vastly underestimated the size of the room and its collection.

We'd come down on the right side of the room. As I turned to face the rest of the library, I realized that there were even more rooms that extended out from the octagon room. The enormity of the task made my spirits sink. The view from the other side of the Caelum door had made it look like a single room in a confined space—not this cavernous, multi-level complex. How on earth were we going to do this?

I hesitated before taking the first step into the rest of the room. I didn't want to repeat the mistakes from the fiasco above. Who knew what unseen obstacles there might be?

I dug in my pocket for the Trollkors ring. I'd remembered it halfway down our climb. I should have used it to check the other side of the wood panel before we opened it. In the excitement about finally entering the library, I'd forgotten about it, and my mistake had almost cost Aedan his life. I cringed.

I took a deep breath. I couldn't change what had occurred, but I could change how I proceeded. Not sure how the ring would even help in the current circumstances, I slipped it on my finger. Perhaps it would show if there were any further obstacles in the library or warn us about Ms. Haugen showing up on the other side of the Caelum door—or something. It certainly couldn't hurt.

The bluish light immediately began to fill the space. It revealed additional rooms behind the bookcases where strange, different-sized objects were stored in boxes or leaning against the walls. Some looked like old vases, jars, or stone crosses. Others were large, towering jade pieces clearly of Asian descent, and what looked like the African death masks that I'd seen in a National Geographic issue. There was one that looked like a Sphinx, and its eyes seemed to glow every time the Trollkors light hit them. Whatever their purpose or significance, it was beyond me.

"Hey, what're you doing?" Aedan asked me in a whisper as he unclipped himself from the ropes.

"Just checking that the coast is clear before we start searching. Don't want a repeat of the above. I should've thought of the ring earlier...I'm so sorry...you could've died," I whispered, looking up at him.

"It wasn't your fault. I should've remembered the ring as well," Aedan responded, lightly squeezing my shoulder as his eyes met mine. My breath quickened. He seemed to hesitate for a moment. Then he quickly dropped his hand and stared around the room as if fascinated by it.

I swung the blue light away from the hidden alcoves and towards the center of the room. Large stone slabs similar to the ones in the tunnel walls covered the floor. As the Trollkors light penetrated them, it revealed yet another alcove below our feet.

"This is impossible. How are we going to be able to search this place in time?" I glanced at Aedan.

"All we can do is try," he said, equally dumbstruck.

As I moved the blue light back up from the floor, it hit the stone table in the middle of the room. Unlike the last time I'd had a glimpse of the library, there were several objects scattered on the table. A few books open to varying degrees, a large magnifying glass, what looked to be an old map, and an intricately carved wooden book pedestal.

On top of the large pedestal lay a giant, open book. As the Trollkors light seeped through the surface, the book began to glow with white light. Both Aedan and I looked at each other in surprise.

"Should we see what the librarian has been reading?" Aedan asked, smirking.

I quickly swept our path to the table with the Trollkors light.

Nothing. I tentatively stepped forward and then took more confident steps as it became apparent that no boobytraps awaited us. Aedan followed close behind.

I cozied up to the table and pedestal, studying the large, open book. Its pages were thick, yellowed with age. Their corners had curled inward from the multiple hands that had turned them.

The open page had writing on it in a language I didn't recognize. The initial word on the page had the first letter decorated in a gold color with an indigo-blue box around it. The letter's arms extended into curls and wisps, giving it the appearance of movement. The opposite page had a picture of a large ash tree with single names on the leaves that hung from its branches. There were so many of them. As I peered more closely, I recognized some of the names. There was Mozart, da Vinci, Einstein, Curie, Darwin, Cleopatra, Franklin, Shakespeare, Newton, King, Gandhi, Gutenberg, Brändström, Nansen, Tesla, Nightingale, Edison, Pasteur, Lister, Parks, Tubman, Lovelace, Chopin.

"Should we see what the book's title is?" Aedan asked as he reached to close the oversized book. He had to use both hands to succeed.

The cover was an old leather binding with a gold border. The front of the book was blank. We peered around the side to the binding. There was a worn title—*Sopitam Hominibus*—but no author.

"What do you think it says?" I wondered out loud.

"I recognize the word *Hominibus*, which is Latin for 'mankind,'" Aedan replied. "But I don't know the other word."

"Let's go back to that tree page..." I said as I touched the book for the first time.

Something strange started to happen as my fingers flipped the pages. It was as if the book was starting to hum.

"Do you hear that?"

"Hear what?" Aedan asked.

"That humming...there's definitely humming...it's growing louder," I said as I turned my head to look around the room and make sure it wasn't coming from somewhere else.

By the time I finally reached the page with the tree, the humming was so loud I could barely hear Aedan's response, saying he didn't hear anything. Then the pages began to glow and get warmer under my touch.

"Do you see that?" I yelled at Aedan.

He looked dumbfounded as he shook his head. Thinking perhaps it was some sort of reaction to the Trollkors ring, I took it off quickly and handed it to Aedan. I bent over, covering my ears as the humming became unbearable. Aedan was shaking me gently, trying to get my attention.

"Elin...Elin, are you okay? What's happening?" he shouted. But his voice was drowned out by another now.

"*Salve sopitam homo...*oh, *femina.*" It coughed a little and cleared its throat.

I raised my head to look up at the book. A small hologram of an old man with a white beard, dressed in gray robes, was projecting from the book. His arms flailed about as if wiping away cobwebs.

At my puzzled expression, he tried again, this time in English. "Hello, Dormant Lady. I am Gnaritas. How can I help you?"

"Who are you?" I shouted as the humming was still continuing.

Visibly concerned, Aedan was trying to shout something at me, and he was looking around the room for an intruder.

"I am not a *who* but actually a *what*. I'm all knowledge for the *Sopitam Hominibus*. As you can see from my pages, they are already filled to the brim. Thus, my creator saw fit to program me to assist future *sopitam homimes* or *feminea*," it replied matter-of-factly.

"Can you turn down that humming noise?" I yelled at the book.

Aedan looked at me like I'd lost my mind.

"Apologies, my lady. It has been a while since someone woke me for assistance. My rebooting and updating process should be in ending in a few seconds," the little man responded as his arm-waving seemed to slow down.

Before he finished his sentence, the humming began to subside. I could finally remove my hands from my ears.

"Gnar...Gnaritas." I struggled to pronounce the little hologram's name. "Why can't my friend see or hear you?"

"I only wake and am audible or visible for *sopitam homines* or *feminae*. Your friend must not be one," Gnaritas answered, peering about as if looking for someone else.

"I see...and nothing we can do about that?" I asked.

I pointed to the book, hoping Aedan was catching on that I hadn't completely lost it.

"I'm afraid not. It is a security protocol that is strictly enforced. In fact, before we continue, I will need you to put your thumb imprint here and promise not to divulge our secrets to anyone else," Gnaritas responded, indicating a blank space on the page.

I hesitantly did as he asked. There wasn't much choice, really, if I wanted to know more.

"What is your definition for *sopitam homines* or *feminae*?" I asked, trying to confirm that we were on the right track—or rather, book.

"*Sopitam homines* and *feminae* are individuals who have a unique latent gene that instills the carrier with special abilities. This *ingenium superno*, however, is currently in a dormant state. *Sopitam homines* or *feminae* translates to... 'dormant men or women'," Gnaritas said as he sat down in a chair that magically appeared behind him. "You see, all of humankind has been given gifts. It is just a spectrum of activeness. Some individuals with practice or effort can achieve wondrous things with their talents even without an active state. This can be observed in humankind's achievements in math, science, music, art, politics, etc. However, *sopitam homines* or *feminae* can awaken their *ingenium* further where it becomes *superno*... supernatural. Their ability can become active instead of passive," Gnaritas explained, stroking his beard as he talked.

"Oh...so everyone has an ability." I pondered for a moment. "Do the *Sopitams* get to select what their active ability is?"

"No, my dear. You do not get to choose. It is a gift that is given and innate in your very person." A pipe materialized in Gnaritas's hand as he contemplated me. He proceeded to puff on it contentedly.

"How do you know what *it* is, then?" I frowned over my lack of an apparent talent.

"Do not fret, my dear. *Sopitam homines* and *feminae* often do not know what their active ability will be, as it is quite literally in a 'dormant' state."

Aedan put his hand on my arm to gain my attention and motioned to his watch. Time seemed to be running out.

"One moment, Gnaritas. I need to talk to my friend for a minute," I said to the old man in the book.

"Standing by. Just remember your oath not to reveal our secrets." Gnaritas looked at me. I nodded in acknowledgment.

"Seems that Ms. Haugen has been reading about Dormants," I said to Aedan, smiling. "I can't tell you much more. I'm sworn to secrecy, but I need a few more minutes."

"Well, thank you, Ms. Haugen! At least this part turned out to be a little easier," Aedan responded, grinning. But he added a bit more anxiously, "Okay, but we have about twenty minutes left before our forty-five minutes are up, and we have to go."

Moving the book wasn't going to be easy. It was too large and heavy an object. I decided to ask Gnaritas my most urgent question.

"Okay, I'll try to make it quick," I replied, turning back to the book. "Gnaritas, how do I awaken my ability?"

"Straight to the point, I see," the little man answered with a laugh.

"I'm pressed for time," I explained, smiling apologetically.

"Well, in that case, it is easier to show rather than tell," Gnaritas answered.

He melted back into the book as the pages flipped to the blank inside-back cover. A small dot began to form on the page. I leaned over to take a closer look. The dot began to grow as wisps of rainbow colors emerged from the page, encircling me. Slowly, the world around me began to shift. It was blurry at first as images swirled around me. Then suddenly their movement stopped.

An evergreen forest with its dark-green needled branches now surrounded me. I could no longer see Aedan or the library. I looked up to see a night sky full of twinkling stars beyond the treetops. Down at my feet, a sparkling brook appeared, beckoning me forward as it flowed toward an uncharted destination.

I followed it, brushing aside the fir and pine branches. I could see something shimmering in the distance. As I got closer, I could hear a chorus of ethereal voices repeating phrases as if reciting a poem. I hurried forward.

The pine branches gave way, and I stepped into a clearing where a large ash tree stood. It felt familiar yet so very strange. Its large leaves were silver in color, reflecting light from an unknown source. I could see its branches extending up into the heavens while its roots extended into the depths of the earth. The tree seemed almost like a sentient being.

The surrounding voices grew louder and clearer. The words of the poem they sang started to make sense.

Those who seek in company,
will not find its harmony.
No key exists to this door,
you must give to receive more.
Once you say these chosen words,
Your path forward affirms.
If the shimmery leaves deem you worthy,
you will begin your journey.
No backward glances now,
Those ancient branches do not allow.
Ek kalla á Askr að vekja blóð minn
Ek kalla á Askr að vekja blóð minn
Ek kalla á Askr að vekja blóð minn

The last refrain of the poem kept repeating over and over, fading into the mist as the shimmering leaves began to swirl around me. It seeped into my head, repeating like the words of a favorite song. Slowly, as if I was waking from a dream, the colors disappeared, and I became aware of Aedan urgently shaking my arm.

"What?" I asked, annoyed, as I shook the last of the mist from my head.

I was still trying to digest everything I'd seen. I turned to look at Aedan but never quite made it. Directly in front of me, walking up the short tunnel from the Caelum door, was Ms. Haugen and Tristan. I quickly closed the back cover of the enormous book.

"I see you've been reading *Sopitam Hominibus*. Find anything interesting?" Ms. Haugen asked in an icy voice.

Her manner was collected and controlled as if she'd just come upon Aedan and me at the town library and was inquiring how we liked a favorite book. It was unnerving.

"Nothing in particular," I responded, trying to match her confident, casual tone.

My brain was on fire as I tried to evaluate our escape routes. Our climbing ropes were too far away. Plus, Tristan was starting to circle the large stone table from that direction while Ms. Haugen was coming from the other.

Aedan was watching Tristan. He pulled me behind him so that he stood between me and Tristan. Tristan's mouth stretched into a sneer.

Ms. Haugen smiled cruelly as she continued to advance. "Oh, what a shame! I'm sure we can find some time to discover an interesting passage together. In fact, I insist upon it. I suspect there are secrets that I haven't unlocked yet."

I could see no better alternative. We either had to go up and cross the stone table or crawl underneath to get to the tunnel that led to Ms. Haugen's house. The tunnel was our only hope for escape.

Crawling would be too slow. Up and over was the only option. I leaned towards Aedan's ear and whispered the plan to him. He nodded.

"Oh, come now, Ms. Bodil...yes, Tristan has told me all about you...don't you know it's rude to whisper in company?" Ms. Haugen chided me.

They were getting closer to us. We couldn't wait another second. We had to go now.

I squeezed Aedan's hand as a signal. We both quickly, although clumsily, scrambled on top of the round stone table. Once on our feet, we ran, knocking books and other papers aside.

Aedan was quicker, taking the lead. He took my hand to help me along. I could hear Ms. Haugen yelling furiously at Tristan to stop us. I saw Tristan madly mounting the table.

Tristan was now on my heels. With the efficiency of a seasoned football player, he launched himself, tackling my legs. He brought me down on the stone table with a thud.

My hand slipped from Aedan's grasp. Pain vibrated through

my body at the hard landing. I saw Aedan hesitate as he witnessed what happened.

"No! Go, Aedan, go!" I managed to yell as I squirmed under Tristan's grip. I could see how conflicted Aedan was. He started towards me. "No, go! Get help."

Finally, he seemed to listen. He closed the distance to the table's edge and jumped down. He was running as fast as he could towards the open tunnel in front of him.

Still struggling with Tristan, I managed to kick him in the groin, getting a satisfying groan. But he was so much stronger. He pinned me on my stomach with my arms behind me in a few seconds.

I turned my head from the awkward position to witness Ms. Haugen reaching for a large knife on her belt. She loosened it and held it in a throwing position. With a glint of the steel, it sailed through the air after Aedan.

"No!" I screamed as I prayed for it to miss its mark.

Aedan was nearly at the Caelum door. Only a few more steps and he'd be past it into the safety of the dark tunnel. The knife rotated as it flew right past Aedan's head, hitting the wall beside the Caelum door. The door slid closed in front of Aedan, causing him to slam into it with his hands outstretched.

Recovering from the impact, Aedan tried furiously to press the same spot on the wall, but nothing happened. He was stuck on the same side as the rest of us. Out of frustration, Aedan slammed his fist against the door.

"Now, now, young sir. I'm afraid that door will not open without a key," Ms. Haugen crooned as she approached me on the table. "As for you, Ms. Bodil, we can have no more of this foolishness." She pulled something from her pocket that looked like a long syringe. "This should settle you until we are better situated."

Tristan held my hands behind my back with one hand and

placed his other on my head to stretch out my neck for his aunt. I tried to squirm out of his grasp, but he only pressed me harder against the table.

I saw Aedan pick up the knife from the floor and start rushing back towards me. But it was too late. Ms. Haugen injected whatever was in the syringe into my neck. I felt burning, and then my body went limp. It was not responding to any of my commands as my mind began to grow fuzzy.

I felt Tristan's bodyweight lift off me as he went to confront Aedan. Aedan was no match for Tristan's Hunter training—at least, not without his *megin*. Tristan had him disarmed and pinned against the wall in a few movements. I saw Ms. Haugen approach Aedan with the same syringe. All I could do was watch as Aedan's body went limp against the wall.

My mind became cloudier as the drug took further hold. The last thing I saw was Ms. Haugen approaching the Caelum door, holding a small device in her hand. She momentarily pressed it against the door. Then she exclaimed in surprise, looking down at the device.

"Why, he is an unregistered Clan member! What a catch...a Dormant and an unregistered member! The Chairman will be so pleased."

Then, like curtains at a theater, my eyelids closed on the image of her unnatural smile stretched thinly over her face.

TWENTY-FOUR

The journey

ELIN

O h, my head ached! I felt something cool against my forehead. My body was lethargic and stiff. It protested any movement.

I managed to wiggle my fingers. I tried my toes next. Yes, they seemed to be working. With some effort, I was able to open my left eye, since my right seemed to be pressed up against something. I saw glass and quickly moving scenery.

The right side of my face was pressed against a car window. It was still dark outside, but I could make out the familiar landmarks of the main road. We were still on Auor Island.

Slowly my thoughts started to collect themselves. We'd been in the Clan library. Gnaritas had shown me how to waken my ability. But I hadn't really had time to process what the images and poem meant. Something stirred at the back of my mind.

Those strange foreign words in the ethereal voices started to echo in my head. Now if I could only remember the rest of the poem.

Ouch! The car hit a bump, knocking my head against the glass. My neck muscles were still not responding, and there was no hat to cushion the blow. Apparently, I'd lost it somewhere along the way.

Where were we going? And where was Aedan? The rest of my memories flooded back from the library. My whole body seemed stiff and sore from Tristan's tackle. What had they done with Aedan?

My hands and feet were experiencing the sensation of pins and needles. Their feeling was starting to come back. I managed to crawl one hand up along the car door, using it to push against, hoping to end up in a more upright position. My body held the upright position for a few seconds before flopping over to the other side.

My head landed against Aedan's shoulder. Well, at least I knew where he was now.

His head was dangling unnaturally forward, his chin resting on his chest. His arms dangled freely by his side. I couldn't see his feet, but his legs didn't seem to be bound. I guess Ms. Haugen was counting on the drug to keep us compliant.

I could hear Tristan and Ms. Haugen arguing in the front seat over who was going to get the recognition for our capture. Ms. Haugen seemed to be threatening Tristan over his past misdeeds in trying to get into the library. But Tristan was countering with a threat to expose the fact that intruders had gotten into the Clan library. Lack of foresight into possible trespassing seemed to be a higher crime since Ms. Haugen sounded like she was backing down from her position.

While they were distracted by their petty grievances, I needed to wake Aedan up. I inched my face up his shoulder until my mouth was close to his ear. I'd never been this close to Aedan. I tried to squash the little flutter of excitement in my stomach.

"Aedan!" I whispered as loudly as I dared. "Aedan, wake up!"

We hit a pothole in the road. My head bounced right into the side of Aedan's face. *Oh, ow!* That was unpleasant.

Slightly troubled by the thought that I might have just given Aedan a black eye, I tried again. "Aedan...Aedan." He mumbled something. "Shh...it's Elin. You have to wake up...but quietly. We're in the back of Ms. Haugen's car."

My head dropped to his chest again. I tried to shimmy up the front of his shoulder. This time it was a little easier. I was starting to get more mobility. The tingling had moved up into my arms and legs now.

"Elin?...Elin, where are we?" Aedan asked in a hushed voice, slurring his words as if he was drunk. "Why can't I move?" I could hear the panic in his words.

"It's the drug Ms. Haugen gave you. Remember?" I whispered, trying to reassure Aedan that it was temporary. "It'll start to wear off. It helps to move around a bit. Try wiggling your fingers and toes."

"They feel all tingly," he whispered back, a bit more clearly now.

"That's good. Keep doing it," I said as I tried rotating my own wrists and ankles. "We've got to get our movement back before the car stops. I have a feeling wherever they're taking us next won't be that pleasant."

Aedan and I slowly worked on getting our mobility back while pretending to be asleep for the front-seat occupants. Our best chance was to take them by surprise and make a run for it when the car stopped.

I caught a few phrases from Ms. Haugen, telling Tristan that they were meeting some sort of transport at the Ash Park parking lot. Apparently, it was the only empty and large enough space nearby that could accommodate the transport. In addition, the parking lot was surrounded by a thick evergreen forest that would be the perfect cover for the landing.

I leaned back over towards Aedan and whispered that we

should run for the forest as soon as the car stopped. It would be our best bet for getting away. He gave a quick confirming nod.

By the time we reached Ash Park, I'd regained all of my movement. Aedan seemed to be more affected by the drug and still had some tingling in his arms and legs. However, he assured me he'd be able to run.

Ms. Haugen pulled the car to a stop by the northern edge of the parking lot, directly beside the forest. We were in luck!

Ms. Haugen and Tristan glanced back towards us. Aedan and I both slumped, trying to give our best performance of being immobilized. Once they turned around again, I wrapped my hand as quietly as possible around the door handle and tried to push it open. Locked! My heart sank.

Aedan signaled to me to just be patient. As if on cue, Ms. Haugen said something about the Black Moon and told Tristan to get out and help the transport land. She tossed him a flashlight from the glovebox and unlocked the doors. Aedan motioned for me to keep still.

We watched as Tristan walked to the center of the parking lot and started waving the lit flashlight toward the sky. Straightaway, a strong wind started whipping his hair this way and that.

Aedan squeezed my hand as the signal to run. Both of us opened the car doors and got out. There was a loud whirring sound. Whirlwinds raced through the parking lot, whipping my ponytail into a frenzy.

I ran—managing a quick glance upward to witness a large aircraft descending straight down with remarkable speed and precision. It was like nothing I'd ever seen. The sounds from the aircraft swallowed up Ms. Haugen's screeches for help as we disappeared into the forest.

Blindly, we ran forward, not caring in which direction as long as it was away. Our breath came out in clouds in front of us. It was bitterly cold—probably the first freeze of the winter season.

The empty lower branches of the dense evergreen trees tore at our clothing as we pushed through. The mossy floor of the forest made our path difficult as our feet sank deep. We climbed over rocks and rotting logs when an easier way was not available.

After a while, Aedan started slowing down, his legs still not quite up for the task from the drug. I grabbed his hand and tried to help him along. Somewhere behind us, we could hear shouts. It was clear that whoever was tracking us was gaining ground.

"Aedan...I think...I should try...to draw Tristan and Ms. Haugen to chase me," I said, breathing heavily. Aedan shook his head.

"No, Elin...It's too...dangerous...They want you... not me," he answered, also gulping for breath.

"Precisely...That's why they'll...follow me. Your legs...just aren't back...to normal yet. Mine are. We've got to...do something or we'll...get caught," I replied.

Aedan looked embarrassed but exhausted. I could tell he knew I was right.

"There's...a road a mile...or two north of here. It should be...a lot easier to traverse...than the forest. If you go north...then I'll lead them south. Do you still have...the Trollkors ring? I can use the light...to draw them away from you."

Aedan reached into his inside pocket to see if it was still in its hiding place. Either Tristan or Ms. Haugen had been smart enough to take our cell phones, but I was hoping that they hadn't thought to look for other smaller items. He opened his fist and showed me the ring. Sighing with relief, I took it from his palm.

"Elin, we should aim for my family's emergency meeting place. Our homes won't be safe anymore. I'm sure Mia and Joel will have gone to my sister by now. Do you remember where?" Aedan asked, breathing more steadily now. I nodded.

"Arne Point, right?" I replied.

"Yeah," Aedan responded. The shouts were getting closer. We looked at each other. "See you there, Elin!"

"See you there!" I responded.

A little awkwardly, I leaned over to hug Aedan. The butterflies in my stomach started to flutter. He wrapped his arms around me and gave me a tight squeeze. Our cheeks gently brushed as we drew apart. Impulsively, I leaned back in and gave Aedan a kiss. A tingling warmth ran down my spine as our lips met and my heart started to race. Having no idea what had compelled me to do it, I quickly drew back and stammered out, "For luck."

I didn't wait for Aedan's response as I could feel the redness creeping deeper into my already-rosy cheeks. Instead, I slipped the Trollkors ring on my finger and started running in the opposite direction from him.

The blue light showed me the way. The forest was just as dense as before, making it difficult to go very fast. I was hoping to make it to Torne Stream. Its wide embankment would make for a faster path.

We'd been at the northern end of the parking lot, so I estimated that I needed to keep running south and a little east to come to the stream. I stopped for a moment, listening for any sounds behind me.

It was quiet. My harried breath came out in puffs in the cold air. I heard two small rustles to my right. I froze. I turned my head and saw the beady eyes of a nocturnal animal reflected in the Trollkors light. I let out my breath.

Then without warning, I heard crashing and breaking of branches some ways behind me. Something much larger was coming—and at great speed. I ran as fast as I could. Whoever was behind me was definitely gaining on me.

I knew I was getting closer to the stream when the fog began to fill the gaps between the trees. The stream ran directly into the inlet where the water tended to be warmer, causing a nighttime fog to sweep into the forest in cold weather. It gave me an idea.

I could lure whoever was chasing me into the fog with the Trollkors light, then take off the ring. It might leave them disoriented for long enough to where I could escape up the stream bed.

The fog became even thicker as I got closer to the inlet. I could barely see the trees in front of me now. The light from the ring was creating a blue halo around me.

I stopped and waited. I dropped into a runners' squat as the noise behind me entered the thick fog. I pulled off the ring, extinguishing the blue light. The person behind me cursed loudly. Then he called my name.

"Elin...Elin, where are you? I know it's you."

Tristan. I started to crawl along the bottom of the forest floor towards the stream embankment.

"I can hear you, Elin! Stop this now and come with me," he insisted in a threatening way. "Why are you playing these games? We want the same thing. Show yourself!"

I continued to inch my way forward, trying to avoid twigs and fallen branches. I was almost to the lip of the embankment. I could hear Tristan taking steps in my direction.

Suddenly, he yelped in pain, followed by cursing. He must have walked into something. The fog was so thick at a standing height that you couldn't see your own hand.

I took advantage of the moment and slipped over the embankment, bracing for the cold water. Instead, I landed on something hard. Ice.

This part of the stream was wide and shallow. The water must have frozen in the wintry night air. I pulled myself as close as possible to the muddy bank, hiding underneath its small ledge.

I lay as still as I could, listening to Tristan fumbling in the forest. I could hear him getting closer as twigs and leaves snapped under his feet. He was nearly to the edge. I tried not to move a muscle.

Crumbles of dirt fell on me from Tristan's weight. He was right above me. He called out my name a few more times. Then silence. I didn't dare breathe. Slowly, his footsteps faded back into the thick forest.

When I judged that enough time had passed, I rolled away from the bank. My body was stiff from lying on the ice. Gingerly, I stood up. I took a few steps back to the side, where the ice seemed sturdier. I rubbed my arms, hoping to get some warmth to seep back into them. Winter had definitely arrived. The snow wouldn't be long now.

I noticed that I'd torn my pants leg further at my knee, opening the scrape wider. It was bleeding but not badly. The rest of my body ached from all the running and Tristan's tackle. But I couldn't stop now. I had to keep moving.

I followed the stream north again away from the fog. I hoped to find a trail that would be easier to follow out of the woods. I knew the danger wasn't over yet, but perhaps I had put enough distance between Tristan and myself that I'd be able to get to a road unseen.

I wondered how Aedan was doing. I hoped he'd made it to the northern road safely. I felt a little flutter in my stomach as I thought of the kiss. I wasn't sure what had compelled me. It was not like me—I wasn't that bold. A little bit of doubt wormed its way into my heart over what Aedan thought about it. I felt the redness rush back into my cheeks.

I took a deep breath of the cold night air and looked up at the sky. It seemed like a million little stars twinkled back at me through the treetops. You could see them so clearly without the moonlight. Something tickled the back of my mind.

As I progressed up the stream, I thought I saw something

shimmering from among the trees up ahead. I paused. I was having a strong case of déjà vu. I'd definitely been here before.

I walked towards the shining light. It wasn't long before I emerged from the evergreen forest into a clearing, where the great ash tree stood. I'd been here on numerous picnics and hikes, but the tree had never looked like this. Its leaves were glowing silver and moving as if there was a breeze. But there was no wind in the forest.

I was curiously drawn to it. I felt like I'd entered some sort of gravity bubble where it was the center. The poem from Gnaritas started to repeat in my head, almost as if my subconscious had been triggered to recall it at the right moment.

> *Those who seek in company,*
> *will not find its harmony.*
> *No key exists to this door,*
> *you must give to receive more.*
> *Once you say these chosen words,*
> *Your path forward affirms.*
> *If the shimmery leaves deem you worthy,*
> *you will begin your journey.*
> *No backward glances now,*
> *Those ancient branches do not allow.*
> *Ek kalla á Askr að vekja blóð minn*
> *Ek kalla á Askr að vekja blóð minn*
> *Ek kalla á Askr að vekja blóð minn*

Something compelled me to whisper the words as I approached the tree. Almost in a trance, I repeated the last refrain as I reached out to touch the tree trunk. Simultaneously, my foot caught a tree root, and I fell to my knees. My injured knee came to rest on the root itself. The friction tore my gash open a little further, which made it bleed more.

A sparkling blue light started to quickly crawl up the tree from the root where my injured knee rested. The branches with their silver leaves began swaying almost violently around me. I ducked my head, trying to avoid getting hit. I clutched the root with my hands, praying that whatever was happening would end. It felt as if the tree was lifting me off the ground as the windstorm intensified. I closed my eyes.

Then sudden calmness. The frenzy had stopped. I opened my eyes in time to see the glimmering blue light melt back down the tree trunk. But it didn't stop at the root. It seeped into me through my injured knee.

I could see all the little veins and capillaries in my hands glowing with the blue light. I could feel the light making its way through my entire body. It was a warmth spreading from my head to my toes. My jacket started to feel like it was too warm.

Then as quickly as it had started, it was gone—the warmth, the blue light, the shimmering leaves, and the feeling of being in a bubble. Now the ash tree was just an ash tree. I was dumbstruck. What had happened?

I stood up slowly, inspecting my body to make sure everything was still where it belonged. As I got to my knees I noticed that the wound on my left knee had completely healed. In fact, all of the pain from my night's struggles had disappeared. I felt completely restored.

As I thought about the events, there was really only one explanation—the awakening. The poem and the images that Gnaritas had shown me all made sense now. I'd followed the stream to the shimmering tree alone. I'd repeated the chosen words —even if I was unsure of their meaning. I'd given some of my blood to receive something more from the tree. The branches had conducted their evaluation and found me worthy. I assumed the bit from the poem about backward glances meant that it was a one-way trip. I couldn't go back to being normal. As Gnaritas would have put it, I'd awakened the *superno* in my blood. I'd begun my journey in a new world.

Everything looked normal on my body—I sighed in relief—and I didn't really feel any different. I tried to flick my wrist like Spider-Man to see if something might happen. Nothing. I concentrated on a nearby rock, trying to move it like Aedan could. Still nothing. I tried jumping into the air. But I just reached my normal height. Then I remembered the Black Moon. Of course, my *megin* was asleep just like everyone else's. I laughed at myself.

My joyous feeling was quickly dampened as I heard noises and shouting again. Time to leave. I whispered a quick thank you to the tree. Then I jumped over the stream to head in the opposite direction from the voices.

At first, I thought it was just easier to run since I was now on a trail and nothing hurt. But as I was passing familiar landmarks on the trail a lot faster than I should, I realized that my pace was way beyond my normal top speed—and I wasn't even trying that hard yet. It felt like I was flying. How was this possible?

A little bit of panic and exhilaration took hold. Aedan had been clear. All of their powers, including speed, were gone during a Black Moon.

As I kept running, I realized that I could also see really well in the dark—without the aid of a light. This wasn't supposed to be possible! Maybe something had gone wrong in the awakening.

Doubt and fear started to circulate inside me. Something must be wrong with me. I went through the sequence of events at the ash tree over and over again as I ran. What had I missed?

Before I knew it, I'd run the five miles all the way to Arne Point. I stood catching my breath in the middle of the clearing by the abandoned boat landing. I guessed my subconscious had known where it was taking me.

Suddenly, headlights appeared from the forest, bouncing up and down over the dips and bumps in the neglected road. I was like a deer in the headlights. They'd caught me. How did they know where I'd be?

I was about to bolt back into the woods when Mr. Grady's familiar Land Rover pulled to a stop a few paces away. I let my breath out. All the car doors opened in unison.

Mr. and Mrs. Grady exited from the front seats. Claire, Edvin, and Mia appeared from the back doors, and Joel tumbled from the trunk. He picked himself up from the ground, dusting his pants and mumbling that he was all right.

I felt my shoulders relax as I could finally take a deep breath. My eyes got a little watery at the sight of them all. They walked towards me, talking at once and posing questions. I couldn't understand a single one, but I was so relieved that I didn't quite care in the moment.

Mia, Claire, and Mrs. Grady gave me big hugs as they reached me. Even Joel came up and squeezed me for what felt like a good minute. Finally, the fuss settled down.

Mrs. Grady took in my appearance and asked, "First, Elin are you all right? Second, where's Aedan? And third, what happened tonight?"

"Yeah, I'm fine. A bit muddy and with a few torn pieces of clothing, but overall, I'm fine," I answered. I was sure I was quite a sight, with my ripped, muddy clothing and twigs in my hair. "Aedan is supposed to meet us here. We had to separate. Aedan wasn't recovering from the drugs as quickly. I tried to lead Ms. Haugen and Tristan away so he could make it to the closest road."

"*What?* Aedan was drugged?" Mrs. Grady was horrified.

"Yes...we both were...by Ms. Haugen. It was some sort of immobilizing injection. They caught us in the Clan library," I explained.

I filled in the details of the night's adventures for the curious crowd. However, I stopped short when I got to the awakening part as it finally sunk in that both Mia and Joel were eagerly listening.

I'd revealed too many details already. They'd have a lot of questions that I wouldn't be able to answer.

"Yes, what happened then, Elin? How did you make it all the way here from there?" Mr. Grady asked.

"Why don't we wait for Aedan to get here before I explain that part," I said, hoping to buy some time. "Do you have anything to drink?"

I was parched from the talking and running. Most likely the drug hadn't helped either.

While Mrs. Grady and the others went to unpack the Land Rover and find a bottle of water, I turned to Mia. "How'd you and Joel end up here with the Gradys?"

Mia started to explain how she and Joel had sat in the boat bobbing in the freezing waters for two hours waiting for Aedan's and my call. When it never came, they'd hightailed it to Aedan's house, where they'd found Mr. and Mrs. Grady and Edvin just arriving from their mainland trip.

They'd tried to explain what had happened, but things didn't get serious until Mia showed them Aedan's cuff and said that it was time to go sailing. At that point, the Gradys had apparently gone into operation mode. They had started packing at a furious speed and running around the house to make sure it was shut down.

She and Joel had stared in amazement. Mia had been under the impression that they'd be heading to the police station. But when it seemed like that wasn't the case, Mia had insisted that she be taken along to wherever they were going to meet Aedan and me.

The Gradys had finally relented after Mia had threatened not to give Aedan's cuff back. Claire had also apparently made the point that they couldn't just leave Mia and Joel at the house for the bad guys, whoever they were, to find.

As Mia was finishing her story, a throbbing pain started behind my right eye. It was growing so intense I could barely concentrate on what she was saying anymore. I pressed my hand against my eye to try to stop the pain. It only got worse. Then a small white dot began to grow in my vision until I could no longer see Mia.

For a few seconds, I was lost in a sea of white. Then suddenly I was hovering above Aedan in the forest, watching as Ms. Haugen cornered him with two flying metal balls. The metal balls closed in with their central red light facing Aedan. One of the little balls fired something at him.

I screamed for Aedan to watch out. But he didn't hear me. The small dart hit him in the neck, and he fell to the ground. I screamed again, but the searing white light had returned.

Mia was hovering above me. She shook me gently, saying my name. "Elin...Elin...can you hear me?"

I nodded slowly, sitting up. Apparently, I'd fallen to the ground. The rest of the group was gathered around me with concerned looks on their faces.

"You were screaming. Are you okay?" Mia asked, worried.

I looked up at Mrs. Grady and tears began to fall down my cheeks. "They caught him," I sobbed. "They caught Aedan."

"I don't understand. How can you know that?" Mia asked, trying to comfort me with a hug. "How can she know that?" she asked, looking at the rest of the group.

Mrs. Grady was leaning on her husband for support with a terrified expression. I saw Claire and Edvin exchange a knowing look.

"It isn't possible...it's a Black Moon..." Mr. Grady said, looking bewildered and holding on to his wife. "What kind of trick is this?"

Before I could stand up, the pain started again behind my eye. Followed by the blinding white light. This time I was hovering above our small group, watching myself lying on the ground.

All of a sudden, the second me on the ground sat straight up and shouted something about metal balls. Moments later, as Mr.

Grady was yelling for everyone to run, the now-familiar metal balls with the red lights emerged from the woods right above the Land Rover. The hovering me tried to warn everyone but once again no one heard me. Then the white light blocked my vision, and I was back with the group lying on the ground.

"The flying metal balls...they're coming!" I exclaimed as I brought myself to a sitting position. The group looked stunned.

Finally, Mr. Grady broke the silence. "RUN! Run into the woods and hide. NOW!"

But it was too late. I could see the glowing red lights of the metal balls as they flew down the old road toward us.

Before any one of us had made it out of the clearing, a black speedboat pulled up by the dock. I thought I was hallucinating as Monsieur Tibadeau jumped out of the boat and onto the dock, carrying what looked like a rocket launcher.

He positioned himself at a distance but in front of the metal balls now hovering above the Land Rover. He fired. A large net with weighted ends erupted from the launcher, flying through the air. The net hit its mark, wrapping around the metal balls and dropping them onto the Land Rover's roof.

A few more people disembarked the boat. One of them climbed on top of the vehicle. He quickly did something to the metal balls with a small tool he pulled from his pocket. He then celebratorily held up two small chips in his hand. "Got them! We're clear."

The only person who did not look astonished by the developments was Claire. She turned to her parents, cleared her throat, and a bit mischievously said, "Welcome to the Resistance."

TWENTY-FIVE

The neophyte

ELIN

There'd been a lot of confusion and chaos at the boat landing after the Resistance's arrival. The Gradys had been caught up in trying to understand who the Resistance was and Claire's relationship to them. Joel and Mia had been completely bewildered as to why there was a Resistance in the first place, who had taken Aedan, and generally what the heck was going on.

Questions had poured from every direction. It had all been too much for me. Between all the excitement, my painful visions, being drugged, a sleepless night, and guilt at leaving Aedan behind, I'd sunken to the ground, the earth spinning. Then blackness had enveloped me.

I woke back in my own bed with Mrs. Grady sitting by my side. Anders was hovering in the doorway. They informed me that I'd pretty much slept for the remainder of the day.

Anders was full of questions and admonishments. He'd thought that I was having a sleepover at Mia's. He'd been completely taken aback when, in his pajamas, he'd answered the 4am pounding at the front door and found Mr. Grady and posse standing on the porch carrying a passed-out me.

"Elin, what happened? Why weren't you at Mia's for the sleepover?" Anders asked, caught somewhere between furious and concerned.

I was at a loss for words, not knowing how to explain to Anders the events that had occurred the previous night.

"Now, now...let's not pester Elin with too many questions. I'm sure everything will be explained in due time. What she really needs right now is some hearty food and some more rest," Mrs. Grady said, coming to my aid. She gently patted my arm in a comforting manner.

When I went to the bathroom to clean up, she ushered Anders downstairs in search of something to eat. I could hear them in the kitchen shuffling pots and pans.

I stared at myself in the bathroom mirror. Someone had done a decent job of getting the twigs and leaves out of my hair. They'd even sponged most of the mud from my face.

Deciding I was still too tired for a full shower, I reached for my brush and attacked the tangles in my hair. Then I washed the remaining mud specks from my face. Once finished, I turned this way and that, looking at myself in the mirror and trying to decide whether I appeared different somehow. I knew, of course, I'd been irrevocably altered on the inside. My genes were transformed, and I now had active supernatural abilities. But nothing in my reflection betrayed any sign of my new status.

I sighed in relief. There was only so much change a girl could take at one time. Besides, as it was, I wasn't sure how I was going to explain to my family the pain and fainting that came with my gift. At least I now knew what my special talent was, even if it was something I couldn't put on my college applications.

I tucked myself back into bed, pondering the strange visions that I'd seen at Arne Point. I really hadn't had a moment to try to make sense of what had occurred. It seemed to me that what I'd seen was a glimpse of the future. The second vision had become real within mere seconds, which would suggest, especially since Aedan wasn't here, that the first one had also happened.

Heat rose to my cheeks. What had I done? It was *my* suggestion that we separate—and instead of helping him, I had sent Aedan straight to his capture. It was all my fault. My stomach twisted and tears started to flood my eyes. I drew the covers closer to my face.

All the consequences of the last few weeks started to flash through my mind. Finding the book and getting my abilities were supposed to protect everyone. Instead, I had endangered my family, friends, and Aedan—and now his family. I quickly sat up. His family was still here. Aedan had been adamant that they leave. Wouldn't the Clan Hunters be coming—if not already here? Were any of us safe?

Mrs. Grady interrupted my thoughts as she appeared in my doorway, carrying a tray laden with a bowl of stew and some thickly sliced bread. I quickly wiped my tears on the bedsheet and straightened up further in the bed. Between spoonfuls of stew, I managed to ask her whether it was dangerous to be in our homes.

"Won't the Clan try to come back for me—and your family as well?"

"You don't need to worry...at least for now. We're safe in our homes. The Resistance set up a Shield Wall, which stretches an invisible barrier around our property and yours. The wall only allows authorized individuals through it. We're very lucky and grateful to the Resistance. Those were the last Shield Wall 'pucks' they managed to smuggle out of Falinvik.

"But," Mrs. Grady warned, "outside the Shield Wall, you need to be accompanied by a *Mannlegur*—at all times. Regardless of where you go—coffee shop, park, or even bathroom. The Clan Hunters will be waiting for any opportunity to find you alone. The one saving grace is that they'll not attack when a *Mannlegur* is close by. They know they'd be severely punished for revealing the Clan's existence to any *Mannlegur*. And now that you have abilities, a public display will be even harder to avoid if you're accompanied everywhere."

The Resistance, on the other hand, was less concerned with that particular Clan edict, according to Mrs. Grady...at least, when it came to *Mannlegurs* who'd learned about their secret or were on the brink of it. In fact, they saw them as key allies.

I could see Mrs. Grady's hesitation as she told me that Mia and Joel were now considered such individuals. I could tell that she wasn't fully comfortable with the idea, but apparently, Mia and Joel had too many questions. Either they'd become inadvertent liabilities or they had to be adopted into the fold.

"When will they be told?" I asked, excited by the prospect of being able to discuss with my best friend and Joel what *really* happened.

"Soon...I think. The Resistance just needs to run some background checks to make sure they are who they say they are. I have a feeling that you'll know rather quickly once your friends are up to speed. I can't imagine they'll be able to resist talking with you once they know." She smiled, but it was tinged with sadness.

I guessed that she was thinking about Aedan. I suddenly felt guilty for not having brought him up sooner.

"I'm sure what I saw with Aedan was just from another sleeping drug."

Mrs. Grady's eyes quickly found mine. "What exactly did you see, Elin?"

I related to her in detail what I'd witnessed in the vision. "It really wasn't that much, since it only lasted a few seconds."

"It was enough," she said, dabbing her damp eyes with a handkerchief. "At least we now know what happened to him."

It felt awful to watch her worry. It really was all my fault. Aedan would've never been at the Clan library or Ash Park if it wasn't for me and my Clan gene. I needed to do something to fix things, but I wasn't sure what...at least, not yet.

After a few moments, I said, "Mrs. Grady? Are the visions my unique ability?" I wanted some confirmation to firmly settle the matter.

"It seems that way. Although I think there's still a lot to be learned, not only about your visions but also the fact that you can have them during a new moon—and even more surprisingly, a Black Moon."

"What do you think it means?" I asked.

"I'm really not sure. Maybe something...or maybe nothing. I've never interacted closely with a Dormant, so my knowledge is limited."

"What about triggering my ability? How do I get my visions to come?"

"All excellent questions, Elin. But I don't have good answers for you. Most powers are triggered either by emotion or action. Usually, we have the advantage of watching the person grow into them since childhood. With you...well, you're essentially a neophyte. We're starting from scratch," Mrs. Grady said, looking at me thoughtfully.

At that moment Anders appeared in my bedroom doorway. "Everything good in here?"

"Yes, everything's fine. I was just about to leave, seeing as Elin has finished her food." Mrs. Grady smiled at Anders, stood up, and reached for the tray on my lap. "I'll be by tomorrow to check in on you...both of you."

"Thanks, Mrs. Grady," I responded, yawning and sliding underneath my blanket.

◆

A few days later, I wasn't sure how I felt about my unique ability anymore. I had absolutely no control over my visions' timing—or anything else about them, for that matter. They came at their own will and showed me whatever they wanted. Some days I'd have several attacks, showing everything from insignificant things like Anders and me having breakfast, to more important things, like Aedan lying on a green plastic mattress in a small, nondescript room.

The one vision that did seem to repeat was of me standing in the dark outside our home, watching through a window as my family prepared dinner. They were laughing merrily in the warm light of the kitchen as I turned to walk away over crunching snow. I guessed that it must be a future event because the snow had yet to stick to the ground, but any further significance eluded me.

Other days there was nothing. Anders became a nervous wreck on the days when my screams of pain blindsided both of us. He kept insisting on taking me to the doctor. It was becoming increasingly difficult to convince him they were just migraines.

The next day when Mrs. Grady came by to see if I had any news of Aedan through my visions, I told her about my dilemma. She dug in her purse and pulled out Aedan's cuff. She held on to it tightly like it was the most precious thing in the world.

"You need a medallion, Elin. It's what centers all of our *megins*...especially when we're just starting to learn how to use them. Usually, there's a beautiful Nordri Clan ceremony where your runes are discovered and your medallion is crafted. We have no such luxury here. We can't even forge you one. They're made of a special metal only available in Falinvik," she said with sadness in her voice. "I think Aedan would've wanted you to have this until we get him back. I have no idea if it'll help since the runes aren't yours, but it's worth a try." She exhaled and a few tears formed in her eyes as she offered the cuff to me.

"Oh, Mrs. Grady...I couldn't possibly," I answered, swallowing hard to avoid my own tears. I knew what the cuff meant to Aedan's family. It was his sacrifice for keeping them safe and a last tangible link to him.

"I insist," she replied, looking at me as she pressed the cuff into my hands. "Someday you'll get your own, but for now hopefully this one will help."

"Thank you," I said, accepting the cuff. After a moment's pause, I asked, "What's the plan for Aedan's rescue?"

I knew the Gradys weren't just going to let Aedan wallow in some Clan prison for very long. There had to be a plan—and I wanted in. I owed Aedan that much.

"Well, the good news is that the Resistance has agreed to help us, but the bad news is that we'll have to wait until the deep freeze of the fjord. The snow has already started to fall up in the mountains, so the few roads that lead to Falinvik are impassable. The fjord is our best option for getting there in the near future... but we need the ice to freeze so it'll be safe to cross," Mrs. Grady explained.

"When do you think that'll happen?" I asked.

"We're hoping in the next month or so," she answered, obviously disheartened at the prospect. "I hate waiting so long... but there is a small silver lining. Many of our beliefs have been shattered in recent days. And having the extra time to process and formulate a foolproof plan is to our advantage."

"What do you mean? What beliefs?"

"I thought I had seen all the Chairman's betrayals, Elin...but this might be the worst," Mrs. Grady said sighing. "He led us to believe that the other three Clans had died...but it's all lies."

She looked empathetically at me as I tried to process the revelation. I felt like my head was spinning.

"For years, we have thought the Nordri were the last... but in recent days, the Resistance has definitively proved that we were just kept isolated and afraid. The full impact is hard to comprehend...families kept apart... the needless grieving... and us... we could've been safe with another Clan this whole time—" Her voice trailed off. She continued with a trace of anger in her voice, "but for now, our focus has to be Aedan...the rest can wait."

I agreed with Mrs. Grady—rescuing Aedan couldn't happen soon enough. He'd been there for me in ways no one else had. I shivered at the thought of him stuck in some Clan cell.

Waiting a month felt like a long time. But as it gave the Gradys a chance to process their new reality, perhaps it would give me a chance—a chance to learn how to control my ability and become an asset rather than a liability. So many things had changed now— well, frankly, everything. Any plans that I had in my former life were now upside-down.

I wasn't quite sure when I accepted that my future lay in this new, unknown world. But since I had, I needed to learn how to survive in it. Not only for myself—but for Aedan as well.

I smiled at Mrs. Grady. "Will you teach me? Will you help me learn how to use my *megin*?"

Epilogue

I returned to the transport. There was no point in wandering around in the thick fog any longer. Elin was gone. I prayed that my aunt had been more successful in her endeavor than I had been in mine. Both of our lives depended on it.

"Tristan, what took you so long? Where's the Dormant Descendant?" Aunt Adis asked with a stern look.

She was helping one of the OATC crew members guide a hover-stretcher through the rear cargo door of the transport. On top of the stretcher lay the unregistered Clan member. He looked to be asleep. I sighed with relief. We were not going back empty-handed.

"She managed to escape," I replied, not bothering to explain further.

"*What?*" My aunt exclaimed with strong disapproval.

"Well, it's not like I don't know where she lives. I'll get her eventually," I answered, trying to appear confident as I strode past her on the cargo ramp.

The truth was that I would have to come back soon if I wanted to be the one to capture Elin. News of my discovery was sure to spread like wildfire once we were back in Falinvik—and every Hunter would be angling to procure her.

"It appears that your 'magic touch' in getting her to come willingly wasn't quite that powerful after all." My aunt smiled smugly. I could see the figurative wheels turning in her head, making her believe she had gained the upper hand.

"Do not think this changes anything in our agreement," I said, pivoting more fully to face my aunt on the cargo ramp. "You still let them trespass in the Clan library."

I was further up the incline than my aunt, so the light from the transport's cabin illuminated her face clearly. I could see hesitation enter her eyes.

"Yes...well...we will still have a lot to explain to the Clan Council." She swept by me to find a seat inside.

Once the OATC crew member finished securing the floating stretcher and its passenger in the cargo bay, the rear doors closed and the transport began to rise. From the window, I could see the first slivers of dawn begin to show at the edge of the horizon as we rose above the mountain tops. The orange and yellow light danced on the wavelets of the sea. The colors reminded me of Elin's dress from the dance.

I could not understand her. Why had she betrayed me? I had risked everything for her. Done everything for her. I was the one who told her about the Clan gene, the awakening, the book, the library, the Clan...about everything. And she...what had she done? Told it all to someone else and then found another way into the library without me. Adding insult to injury, she now acted as if I was the bad guy.

I was willing to admit that perhaps the events at the library could have been handled better, but neither my aunt nor Elin had really left me much choice in the matter. I had done what was expected of a Clan Hunter and assisted in capturing an escaping prey. Thus, it really was a perfectly reasonable act.

Yes...I was sure once I explained the situation to Elin, she would understand. After all, she still had the opportunity to convert and become a *Stór-menni* Clanswoman. And what could be a higher honor for a *Smá-menn* than that?

I wasn't entirely sure what the Clan Council's plans for Dormants were, but what I did know was that they were desperate for them—making Elin enormously valuable. And a prize I deserved after everything I had sacrificed in the last weeks.

Returning to Falinvik and bringing news of her existence and the unregistered Clansman would already be enough to promote me. I was sure of it. But whether those two bounties were sufficient for me to achieve the rank of Captain and command of my own squadron was a different matter.

It was settled. I would be back for her. It was only a question of opportunity and time.

Extras

Translation Dictionary

Old Norse Words

AUSTRI: one in the East

LEYNASK: hide oneself, be concealed

MANNLEGUR: human

MEGIN: ability, might, power; strength; supernatural strength

NORDRI (also Norðri): one in the North

SMÁ-MENN: insignificant men, men of little power

STÓR-MENNI: big men, men of rank

SUDRI (also Suðri): one in the South

VESTRI: one in the West

Latin Words

FEMINA: woman

HOMO: man

INGENIUM: talent, ability

SALVE: hello

SOPITAM HOMINIBUS: dormant mankind

SUPERNO: supernatural

Þ	Self-Discipline	↑	Shield, Guardian
ᚲ	Revelation	M	Motion, Energy
ᚠ	Leadership	R	Journey
ᛒ	Dreams	ᚾ	Physical Strenght, Speed
ᛞ	Awakening	ᚷ	Personal Relationships
ᛉ	Dual Nature	◇	Legacy, Group Order
ᛃ	Fire, Flame	†	Determination, Patience
ᛗ	Communication	ᛇ	Honor, Life Force
ᛜ	Productivity	↑	Justice, Authority

Thanks for reading!

I hope you enjoyed *The Undiscovered Descendants*! Writing the book has been a labor of love over many years where I've found small moments to breathe life into the Four Clans, Auor Island, and its inhabitants.

If you'd like to support the continuation of the Nordri Series, the best way is to help other readers discover the book. Share your enjoyment of the book with your friends and family, and please leave a review on Amazon, Goodreads, and Bookbub.

To hear news and updates on Book #2 of the Nordri Series, sign-up for my author newsletter at: www.jovisuri.com/signup

Or follow me on:
Twitter @auorauthor | Facebook auorauthor

COMING 2022

Sign-up for Jo's newsletter to be the first to hear when **BOOK #2 OF NORDRI SERIES** is available.

Also, get exclusive deals and sneak previews before anyone else!

www.jovisuri.com/signup

Acknowledgements

As all authors know, a completed book is a labor of love—but one does not labor alone to accomplish it.

First and foremost, I would like to thank my family and friends who believed in Auor and the Four Clans from the start. Your support and encouragement helped mold and shape the story into so much more than it was.

To my Beta readers, thank you so much for finding all the little flaws, lending me your thoughts, and being relentless cheerleaders. Auor, its inhabitants, and I are forever grateful for your feedback.

To my wise and eloquent editor Susan Grossman, you smoothed out the wrinkles and helped give each character a distinct voice. I am beyond grateful.

Finally, I would be especially remiss if I didn't thank my youngest Beta readers, Isabella and Samantha. Your giggles and comments helped me understand how readers of all ages could delight in Elin, Aedan, and Tristan's adventures.

About the Author

Jo Visuri was born and raised on an island in Finland's famous archipelago, where she found her one and only Viking coin at the age of six. After spending a few formative years living by a Norwegian fjord, Jo's family uprooted to the sunny beaches of Los Angeles, CA.

A graduate of Brown University, Jo has privately written stories since she could read one and launched her debut *The Undiscovered Descendants* in Fall 2021. She now lives and writes in San Diego, CA, when she isn't distracted by her very cuddly and demanding senior dog.

To catch up on the latest news and updates, join Jo Visuri's newsletter at: www.jovisuri.com.

facebook.com/auorauthor

twitter.com/auorauthor